# CHOSEN
# CHILD

by

LINDA HUBER

# ACKNOWLEDGEMENTS

Very special thanks yet again to my editor Debi Alper. Her help and encouragement with this book were, as always, invaluable. Thanks also to Julia Gibbs and Yvonne Betancourt for their proofreading and formatting skills, and to Debbie Bright of The Cover Collection for the amazing cover artwork.

Many thanks to my sons Matthias and Pascal Huber and my nephew Calum Rodger for technical help and information, and to Pascal for his work on my website and book trailers. Thanks, guys – couldn't manage without you!

Special thanks go to Eileen Shannon. A chance conversation with her at a wedding gave me the original idea for this book. I still have the paper serviette with scribbled information.

Yet more thanks to Di Napier, for information and advice on garden plants, and to Bea Davenport for her help with the blurb.

And to the many, many people who have helped and supported me in so many ways, with this book and my others, both in real life and on social media – thank you SO much!

Information about adoption and adoption parties (adoption activity days) in the UK can be found at: baaf.org.uk

To Anne, Evelyn, Ann, Fiona and Hilary

Linda Huber grew up in Glasgow, Scotland, where she trained as a physiotherapist. She spent ten years working with neurological patients, firstly in Glasgow and then in Switzerland. During this time she learned that different people have different ways of dealing with stress in their lives, and this knowledge still helps her today, in her writing.

Linda now lives in Arbon, Switzerland, where she works as a language teacher on the banks of beautiful Lake Constance. *Chosen Child* is her fourth novel.

Visit Linda at www.lindahuber.net
Follow her on Twitter@LindaHuber19

Also by Linda Huber

*The Paradise Trees*

*The Cold Cold Sea*

*The Attic Room*

# PART ONE
# THE WAITING

# CHAPTER ONE

Saturday 3rd May

Ella held her breath, squinting at Rick as he inched the Peugeot into the narrow space between a battered Clio and a shiny new BMW. He was nervous – of course he was, she was too – and it didn't make the manoeuvre any easier. The Peugeot crept forward until Rick yanked the handbrake up, and Ella's shoulders sagged in relief. A scrape on anyone's car would have been the worst possible start to their first adoption party.

'I'll need to get out your side,' said Rick, glaring at the Clio. 'What a cattle market. I can't believe we're doing this – we'd be much better waiting for Liz to find us a kid the traditional way.'

Ella opened the passenger seat door. Rick was a planner; he'd never been the kind of person to simply have a go and see how things turned out. She tried to sound encouraging. 'Liz said these parties were a great place for people to find a child they were – attracted to.'

It was the wrong choice of words.

'I don't want to be attracted. You don't get to pick out an attractive baby when you have one of your own, do you? I don't care if he's blonde like you or dark like me, or whatever. All I want is a nice little kid – a boy, preferably, one we can give a good home to and enjoy as he grows up.' He struggled across the passenger seat and emerged beside Ella in the car park, crammed today with a motley selection of vehicles, including a tandem. People attending adoption parties seemed to be a varied lot.

Ella took Rick's arm as they walked towards the entrance. The Majestic was the largest hotel in St Ives, a relic from a slower, more elegant era, its white walls dazzling in the warm spring sunshine. She was conscious of the nervous churning in her stomach – this was the first time they would come face to face with children who were up for adoption. It was the dream of a lifetime for Ella – how very much she wanted to read bedtime stories and mop up tears and be frustrated because they couldn't find a babysitter. And this afternoon could bring them a huge step closer to doing just that. As of last Thursday, they were panel-approved to adopt, so 'all' they needed now was a child.

Ella was astonished when she learned about the adoption party project. It sounded so lightheaded, like going to a salesroom and picking out a new car.

Liz, their adoption society worker, had explained. 'It's organised as a fun afternoon for the kids, with loads of games and activities. People who're panel-approved can meet the children in an informal setting. There've been several successful events around London, though this one's the first in our part of the country.'

Ella wasn't sure she'd understood. 'So we have a look

and see if there's a child that might suit us?'

'It can make a difference when you see a child in person. I've known several instances of a couple saying beforehand they'd only consider a baby, or they must have a girl – and then they go to a party and fall in love with a completely different child. Of course you still need to go through all the normal channels afterwards.'

'Sounds a bit plastic to me,' said Rick, and Ella knew by his tone if he hadn't respected Liz so much he'd have called the idea something a lot worse than plastic.


And now it was party day and Rick was showing his nerves, so Ella had to be the calm one. She took a deep, steadying breath as they joined the other prospective adopters in the dining room. A woman name-badged Kirsty stood up and went on to tell them everything Liz had already gone through. Ella could feel Rick twitching beside her. Why was this so hard for him? It wasn't as if they had to make a decision today.

'And of course, the most important thing about this afternoon is that the children have fun. So on you go and have fun with them,' said Kirsty, gathering her papers at the end of her talk. 'The foster carers will be available for questions, and this room can be used if anyone wants a quiet place.'

Ella squeezed Rick's hand as they joined the general shuffle towards the door. This was it. The search for their child had begun. The sound of excited young voices floated across the garden, and anticipation fizzed through Ella. Any second now they might come face to face with the little boy who'd be their son.

'It's well organised, isn't it?' Her eyes flitted across the garden, where a bouncy castle, a couple of donkeys, and a clown were already in action. A marquee with games was set up to one side, and the smell of coffee came wafting over the grass.

'Hm. So we find a kid and start talking?' said Rick, and Ella gave his arm a shake.

'Yes – and give it a proper chance, please,' she said briskly.

Rick shot her a hunted look, and Ella felt the tension creeping back into her shoulders. She fought against rising resentment. This was supposed to be a fun day and she wanted to enjoy it. But if Rick went on like this he would ruin it for both of them.

After a few minutes the procession of adults dispersed around the garden, and the children became more visible. Some were clinging to foster carers, more were playing independently. A lump rose in Ella's throat – all these children needed a forever home, and all these 'parents' wanted a child. Surely some of them would find what they were looking for.

They stopped by a dark-haired boy of about three and Ella crouched down. 'Having a good time?' she asked, patting the plastic tractor the child was riding.

'I'm a farmer,' said the boy, whose name badge identified him as Joey. He pedalled his tractor over the grass, and Ella smiled as he swung it round and parked beside Rick. This little boy was just what they were looking for – could they have struck gold already?

A woman with a foster carer's badge appeared and

handed the child an ice cream.

Ella stepped across and spoke in a low voice. 'Has Joey been with you long?'

'Eighteen months,' said the woman, taking Ella a few steps to the side. 'Lovely kiddie. He has epilepsy but it's well-controlled.' She turned to smile at another couple who were hovering.

'Oh,' said Rick blankly when Ella told him what Joey's foster carer had said. 'I'd wondered if we might consider him, but now – no way. I wouldn't cope with that.'

Ella nodded. Rick had said right from the start that he didn't want a child with a disability, and she'd accepted it.

They stood for a while with a group watching the clown, then moved inside the marquee to help two small boys build a tower with wooden bricks. Disappointment and frustration were gnawing away inside Ella. She'd been imagining the equivalent of love at first sight bowling both her and Rick over – that they would see a child and know immediately 'that's the one'. And it wasn't happening. The little boys jumped up and down on the wooden marquee floor, and the tower swayed elegantly before crashing to the ground amid shrieks of laughter.

Rick was grinning too as they turned away. 'Fun, but not quite what we're looking for.' He pulled her towards the queue for coffee.

'We'll probably feel this way when they find us a child on paper,' said Ella, when they were sitting at a table overlooking the inside play area. 'It's normal.'

'When they find us a child the usual way, at least we'll know he ticks the important boxes. And we'll be able to get to know him in a quiet place, not in a bloody rabble.' Rick jerked his head to the corner of the marquee where two small boys and a thin little girl were quarrelling over an electric racing car track. The boys weren't letting the girl have a turn, and she wasn't taking it quietly.

Ella sipped slowly. Rick had given up on the afternoon. Why was he being so defeatist?

The racing car dispute came to a sudden end when one of the boys ripped up a piece of track and threw it at the girl before running off with his friend. The girl stared after them, blinking hard and pushing long dark hair behind her ears.

'Oops,' murmured Ella, and went over to the child, who was fitting the track together again, her eyes bleak. 'Want a hand with that?'

The girl looked about six or seven. She wasn't wearing a name badge, which made Ella wonder if she was up for adoption. Not that it mattered; this child ticked none of their boxes. Ella watched as she banged the track into place.

'I can't do it anyway,' she said, her voice trembling. 'But they should have let me try.' She slotted a car into place and lifted the hand control to demonstrate she really couldn't do it.

Rick crouched down and picked up the second control. 'I used to have one of these. Wonder if I can still make it go.'

'Who's that on there?' said the girl, pointing to the medallion round Rick's neck.

Ella laughed. 'St Christopher. He brings good luck to travellers. Just right for this game, isn't he?'

'It's got a bash.'

'That's because Rick dropped it one day and then drove over it. So maybe it's not so lucky after all.' Ella knelt beside the track. 'Let's have a race. You and me on the red car, Rick on the yellow one.'

The girl slid over and together they grasped the red control stick. A whiff of peach shampoo tickled Ella's nose, and tears welled up in her eyes. Why, why couldn't she have a child of her own? Life was cruel, and there would be no happy end for them this afternoon. All Rick wanted was to go home and let Liz get on with the task of finding them a little boy. Swallowing her disappointment, Ella held the girl's hand over the control and tried to keep the car on the track.

'Faster!' cried the child, pressing harder, and inevitably the red car spun off course.

Rick swept past with the yellow one and stopped. 'Have another go. The trick is to slow right down when you go into the curves.'

The girl gave him a suspicious look, then tried again. The red car crept along the bottom curve, accelerated briefly on the straight, then drove sedately round the top bend and into the garage area.

One of the foster carers came into the tent, relief on her face as she hurried towards the girl. 'There you are! Oh – you're playing cars? Where's your name badge?'

'I took it off,' said the girl. 'Kids were being stupid.'

Ella almost laughed. The words were so direct, and the woman clearly hadn't expected to find this child playing cars or anything at all.

The girl waved the handset towards Ella and Rick. 'Then *they* came and *he* told me how to do it and I drove a round by myself!' Her voice was positively triumphant. She gazed from Rick to Ella and beamed suddenly, showing a gap where a bottom front tooth should have been.

Oh my God, thought Ella, her breath catching in her throat. Oh my *God*.

# CHAPTER TWO

Friday 9th May

Butterflies crashing around in her tummy, Amanda Waters picked up the pregnancy test and re-read the instructions. It was pretty straightforward – all you had to do was pee on the stick and wait for three minutes. Then, if a blue line was showing in the window, you were pregnant. Early morning was best, apparently, so she was spot-on there; it was only half past six. She took it through to the bathroom, sighing when the first thing she saw was Gareth's SOS pendant by the basin. How many times had she told him there was no need to remove it when he showered? One of those days he'd have an accident without it and if anyone tried to give him penicillin they'd make things a whole lot worse – and it would be Gareth's fault, not hers. There was no point having the stupid thing if he wasn't going to wear it.

Now for the test. Amanda smiled wryly as she remembered how she'd found out she was pregnant with Jaden. She'd fainted in the middle of Marks and Spencer's food hall, and when she didn't come round straightaway they called an ambulance. The doctor at A&E asked a few questions, then insisted on doing a pregnancy test. They'd had a big celebration that day, her and Gareth. This time, everything was different.

Amanda left the test stick on the window ledge and went to make coffee while she waited. Jaden would be up soon and the peace would be shattered, but at least he hadn't wakened when Gareth left. She hated it when that happened; starting the day at six-fifteen put poor Jaden out of sorts all morning.

She set the kitchen timer for a full five minutes to be sure and stood watching it, hands clasped under her chin and stomach churning. What would she do if it was positive? Hell, she didn't even know who the father would be. James was a lot more likely. Gareth had been so involved in looking for a new job he'd barely had time to come home recently, never mind have sex – but she couldn't be sure, that was the problem. Was it possible to predict to the day when a child was conceived? Somehow, Amanda didn't think so.

But thinking about James made her smile in spite of the nerves. It was one of those crazy things. She'd been drafted in to serve coffees at a conference Gareth's company'd held three months ago, and James came to her aid when she was trying to carry too many empty cups. He swooped up, relieved her of half her armful, and followed her out towards the kitchens.

The few minutes they'd spent chatting were enough to ignite something that had been missing in Amanda's marriage for a long time. James was funny in a clever, sarcastic way and he made no secret of the fact that he was attracted. Against her better judgement Amanda agreed to his suggestion of dinner the next evening. She told Gareth she was going out with the girls, then met James in the new Italian restaurant in Hayle where she confessed that she was married and a stay-at-home mum to her eleven-month-old son. Rather to her surprise he didn't mind.

'It's better to be married to your kid's father, makes it easier for the kid,' he said, leaning across the table and taking her hand. 'But most relationships are pretty open nowadays, don't you think?'

Amanda was happy to be swept away, and three months later they were still meeting regularly. James' small flat in Hayle was within easy driving distance of St Ives but far enough away for discretion, and 'nights out with the girls' had become weekly occurrences. Sometimes they had an afternoon together, when James wasn't working and Jaden was on a play date. It was 'just an affair' for them both, but it was the most fun Amanda'd had for, oh, for months. James came to the house occasionally too, but Amanda didn't enjoy these dates as much. Sleeping with James in her and Gareth's bed, Jaden napping in the next room – it didn't feel right. The good part was watching James play with Jaden – he was great with kids; it was lovely to see the little boy's face light up when James started another silly game for him.

The timer pinged and Amanda went back to the bathroom. Her instincts had been right; she could see the blue line from the doorway. Another baby was on the way, and when this child was born she'd have two under-two-year-olds. Golly. She'd always wanted a big family, but oh, dear, this wasn't the best way to go about it. This was plain messy. And yet – she was pleased, wasn't she? Yes, of course she was pleased; she loved kids – but what was she going to tell James – and Gareth?

Nothing yet, she decided, as Jaden yelled from his room. She would see a doctor, if possible work out who the father was, and take it from there.

It wasn't until she was clearing up after Jaden's breakfast that reality hit Amanda. She sank down on a chair and stared at the fruit bowl. There had never been any talk about her relationship with James being anything more than a fun-filled couple of dates a week. How would he react when she told him she was having a baby? And what did she know about the man, anyway? He worked as an IT specialist in Brompton & Son, a local company who designed aircraft engines and provided half the region with jobs. He was a minimalist. He liked red wine, Greek food, and sex... and for all she knew, she could be one of a string of girlfriends. In fact she probably was, you couldn't call two dates a week spent mostly in bed a relationship.

And he was way more likely than Gareth to be the father of her baby. Her new baby.

Amanda shivered, settled Jaden on the floor with a saucer of raisins, and lifted the iPad. The World Wide Web would tell her when the baby had started – maybe James wasn't the father.

Okay, she'd had a period on the 2nd of April so she was more than a week overdue. Amanda googled 'estimate conception date', and typed April 2nd into the box on the first site she came to. She peered at the result. So her probable ovulation date had been April 16th, and according to this, the 'window of conception' fell between April 12th and 20th – a whole week. This wasn't going to work, she could tell.

Sick at heart, Amanda reached for her phone and went into her appointments diary. Those dates included not one but two weekends, one of which was Easter, so she must have slept with Gareth at least once during the 'window'. And she had certainly slept with James.

A heavy, dull feeling in her middle, Amanda read further into the website. There in the FAQ section was the very same problem, and the answer was exactly what she didn't want to hear. *When you have intercourse with more than one partner around the time of ovulation and a pregnancy results, it is impossible to determine who the father of the baby is based on dates alone.*

Amanda bit her lip. A paternity test was the only way to find out who the baby's father was. That wasn't going to help her any time soon.

Jaden was toddling around the room, putting a raisin on every piece of furniture. Amanda sat watching him, lethargy sweeping through her. Poor little boy – what would happen to them all? They'd had such plans, her and Gareth. This house, a rented semi on the edge of town, was to be home until they'd saved enough for the deposit on a place of their own. Amanda didn't care where they lived, but Gareth was hankering after a cottage in one of the villages further up the coast. Her husband's life had turned into a vicious round of saving, job hunting and doing courses to make himself eligible for a better-paid position. Which he'd found last week. But somewhere along the way the passion had gone out of their marriage.

Jaden arrived at the bookshelf and deposited a raisin beside a framed photo of the three of them last Christmas. Smiling faces, a happy family. A lie. Tears ran silently down Amanda's cheeks, but Jaden noticed. He hurried over and pressed a hot, sticky raisin into her hand.

'Mum-mum-mum,' he said, and Amanda had to laugh. Did he mean 'Mum' or was he encouraging her to eat up? As soon as she laughed he did too, and Amanda lifted him and danced him round the living room, new strength sweeping through her.

A baby was good news no matter what and she would get this sorted. The first thing to do was see how James – the probable father – reacted. Then she would decide what to do about Gareth. It might be best for them all if she and Gareth put some work in to save their marriage. But was that what she wanted?

Early afternoon was the best time to get hold of James. Amanda waited until Jaden was napping, and settled into the corner of the sofa to phone. She would tell him there was something important they had to talk about tomorrow; she didn't want him to pick her up expecting a quick drive to Hayle and their usual romp in bed.

'Amanda, hi – I was just about to call you. I'm afraid we'll have to cancel tomorrow's appointment.' James sounded bright, and she guessed he was in the office.

Amanda's heart thumped in her chest. 'Oh no, James.'

'Sorry, but the boss has sprung a meeting on us and I can't get out of it. We'll reschedule – how about Tuesday?'

He was definitely being overheard. But no way could she wait until Tuesday to tell him what was going on. Breaking news like this on the phone wasn't ideal, but what else could she do?

'I'm sorry, but there's something you should know.'

He made an inquiring noise in his throat and she took a deep breath. Now for it.

'I'm pregnant.'

He was silent for several seconds, and she could hear that he was walking now. The sound of a door closing came down the phone.

'Are you sure? Whose is it? His voice was low and guarded.

'Of course I'm sure. But I have no idea if it's yours or Gareth's. It's about a million times more likely to be yours if we're talking about numbers of sperm, but there's no way to tell yet.'

'How the hell did it happen? You said contraception was no problem. What are you going to do?'

It was the question she'd been dreading. If he tried to make her have an abortion, that was them finished. End of. 'My coil must have failed for some reason. And I'm not getting rid of it – you can't make me.'

He was silent, and she heard the sound of a car down the phone. He must have gone outside. 'James?'

His voice was low. 'Look, I can't talk here. I'll call you,

23

okay? Don't worry.'

Amanda sat clutching her phone, her heart still racing. That hadn't gone well, but he knew now and she could start to plan. She rubbed a hand over the flatness of her tummy. No matter what happened, she was going to have this baby.

# CHAPTER THREE

Saturday 3rd – Friday 9th May

The girl's name was Soraya, and the reason she'd removed her name badge was that the bigger kids took one look and called her 'Sore-eyes'. Ella stood gaping while the child's foster mother re-attached the badge. Soraya promptly dashed off, and the woman grinned at Ella and Rick.

'Speedy Gonzales has nothing on Soraya. Hope you'd finished the game? Sorry, I'd better go after her. Catch me later if you want to talk.'

Ella only just managed to smile and nod.

Rick had seen her face. 'You want to inquire about her, don't you?' he said, pulling her back outside.

Ella felt physically sick. Soraya and the woman were nowhere to be seen, and anyway, she had already agreed to adopting a boy.

'She – struck a chord,' she whispered as they walked across the car park, in silent mutual consent that the party was over.

'Ah. The famous spark of attraction,' said Rick, opening the passenger door and clambering over to the driver's seat. Ella got in beside him. He didn't seem upset that she was making up her mind – because she was, wasn't she? – that a rather cheeky six-year-old girl was the child for them and not the years-younger boy Rick wanted.

She closed her eyes, not speaking as Rick reversed out and drove towards their home, a three-bed semi with a large L-shaped garden within smelling distance of the sea. They'd bought it in the days when they thought it would be the easiest thing in the world to make a couple of kids to fill the bedrooms. Ella stood in the driveway, blinking back tears at the thought of those empty rooms and the tidy, child-free garden. From here she could see all the way up the side, though the back green was partially hidden by the large wooden shed. Would there ever be trikes and scooters in there?

Over dinner they thrashed it out. Rick was still hankering after a son, though to Ella's surprise he didn't dismiss Soraya out of hand.

'I'd prefer a boy,' he said. 'But we want more than one, don't we? We could adopt a boy next time. And I did like Soraya's spunk. You should decide, you'll have more to do with the kid anyway.'

Ella blinked. After all the insistence about young and healthy white boys she hadn't expected this about-turn, but instead of making her feel positive and excited it simply scared her. Rick *hadn't* wanted a child of that age, and definitely not a girl. Did this sudden capitulation meant that, having seen the reality of children up for adoption, he was stepping back from the parenthood idea? Her idea, her child, her responsibility? It wasn't the best way to do this. But – she wanted Soraya so badly; it was an almost physical ache in her gut. Ella stuck her chin in the air. Soraya this time, a boy the next... Why not?

She phoned Liz after dinner, and the social worker promised to arrange a visit to Soraya's foster home for them. Ella put the phone down feeling they'd taken a huge step towards adoption. Soon they'd be able to talk properly with Soraya's foster mother, and have afternoon tea with Soraya and the other children. If they decided to continue, the match would be presented to the adoption panel for approval, and other and longer visits would follow, both in Soraya's home and here at their own place. Ella shivered. This must, it absolutely must work out for them.


And now it was Friday, the day of their visit to Soraya. Ella checked the clock on the microwave for the hundredth time. To say that she was nervous would be a total understatement, she thought, massaging throbbing temples. Would the famous spark still be there when she saw Soraya? Her lips tightened as she glanced outside. It was after two o'clock; they would need to leave soon, and there was Rick, strolling up and down the garden with his phone pinned to one ear. He was one of those people who had problems taking an afternoon off work. Or rather, work had problems when Rick took a few hours off, something he'd had to do several times since they'd started the adoption procedure. To make up the time he often worked for a few hours on Saturdays. Rick's was a good, well-paid job – Brompton & Son had branches all over the globe – all she could hope was it would leave him enough time for fatherhood.

Ella sighed. Whatever this call was, it was important, if the look on Rick's face was anything to go by. She banged on the window and pointed to her wrist, and he gave her a thumbs-up sign. Good.

Upstairs, Ella stood in the doorway of the larger spare bedroom. If things went well, they would need to redecorate in here. What was Soraya's favourite colour? Most little girls liked pink, but something was telling Ella that Soraya wasn't like most little girls. She went into her own room; heavens, what were you supposed to wear for your first visit to the child who might, one day, be your daughter? Ella pulled on black jeans and a green shirt, then fastened a string of onyx beads round her neck. A brooch she'd worn as a child caught her eye; a vivid turquoise enamel butterfly on a gold base; she'd inherited it from her grandmother. Would she be able to give it to her own granddaughter, some day far in the future? Ella hugged herself. In a way she felt like a child this afternoon – such a shivery, magical feeling, like the day before Christmas, or her birthday. She shouldn't get too far ahead here, but oh, this felt right. Soraya was special. Their child, please God their child.


Mel and Ben, Soraya's foster parents, lived in Redruth, a small inland town half an hour up the A30. As usual when they went somewhere together, Rick drove. The sea on Ella's left was deep blue today, tinged with green nearer the beach, and she gloried in the thought that maybe, maybe this summer they could go to the beach and play with Soraya. They'd be able to do all the fun mum and dad things. Rick was silent. He'd been snappy since his phone call, and Ella wondered if he regretted agreeing to visit Soraya. But when he spoke she realised he'd been mulling over the ramifications of becoming a three-person household.

'If we go ahead you'd need to do something about your Smart car,' he said.

'We can sell it. Two cars are a bit of a luxury, anyway. And if we get her, I'll want to give up working for a year or two. I've spoken to Sheila West – the temp we had last year while Jill was on maternity leave would like to come back, so I can stop anytime.'

Rick grunted, and Ella sat thinking about the questions she had for Mel. Soraya had been in care since she was ten months old, but had only recently been released for adoption. Her current foster home was her sixth. It seemed like a lot of being shifted around for a very young child who could have used some stability.

Mel's home was a 1930s, detached house on the edge of the Redruth. Soraya was standing at a downstairs window when Rick pulled up outside. She immediately vanished, to reappear at the front door, and Ella's heart thumped uncomfortably as she and the child faced each other. Soraya's hair was in bunches today, and her black leggings and oversized t-shirt emphasised her slightness.

'Are you going to play with me?'

Her eyes were huge, and the lump in Ella's throat was so big she could hardly speak. Oh yes, this was her child. Please, please, this had to work out for them.

She blinked hard and managed to speak normally.

'We're having a chat with your Auntie Mel first, and then I'm sure we'll have enough time to play.'

'Bum. I wanted a long time.'

'You're here!' Soraya's foster mother came up behind her. 'In you come. Soraya, you've said hello, so off you go and do your homework while we have a chat. I'll call you down when we're ready.'

Ella smiled warmly at the child and followed Mel into a sunny sitting room where three shabby sofas were grouped round a red brick fireplace. The tightness in her middle eased when Ella saw that 'Auntie Mel' was pleasant and informal. The older woman talked about Soraya's life in the foster family, giving Ella the impression that the girl was a handful, but with the right guidance an easy enough child to live with.

'The thing to do with Soraya is set clear boundaries right from the word go,' she said. 'She's been here eight months and she's really come along well.'

'Why has she had so many foster homes?' asked Ella.

'She was unlucky a couple of times – one set of foster parents had to give up because of illness in the family, and in another place Soraya had massive issues with the couple's own child. For a long time the aim was to reunite her with her mother, but she died last year. Soraya was sent to us on a long-term placement, and if she isn't adopted she'll stay here.'

Mel had given them a way out, thought Ella as she and Rick went upstairs to Soraya's room. Knowing the child had a permanent foster home now would make it easier to step away. Would Rick still agree to carry on, knowing Soraya's foster mother thought she was a 'handful'?

The little girl danced around the bedroom she shared with her eleven-year-old foster-sister, showing them her possessions and chattering non-stop. Ella sat on the bed and devoured the child with her eyes. Did Soraya know they were interested in adopting her? If she did she made no mention of it. She produced a variety of soft toys for them to admire, and allowed Ella to reorganise the doll's house. Rick asked about reading and was shown a box of picture books. He pulled out *The Tiger Who Came To Tea*, and Soraya sat on the floor while Ella read aloud.

'Ever seen a real tiger?' asked Ella, after the story. Soraya shook her head.

'Never been to the zoo?'

Another shake. Then, heartbreakingly, 'Who are you?'

Ella reached out and squeezed the small hand. 'We're your visitors. We hope we'll be able to come again, and maybe you'll visit us too.'

'Like Auntie Mel?'

'No, we're not foster parents. We're just – people.'

'Can we go to the zoo, then?'

Ella nudged Rick – this was supposed to be a three-way conversation – but he made no move to speak. She turned back to Soraya. 'That's a great idea and if it's possible, we will. I'll find out and let you know next time, okay?'

Mel called them down for coffee, and Ella watched as Soraya interacted with her foster family. Mel was pleasant to the child but very firm, and Soraya sat nicely at the table, eating her piece of lemon drizzle cake with no sign of the buzz of chatter from upstairs.

'Are you enjoying your visit, Soraya?' said Mel, when

the little girl passed her glass for more juice. Soraya nodded, and Mel patted her shoulder. 'Good girl.'

The words were friendly, the gesture was motherly, but the smile didn't quite reach Mel's eyes. Appalled, Ella realised that the other woman was looking after Soraya kindly and efficiently, but without loving her. And Soraya knew it.

It was hard saying goodbye. All Ella wanted to do was fold the child into her arms and hold her tight, and that was precisely what she wasn't supposed to do yet.

'I hope we'll be able to visit you again very soon,' she said at last, holding Soraya's gaze. The girl stood for a moment without speaking, then turned and ran upstairs.

Ella was silent as they started back to St Ives. After a while she pulled out her mobile. 'I said I'd phone Liz. What do you think?'

Rick's voice was void of expression. 'If you want Soraya, go for it. It's your decision, after all, I - '

He broke off, and Ella stared at him, her thumb hovering over Liz's number.

'You what?'

He rubbed his face. 'I – I'd be at work all day, so you'd be more hands-on than me.'

His expression was guarded. Ella hesitated, then pressed connect. The sooner they got this process started, the better.

# CHAPTER FOUR

Thursday 15th – Friday 16th May

Amanda still hadn't had a satisfactory talk with James about the baby; she had no idea what he was thinking and it wasn't a good feeling. She'd even started biting her nails again, something she'd stopped when she was fifteen. Part of the problem was they hadn't managed to meet since she'd told him, as Gareth was at home with a virus at the beginning of the week. It was horrible, not knowing which direction her life would take. Would her future be with James and excitement, or Gareth and safety and family? Sometimes all she wanted was to turn the clock back to the days when she and Gareth were happy together, and hold on to that happiness as hard as ever she could. But that was impossible. James was part of her life now, and his reaction would shape what she told Gareth, which in turn would shape what became of her life – and Jaden's too. Amanda blinked back tears. She might have destroyed her child's happy little family life.

However you looked at it, her marriage was in

trouble. Gareth was so fanatical about his work, and that would only get worse when he started the new job next month. Tears of self-pity welled up in Amanda's eyes. Her husband would barely notice if she and Jaden packed their things and left today.

On the other hand, if James ran a mile without saying goodbye, it might be best to say nothing about the affair to Gareth. The two men were alike enough that she didn't have to worry about the baby taking after its father. Both were tall and dark, although Gareth had unusual grey eyes that he'd passed on to Jaden, and James' were brown like hers.

Amanda bit her lip. It sounded easy when you thought about it in black and white like this, but James' reaction would probably be somewhere in the middle of the two extremes, which would make everything complicated and messy. The mess was of her own making, she was under no illusions about that, and it didn't make her feel proud. Starting an affair hadn't been her best move as a mother.

Jaden snored gently on the sofa, and Amanda spread her sweatshirt over him and boxed him in with cushions. She usually put him in his cot for his nap, but today he'd fallen asleep where he'd had lunch. Feeding him in front of the TV meant she could sneak some vegetables into him while he was engrossed. Satisfied he wouldn't roll off, she took her phone through to the kitchen. Time to call James and warn him that business, not sex was on the menu tomorrow. They were meeting here; she hadn't been able to find a sitter.

His voice was upbeat. 'Hi, sweetie, are we still on at

your place tomorrow?'

It didn't sound as if he was planning to run off and leave her, and Amanda choked back a sob. The hormones were playing havoc with her already. She didn't usually burst into tears at every little thing.

'Yes. James. I – I want us to have a proper talk about the baby.'

'I know. I've been feeling bad about that. You know I'll stand by whatever you want to do. Will we have time for a long chat tomorrow?'

Relief washed through Amanda like a cool wave on a hot day. It was going to be okay. 'Yes. It's Gareth's last day in his old job and they're having a do for him, so heaven knows when he'll be back.'

'I thought the new job didn't start till June?'

'It doesn't, but he's got so much bloody overtime he leaves tomorrow. He's going on a solo-walking trip next week and then we're all going to Scotland on holiday.'

Now she really was crying as the relief that James was sticking around gave way to resentment that he was asking about Gareth and not about her and the baby.

'Right. So we'll have time to plan while he's away, too.' His voice was upbeat; he hadn't realised she was upset. 'We'll manage something, okay? I have to go, Amanda, but I'll see you soon.'

He broke the connection, and Amanda went back through and flopped down beside Jaden. From a purely practical point of view it would have been easier if James had said, 'Hell, no, I'm out of here.' But she'd known he wasn't that kind of person. She'd never have become involved with someone like that. She and James were both decent people who'd simply wanted some extra fun in life – although the fun was in a grey zone, she knew that. *Did* he have other girlfriends? But even if he did, she was the one with the baby. Could they make a go of it? Did she want to?

She was having coffee and mulling over her options when Gareth arrived home, early for once. He sat playing with Jaden while Amanda phoned for pizza, then they all ate together on the living room floor, Jaden straddling one of Gareth's thighs and *Thomas the Tank Engine* tooting around on the DVD player. Guilt washed through Amanda as she watched her husband cut pizza into bite-sized chunks for Jaden. This was the kind of thing she loved – family fun, a little picnic with them all enjoying themselves. But their days as a family were almost certainly numbered. Gareth must have noticed her silence because he reached out and hugged her, Jaden squealing in protest as his 'horse' slid to one side.

'Steady, cowboy. Mands, I'm sorry I've been so busy lately. The new job'll give us more family time, you'll see. And the holiday will do us good. I'll come back from my walk a new man and we'll all have a great time in Scotland.' He kissed her head.

For a moment Amanda leaned on him. She had loved him so passionately when they first got together – would it be possible to get that back? How very much easier it would be just to forget James and carry on in their own little family, her and Gareth. Of course, that could still happen. James might be happy to forget about her, too. Was he really the kind to settle down and start a family? Although – he had such a knack with Jaden. He did like kids. What a mess she was in.

She was still half-asleep when Gareth put his head round the bedroom door the following morning.

'Last day, wish me luck,' he said cheerfully. 'I don't know when the leaving do'll finish so expect me when you see me, okay? Love you.'

Amanda listened as the car exited the garage and roared off into the distance. How awful; he was clueless about what was going on in his family. And now she had six hours to put in till James came for their talk. She felt like a sixteen-year-old with an important exam ahead of her; her stomach was heaving and she felt... Oh no.

It was morning sickness, of course. She'd had it badly with Jaden; not physical sickness, more a horrible nauseous feeling, and it had gone on for most of the pregnancy. Another eight months of feeling like crap was staring her in the face, and who was going to hold her hand through it this time? Amanda rolled out of bed and went to make tea and toast. They'd been the only things that had helped last time.

Fortunately, a slice of toast and a mug of sweet tea put paid to the nausea for the moment. Amanda woke Jaden to ensure he'd be properly tired at lunchtime, and started to think about what she should cook for James. The few times he'd come here before, they'd had a glass of wine and some finger food and then gone straight to bed, but that wouldn't happen today. Eventually she decided to make apple cake. Then they could have ice cream or just cream with it, and coffee. She bundled

Jaden into the buggy and set off for the local shop.

By twelve o'clock the house smelled like a farmhouse kitchen and Amanda was putting Jaden into his cot. He stared at her, bleary-eyed and thumb in mouth, then rolled on his side and slept. Amanda's heart contracted with love. What a good boy he was. He didn't know his little world was in danger of disappearing forever. Maybe the best thing would be to tell James the baby was Gareth's, end the relationship and make a go of her marriage, but oh, she wouldn't be able to live with the lie, she knew she wouldn't.

James arrived at ten past and hugged her. No smoochy kiss today, no grabbing her the second the front door was shut. His face was serious as he followed her into the kitchen. Heart thumping, she poured coffee for them both and passed him a plate with a chunk of still-warm apple cake. And what were they doing, sitting here playing happy families when they should be discussing their future – and the baby's future? She looked at him miserably.

'Chin up,' he said. 'I've done a lot of thinking, and I've come up with the perfect plan. Two words: you decide. If you want me to stick around and play daddy, I will. If you want me to disappear, I'll do that too. My only proviso is, if I'm going to be paying out hard cash, we do a paternity test.'

The moist apple cake turned dry as dust in Amanda's mouth. So he would do the decent thing if pushed, otherwise he'd let her – and the baby that was almost certainly his – go. Wasn't that telling her something? And he'd said nothing about moving in together; that was significant too. And she still didn't know how many girlfriends he had.

He finished his cake and reached for her hand. 'I know it's a lot to decide, but we don't need to set it in stone today. I won't leave you in the lurch, don't worry – unless you want to be left in the lurch. But that would break my heart.'

He grinned at her, the old sarcastic grin, and Amanda melted. She could never resist him when he was like this. Five minutes later they were in bed together.

And ten minutes later she heard Gareth's key in the door.

# CHAPTER FIVE

Friday 16th May

Ella couldn't settle to anything. It was her day off and normally she'd have had a quick blitz round the house to get it ready for the weekend, or started preparations for any dinner guests they'd invited. But the only visitor they were expecting today was Soraya, and the preparations were complete – weren't they? She opened the fridge yet again.

Soraya's favourite lime cordial – check. Victoria sponge – check, and the vanilla ice cream to go with it was in the freezer. Chocolate digestives in the cupboard – check.

'You'll send her home sick as a dog,' Rick said the night before, when Ella told him the proposed afternoon tea menu.

'I won't. And her first visit's an occasion. We must have something special and Mel said these were her favourites.'

Ella laid out the new plastic place mats she'd bought. It was starting to become real, this thought that Soraya could become their daughter. Liz had put the match in for approval by the adoption panel, and until this came through Soraya would continue to know them as her 'visitors'. They had seen her twice in her foster home now, and there was no reason to think the panel would reject their application; as Liz said, it was a match made in heaven. The anticipation of motherhood was the sharpest pleasure Ella had ever experienced. It was so special, so exciting – did women who were pregnant feel the same way? She turned back to the clock for the zillionth time. Soon, soon, Soraya would be here.

They knew more about the little girl's history now and it had made Ella cry. The mother was a heroin addict, and although she remained clean for most of the pregnancy she'd made some very poor choices afterwards, and Soraya's grandmother was given custody. Unfortunately, the older woman's partner hadn't tolerated the presence of a baby, and Soraya was put in the first of her foster homes well before her first birthday. Ella felt ill just thinking about it. Poor Soraya had never been in a stable home for longer than a few months at a time; she would never have learned to love and trust. Changing that wouldn't be easy, and what it all meant for the little girl's development was something they still had to find out.

The landline in the hall trilled out and Ella hurried through. Surely Rick wasn't going to be late... But no, it was her mother. 'Hi, Mum, how's the Yorkshire air?'

'Funny you should ask that, darling – we're about to swap it for some Western Isles air. One of those last minute trips. We're leaving tomorrow morning.'

Ella grinned to herself. Retirement had given her parents a new lease of life – it was here, there and everywhere nowadays. And quite right too. 'Sounds good. Which island are you going to?'

'Taransay and Lewis, then we're coming home via Aberdeen to give us the chance to catch up with Rowena for a few days. Nothing'll happen about the adoption while we're away, will it? Mobile reception might be a bit dicey in the Hebrides.'

'Liz is hoping for a favourable report from the adoption panel next week, but we'll still be doing visits for a while. Soraya's coming this afternoon. Mum, it's so amazing!'

'I can't wait to meet her and I'll cross my fingers very hard it all works out quickly for you. Have a fabulous time.'

Ella put the phone down feeling warmed, but irritation flooded through her when she saw the time – quarter to two already. Rick should have been here fifteen minutes ago. He had grumbled about the visit being on a Friday, but Soraya was going away for the weekend with her foster family. School had broken up for half-term yesterday, so this was the ideal day.

Determinedly not thinking about Rick's lateness, Ella wandered outside. The kitchen door at the side of the house led out to a generous garden – plenty of room here to put up a swing set or a net for badminton. A Wendy house? It was an idea, but maybe the best thing was to wait until the adoption was approved, and then include Soraya in the new plans. Ella pictured them going to the garden centre to choose a swing; a family of three, and oh, she had waited so long for this. They could grow veg, too – nothing like carrots straight from the garden to encourage kids to eat their five a day. Ella smiled, then grimaced. For all she knew, Soraya could be the biggest veggie-fan on the planet. There was so much they didn't know about her.

Ella slumped as the shivery anticipation gave way to a wave of something like depression, the first since they'd met Soraya. The child was six. Six years of life they knew little about – could they really hope to balance out the effects of all those foster homes, not to mention whatever had gone on in the first months of Soraya's life? The prospect was suddenly daunting. Soraya would always remember she'd had a life before meeting them. But then, this very fact gave them the chance to talk to her about it in a way she'd understand. Mummy and Daddy had so, so wanted a child, and then they'd seen Soraya and *paff*! – they'd known straightaway that she was their little girl.

Ella hesitated, staring at two blue butterflies flitting around the flower border. It was all very well saying 'they' all the time, but in actual fact she was the one who had fallen in love. If she hadn't pushed, Rick would never have considered Soraya. If she hadn't pushed he might well have been content to stay childless.

Young voices floated into the garden from the street and Ella saw a group of mums and kids, on their way to the beach, probably. Anticipation flooded back. Of course she would cope with whatever Soraya might fling at her – that was what parents did, wasn't it? And Rick would cope too.

Of course he would.

# Chapter Six

Friday 16th May

Amanda clapped her hand over James' mouth and they both froze. This was like a bad film, she thought wildly, this should *not* be happening. What the shit was Gareth doing home at this time? Her heart was hammering in her chest and it had nothing to do with James' proximity.

James slid out of bed and grabbed his jeans, stumbling in his hurry to get into them.

'Go downstairs!' he hissed. 'Keep him in the kitchen!'

Amanda fumbled into her bathrobe. Gareth hadn't called out to her; he would know it was Jaden's nap time. She could hear him in the living room below; he was going through to the kitchen now and the coffee mugs and plates were still on the table. The mugs would still be warm... And James' Peugeot was in the driveway, blocking the entrance to the garage.

Gareth was back in the hallway, no, no – what was she going to say to him?

She thrust bare feet into her slippers and ran from the room. Gareth was standing at the bottom of the stairs looking up, and the expression on his face... she had never seen it before.

'What's going on, Amanda?'

His voice was quiet and Amanda clutched the bathrobe round her neck. It must be perfectly obvious what was going on.

'Julie was here for lunch, but I had a bit of a headache so I went for a lie down when she left.' It didn't sound convincing even in her own ears. She started down the stairs, holding on to the banister as if it would protect her from whatever was going to happen. 'I'm fine now. Let's have coffee – there's still plenty of cake.'

He didn't budge from his position on the bottom stair. His eyes met hers, staring coldly.

'That isn't Julie's car outside.'

There was a creak from the bedroom, and Amanda suppressed a groan. James had stood on the loose board by the door. That was it then. Her gut cramped; her knees were knocking together and her thighs hurt.

'Is – is your leaving do over already?' she said, her voice feeble.

Colour drained from Gareth's cheeks and his chin began to tremble. He lurched up two steps until he was towering over her, and Amanda flinched. She could feel the warmth of his breath and the slight spit as he hissed into her face.

'You weren't expecting that, were you? It was a brunch, Amanda. Didn't you know? And *I'd* like to know who's up there in my bedroom.' He pushed past her and strode upstairs, his feet thudding on each tread.

Amanda released her grip on the banister and stumbled after him. She had never seen him so angry;

his lips were white round the edges and his breath was coming in hoarse pants.

Jaden's voice cried out from his room. 'Ma-mama!'

'Gar, it's not – '

Gareth disappeared into the bedroom and Amanda staggered after him. This was the worst, the very worst thing she had ever lived through. What would he do to James – were they going to fight? No, she had to stop that – she had to get them out of this. Grabbing Gareth's t-shirt, she pulled him back. He shook her off and she reeled against the wall, knocking a picture of the three of them to the floor.

James was fumbling with his shirt buttons. Amanda could see the horror in his eyes as he stepped towards Gareth, a trembling hand raised in what was probably meant to be a placatory gesture, but it still felt like a bad film. Gareth balled both fists, and James retreated again.

Jaden's howls were filling the house now but she didn't have time to think about that. 'Gar, no, stop –'

Gareth lunged at James, hands reaching for his throat. 'You bastard! You -'

'Gareth! Leave him! You can't -' Amanda sprang forward then side-stepped as James dodged Gareth, pushing him back towards the door. Gareth tripped over Amanda's jeans on the floor and pitched towards her. Panicking, she shoved him away as hard as she could, sobbing as he swayed, pulling James with him as he collided with the mirror on the wardrobe door. The glass broke with a horrible tinkling sound. A sickening crack as both men hit the floor sent a shiver right through Amanda. She screamed, hearing the echoing shriek from

Jaden.

James leapt to his feet, blood dripping from his arm onto Amanda's jeans on the floor. Too horrified to speak, she stood in the wreckage of her bedroom. Shards of mirror lay in front of the wardrobe door, and Gareth was sprawled in the middle of them. His eyes were open and staring. He wasn't moving.

Amanda sank to her knees beside him, feeling splinters of mirror pierce her skin. Her hand shook on Gareth's chest. Dear God, was he breathing?

'Gar? Can you hear me? Are you -' Panic swept through her and she moaned, shuddering as she scrambled to her feet and staggered backwards, colliding with the door frame. No, no – look how his head was twisted... and there was no expression at all in those terrible grey eyes...

Unremitting screams from Jaden's room made the scene before Amanda a million times more awful. 'He's dead!' Her teeth were chattering.

James was wrapping his boxer shorts round his bleeding arm. 'Don't be so bloody stupid, he's not dead. It wasn't even a hard -' He bent over Gareth, feeling for a pulse as he spoke, and Amanda moaned as his face blanched. He sat down heavily on the bed. 'What are we going to do?'

If she hadn't known it was James speaking she would never have recognised the voice, a grainy, appalled whisper.

Amanda clutched the door frame, panting. 'Call an ambulance! Quick, quick – where's your phone?' She stretched a hand towards him.

'He's dead, he doesn't need an ambulance!' James leapt up and pushed her onto the landing. 'Get Jaden and come downstairs. We have to talk.'

'We have to get a doctor – they might be able to save him!' Aghast, Amanda pulled away from him. Her mobile, where was her mobile? Jaden was still howling, and she called out to him. 'Sleepy-time, lovey! Be a good boy!' Unsurprisingly, this only made him cry harder.

James tightened the bloody boxer shorts round his arm, his face sheet white. 'I reckon his neck's broken. He's gone, Amanda.'

He pushed her towards Jaden's room. Amanda grabbed her son from his cot and dashed down to the kitchen. James was leaning over the sink washing the blood from his arm, breathing hoarsely through his mouth. 'Got a plaster?'

'Boo boo,' said Jaden, and Amanda stared. Up till now his only words had been Mama, Dada and bus. She strapped him into his hated high chair and gave him a generous slice of apple cake to keep him busy. Thank God, oh thank God he was too young to understand what was going on. The nausea had returned, dizziness was coming in waves, and her teeth were chattering. Hands shaking, she reached into the high cupboard for the first aid kit. James rummaged for a strip of plaster and she helped him stick it on.

'We have to call the police, James.' It didn't sound like her voice either.

'Don't be so stupid. If we do that there'll be hell to pay.' He drummed the fingers of his uninjured hand on the table.

Amanda glared at him. What was he getting at? They didn't have any choice. 'We *have* to call them. Or an ambulance.' It was unbelievable. Gareth – her husband – was *dead*. Ten minutes ago he'd been alive, happy to be coming home, looking forward to his holiday... and then his last moments had been filled with such horror.

James leaned forwards. 'We both pushed him, Amanda. They'd arrest us and charge us with manslaughter, even though Gareth attacked me.'

'We can't pretend it didn't happen.' Amanda sank her head to the table top.

'We have to plan what we say, then – we have to make it look like an accident.'

'It *was* an accident!' She was crying now; the sheer irrevocability of Gareth's death was crushing. Jaden's eyes were fixed on her, his lower lip trembling, and she patted his hand.

James scratched his chin. 'You're right. Yes... You could say he was getting changed after work and he fell over something and crashed against the mirror. If we don't tell them about me the police'd have no reason not to believe you. I'll go and you can make the bed and phone -'

He strode out to the hallway and Amanda ran after him. Was he going to leave her to face the police alone in the wreckage of her life? James came to a halt by the hall window, moaning as he stared out. Amanda looked too and saw the reason for his alarm. Bob Charles across the road was out washing his car, and a noisy group of boys were playing football on the deserted street, the goalpost level with James' car. And Mrs Gray next door was sitting in the sunshine beside her lilac tree.

'Fuck, Amanda – they'll see me when I go. When you report Gareth dead the police'll ask around... and my car's been outside all the time. We have to think of a way out of this.'

Amanda sank down on the stairs and sobbed. There was no way back from a dead man.

James sat beside her and hugged her, and for a brief moment she leaned on him. Jaden was howling in the kitchen and Gareth was dead and there was no one else to lean on.

'We have to make this look as if it has nothing to do with either of us. Think. Who's the next person expecting to see Gareth?'

Amanda started back into the kitchen. 'Well – me, and...'

It was difficult to think clearly, but as far as she knew there was no one expecting Gareth to turn up anywhere soon. He was finished at work, next week he had planned his walking tour, and the week after they were going to Scotland.

'We're meeting his mum in Glasgow the week after next.'

'And the walking tour?'

Amanda clutched her head with both hands. She'd been looking forward to Gareth's week away. It would have given her and James a lovely long time of meeting whenever they wanted to. What a terrible person she was.

'He's going alone. He often does that. Sometimes he goes with friends but this time...'

James tapped his fingertips together. 'Okay. So

theoretically he could have an accident out walking next week? He could fall over a cliff, couldn't he?'

Amanda felt stupid and slow; her mind wasn't working properly. Gareth was planning to walk along the coastal path from Lamorna, heading towards Plymouth. They'd done a section of it together before Jaden was born. The views were magnificent, but the path was tricky in places. There was nothing Amanda could think of to say to James. What on earth was he proposing? To throw Gareth over a cliff at midnight? She could feel her eyes widening in disbelief.

James sat staring at nothing, then reached over and grabbed her hand. 'Listen. We'll work something out, but until we do we have to make sure we behave absolutely normally. Give me a couple of large bin bags and some tape. I'll wrap him up and come back later to take him away. I'll go back to – to work now, though how I'll manage anything I don't know. You clean the room upstairs. Next time I come I'll have thought of a plan. I promise. There's no sense us going to prison over this; it wasn't our fault.'

But it was, thought Amanda. If they hadn't been in bed together none of this would have happened. But if the police came here and saw the bedroom in the state it was now... if she was arrested... She looked at Jaden, happy again with his cake. Wiping her nose on the sleeve of her robe, she blinked at James, then pulled the roll of bin bags out from under the sink. He slunk from the room, and she buried her head in her arms on the table, listening as he slow-stepped upstairs. This was surreal; what were they *doing*? But what choice was there? She couldn't leave her boy while she was arrested and proving

51

her innocence. Supposing the police didn't believe it was an accident? Jaden stretched out his arms and she lifted him and tried to hug him, but he wriggled until she put him down.

It was impossible to block out the sounds from upstairs. The rustle of bin bags, then thumps and scrapes, and groans from James. He was putting Gareth into the spare room. His face was like grey marble when he came back down, and Amanda saw blood seeping through his plaster. Not speaking, she pulled out the first aid kit again.

When she was done James hugged her tightly for a few moments, then left. She heard him drive off down the road.

He hadn't been gone two minutes when Gareth's mobile rang upstairs.

# CHAPTER SEVEN

Friday 16th May

Rick's car swung into the driveway, and Ella closed her eyes in relief. At last.

'Sorry, sorry, got stuck on the phone to India. I'll just go and change.' He ran upstairs, barely looking at her.

Irritation gone, Ella stood at the front room window. Ten minutes till Mel and Soraya arrived. Would she stand here one day, waiting for Soraya to come home from school? Or would she collect her daughter? Some of the local mothers did group school runs, she knew. Anticipation fizzed through Ella; this must, this simply must work out for them. If someone came now and said, 'You can't have Soraya,' she would be devastated.

Mel's car pulled up at the roadside and Ella hurried to the door. Mel was standing beside the driver's door, leaning on the roof, so obviously she wasn't coming inside. Soraya emerged from the back and ran up the path, her face one big question mark.

'I'll collect her at five!' called Mel, and Ella waved.

Soraya didn't look back, and Ella took her hand and led her inside.

'What are we going to do?'

Ella laughed. 'Hello to you too. We'll go for a walk first, to look at the sea, and then we're coming back here for the best tea you can imagine, and then we'll play in the garden.'

'I wanted to make a sandcastle and go paddling and have an ice cream on the beach,' said Soraya, her voice disappointed.

Ella remembered what Mel had advised about being firm. 'We'll save that for another time. A whole afternoon at the beach needs better weather, and there isn't much we can do about that, is there?'

Soraya peered up at the sky, where grey clouds were scudding in front of the wind. 'Where's Rick?'

'Right here,' said Rick, running downstairs. 'Come on, I can smell the sea. Put your jacket on, you'll need it.'

They took Soraya to Porthgwidden beach where it was relatively sheltered. It was an odd feeling, thought Ella. Three people who could become a family – but they didn't really know each other yet. The tide was out, but the sea was stormy enough to be impressive, and Soraya squealed in excitement as the wind whipped her hair across her face. On the beach she started to collect shells, her eyes dreamy. Ella and Rick wandered along beside her, Ella pointing out shells and commenting on them. Rick was lost in his own world, staring across the ocean, hands thrust into his jacket pockets. His replies were monosyllabic when Ella tried to draw him into the conversation, and after a while she gave up and concentrated on Soraya, who wasn't saying much either but was definitely enjoying her outing. After a while the rain came on and they ran back to the car.

'Are you okay?' said Ella quietly, when Rick had fastened Soraya's seatbelt.

His face was drawn. 'Sorry. My head's still in India with the contract we haven't got yet.'

He was still lost in thought when they arrived home, and Ella gave his arm a little shake while Soraya was washing her shells in the bathroom.

'For heaven's sake forget about work. We've only got her for another hour and a half. We need your full presence, please.'

He pulled his arm away, and Ella struggled to hide her exasperation. He might make a bit more effort. Dodgy contracts belonged to everyday life, but there would never be another first visit. She called Soraya to the kitchen table, where the girl gobbled down a large slice of cake with a scoop of ice cream on the side.

'Can I have some more? Please?'

'Here you are,' said Ella, providing a sliver with a small scoop of vanilla. When Soraya asked for a third portion, however, she shook her head, mimicking Mel's manner. 'Seconds are fine on special occasions, thirds are mostly too much. But you can take the rest of the cake back with you. It'll still be nice tomorrow if you put it in the fridge. You can have a chocolate biscuit to finish with.'

Soraya took a biscuit. 'Auntie Mel says no seconds,' she said, squinting at Ella across the table, a small smile on her face.

Ella smiled back to gain a few seconds thinking time. Was Soraya being provocative?

'Auntie Mel's right. Seconds are for special occasions,

like your first visit here. Eat up, and when you've finished we can go and look at the garden now the rain's off.'

To Ella's amusement Soraya looked abashed. Little monkey, she'd been testing them. The child passed by on her way to the kitchen door, and Ella hugged her spontaneously.

'I'm so glad you've come today.'

The beam that had first grabbed Ella's heart flashed across Soraya's face before she wriggled away and ran outside. Ella glanced round for Rick, but he'd opened up the laptop in the dining room. Didn't he want to get to know Soraya? Or was this his way of showing her this child hadn't been his first choice? Ella hesitated in the doorway. If she complained too hard he might go off in a huff and spoil the rest of the visit. Even now, her pleasure was marred by frustration at his behaviour.

'Be with you in a minute. I want to check something first,' he said, then pulled a face at her. 'I'm being a pain, I know. Sorry. But there'll be plenty more visits and you're more important to her anyway.'

Ella put that remark away to talk about later. He shouldn't be going into adoption thinking of himself as the less-important parent – that would be asking for trouble. Fortunately, Soraya didn't appear to see things that way. As soon as Rick appeared she dropped the ball she and Ella had been throwing about, and ran up to him.

'Ella says you built the shed.'

'Didn't you believe me?' said Ella, laughing.

Rick laughed too, but Ella noticed the strain on his face. The contract must still be uncertain, which probably meant it would stay that way till Monday. Happy weekend.

Oh well, maybe he'd have snapped out of it tomorrow.

The shed was one of the large-size chalet kind, used to store garden equipment and as a DIY workshop. Ella watched as Rick showed Soraya how the walls and floor fitted together. The little girl was fascinated by his collection of tools, and hefted a hammer which Rick promptly removed from her grasp.

'That one's adults only,' he said. 'But tell you what, I'll get a basket next week and screw it to the end wall, and next time you come we can play basketball.'

The beam was back immediately, and a lump rose in Ella's throat. Poor little scrap she was. If ever a child had been crying out for a home and a family who loved her, it was Soraya.

'What do you want to do with your shells?' she asked. 'You can take them back to Auntie Mel's, or you can leave them with us. You could have a little patch here for a shell garden, if you like.'

'Oh! Can we make it over there? Beside the bush with the butterflies?' Soraya looked as if she'd been given the moon, and tears shot into Ella's eyes.

They spent the rest of the visit constructing the shell garden, which Soraya had definite ideas about. Two of the butterflies came to investigate, and the child's face was a picture. At five o'clock Ella and Rick stood waving as Mel drove off with Soraya, a plastic bag with a few of the prettiest shells safely hidden in the child's jacket pocket, 'in case the others take them'.

Ella sighed as the car turned the corner. How empty she felt now. 'Well, that's that till next week. I'm glad she's coming back so soon, we - '

She turned, but Rick had gone back to the garden. Ella joined him as he stood staring at the shed.

'It's a good place to put up a basket,' she said, slipping her arm through his and feeling him jump in surprise. 'Basketball's the kind of game kids can play by themselves as well as with other people. Great idea.'

'What? Oh – yes. I was thinking about something else.'

Ella left him to it. It was a pity he'd been so distracted, but like he'd said, there would be other visits. She was clearing the kitchen when Rick appeared suddenly in the kitchen door.

'I'll pop back to the office and see how things are going. I'll be back in an hour, max. Sorry, love.'

# CHAPTER EIGHT

Friday 16th May

Amanda stood in the hallway, hands clamped over her mouth, retching as Gareth's phone sounded upstairs. What was she supposed to do now? Where was the phone, anyway? Was she going to have to *rootle through his pockets* for it? She collapsed on the bottom step and burst into tears. She was a widow... She had killed her husband. And she had — two children. It was a blacker nightmare than she'd ever imagined and there would be no waking up in the morning.

Jaden toddled through from the living room, a sweetly concerned expression on his face. 'Ma-mama.' He laid plump hands on her knees, where tiny cuts from kneeling on the floor beside Gareth zigzagged across her skin. 'Boo boo?'

Amanda lifted him onto her lap, soaking up his heavy warmth and baby smell, pulling comfort and strength from her fourteen-month-old son. She had to get a grip, and fast. Gareth was gone and she could never make that right again, but Jaden was here and she had to build a life for him and the coming baby. James was right. There was no way she could go to prison.

But – would she really be sent to prison for something that had been a complete accident? Gareth and James had started the fight... Amanda wiped her eyes with her free hand. She had pushed Gareth. To his death. It was her fault, hers and James'. Would there ever be a way to get past that? If the police were involved, at the very least she'd be investigated and heaven knows how long that would take. They would take Jaden from her until it was all resolved.

And – a shudder ran through her at the thought – the whole sordid tale would come out. The pregnant adulterous wife who didn't know who the father of her baby was. She and James would be on the front page of every newspaper in the country, the talk of the town. Heads would turn every time she walked along the street, curtains would twitch and people would whisper behind her back. The woman whose lover and husband fought to the death.

Amanda stood up, Jaden in her arms. She could *not* let that happen. Her child deserved better.

'Right, mister,' she said. 'Mummy has some cleaning to do upstairs, so you can sit in the buggy down here with some raisins and watch Thomas, okay?'

The novelty appealed to Jaden, and she left him safely strapped in, a saucer of raisins by his side and Thomas and friends tooting around on the television. Soberly, Amanda gathered cleaning stuff for the bedroom carpet – was there blood there? – and a bucket for the broken mirror. Her stomach heaving, she forced her feet upstairs and stood in the spare room doorway.

James had wrapped Gareth in three large bin bags, one over his head, another over his feet, and the third taped round his middle. Amanda dropped the bucket and clapped a hand over her mouth and nose. Shit... it smelled like shit in here. She'd never be able to open that terrible parcel and search through Gareth's pockets. Never again would she touch her husband... Bile rising in her throat, Amanda scuttled across the landing and called Gareth's number from her mobile. Blessed relief washed over her when his phone rang in the bedroom, yes, there it was under the bedside table. It must have fallen from his pocket during the scuffle. Amanda grabbed the mobile and sank down on the bed, her legs suddenly weak.

The call had been from Gareth's mother, a newly-retired hairdresser who lived in the west end of Glasgow. Amanda rubbed her chin; she'd need to get hold of herself before she talked to Susie. Her fingers were all over the place, but somehow she managed to text. *Busy atm, call you later x*.

Trembling, Amanda gathered the larger pieces of mirror from the carpet and vacuum cleaned, hearing splinters of glass tinkle up the tube. Would she have seven years bad luck now? But Gareth had broken the mirror and his was the ultimate bad luck. Sobbing, Amanda pulled the one remaining shard from the wardrobe door and dropped it into the bucket. Had Gareth slipped on the smooth surface of the glass? If so, he might still be alive if she hadn't been vain enough to stick a mirror to a wardrobe door where no mirror was intended... her fault, her fault. She would hear the crack of Gareth's neck breaking every day for the rest of her life.

As far as she could see there was no blood on the carpet, not even at the foot of the bed where James had been standing. Good. She sprayed carpet shampoo over the floor where Gareth had been, then went to check on Jaden and phone her mother-in-law. This was where she had to prove she could act.

Three times she broke the connection before it rang, then she bit down hard inside her cheek and forced herself to go through with it. 'Hi, Suze. How's things?'

'Not so bad. I'm looking forward to seeing the three of you. How's my boy?'

Nausea flooded through Amanda until she realised Susie was talking about Jaden. 'Oh – he's, ah, enjoying the Thomas DVD you sent him. I – I'll take him for a walk on the front soon, get him tired for bed. Suze, Gareth was going to call you back but he's crashed out upstairs. It was his leaving do at work this afternoon.'

Now she had done it. She had passed the point of no return.

Susie laughed. ''Nuff said. I know my son. I wanted to confirm what day you were driving north.'

Amanda's head was spinning and it was all she could do to keep her voice steady. 'Oh – a week on Sunday. Less traffic on the motorway. We're planning an overnight stop in Yorkshire so we'll be with you by Monday afternoon.'

'Are you all right, hen? You sound a bit funny.'

Amanda bit her cheek again and tasted blood. 'Just tired. I need my holiday.'

Susie accepted this and chatted on for a few moments about an exhibition she wanted to take them to, then rang off. Amanda took a deep breath. The cover-up had started. She could no longer claim that Gareth's death was an accident. And now she'd do as she'd said and take Jaden for a walk along the sea front to tire him out. She needed him asleep; she needed alone-time.

The rest of the afternoon passed in a blur. Amanda pushed Jaden's buggy along Wharf Road, then let him toddle along the sand for a quarter of an hour. The outing did nothing for her nerves. Too many other mums and babies were doing the same thing, enjoying a lovely spring day at the beach, breakers crashing in the distance and gulls crying mournfully above them. Shivering in spite of the warmth of the day, Amanda turned back before she met anyone she knew. Home again, she made Jaden banana sandwiches for his dinner and sat beside him in the kitchen while he ate. Poor baby, he hadn't had a proper meal all day; a snack for lunch because James was coming, then cake, and now another snack for dinner because his daddy was dead upstairs. Jaden sat munching with a happy smile on his little face, and Amanda wiped tears from her cheeks.

How was she supposed to get through the next however many days acting as if everything was all right? It was a ridiculous idea, pretending that Gareth had gone on his walk and then disappeared. What if the police found out what had really happened? She would definitely go to prison. It was all so unbelievable and so *hurtful*; she was hurting more than she'd ever hurt in her life, a million times more. She was numb with hurt.

When Jaden finished eating they went back to the living room and she put another DVD into the player for him. Now she was being an even worse mother, but she simply couldn't sit there playing after tea as she normally did.

Cars were passing by as the neighbours came home from work. Amanda glanced outside. Their Ford was still parked on the street; she should move it into the garage. They never left it outside all night.

She was searching for the car key – Gareth usually plonked it on the hallway table but today of all days it wasn't there – when her phone rang. It was James.

'Can you access your garage from inside the house?'

'No.'

'Hell. That would have been too easy. Right. Fill two or three of those big black bags with something – clothes, spare bed stuff, whatever. I'll be with you in ten.'

Amanda stared at her phone, seeing her hand begin to tremble again. Why the bags of stuff? He might have told her more. Resentment rising inside her, she nonetheless went upstairs and stuffed duvets and pillows into three large bin bags.

True to his word, ten minutes later James reversed into the driveway and bounded up the path, looking for all the world like a man come to visit a good friend.

'Here's the plan,' he said, closing the front door behind him. 'If anyone sees us and mentions it later, you say I'm a friend who's expecting visitors and you're lending me some bed things. We'll take the bags out and put them in my car, laughing and chatting, and Gareth'll be in one of them. Okay, Amanda? We want to do this quickly and look natural while we're doing it.'

Amanda's knees gave way and she sat down on the stairs again. 'What are you going to do with him?'

His expression was grim. 'I won't tell you that, because next week you're going to have to act frantic when he disappears. I'll come back tomorrow morning and we'll thrash out the details. The important thing now is to get the body away.'

*The body*... Unable to speak, Amanda followed him up to the spare room. James crouched beside the bundle that was her husband, testing the weight, and Amanda felt nausea rise. The smell was awful, and that was just... body fluids. When decay set in it would be so much worse. What on earth could James possibly do to hide that?

'He's starting to go stiff,' said James in a low voice. 'This is the pits. But there's nothing else we can do.'

He grasped the package, hefting the body into a good position in his arms, his face sheet-white.

'Come *on*, Amanda. Go down and open the boot. Take one of the other bags. We'll put that one and Gareth in first and then come back for the other two, then it'll be thanks and hugs and goodbye out there, and I'll drive off.' His voice was vicious but that was how Amanda felt too.

Almost in a trance, Amanda led the way. James stumbled halfway downstairs, Gareth's foot inside black plastic hooking in the banisters. Shuddering, Amanda jerked it free. It felt nothing at all like Gareth's foot. And the terrible bundle in James' arms obviously wasn't a spare duvet. This was crazy... if anyone saw... But it was way too late to do anything else, wasn't it? She opened the front door.

Bile rose in Amanda's throat as James heaved Gareth into the boot, then she tossed another bag in after him.

James shot her the bleakest look in the world as he flung the remaining bags of pillows in too and slammed the boot shut. He hugged her, a ghastly grin on his sheet-white face, and a minute later the car was turning the corner. Amanda trailed back inside. That was the last she would ever see of her husband.

Jaden was still intent on his DVD, and Amanda stroked his head. He looked up at her, a hopeful expression on his little face. 'Da-dada?'

Amanda burst into tears.

# CHAPTER NINE

Saturday 17th May

Ella waved as Rick drove away. Officially, he was going to the garden centre to get some more compost, and fresh gravel for the driveway. Unofficially he would almost certainly call into work first, because he hadn't wanted her to come with him. She sighed. He'd been gone well under an hour last night but returned looking grim. Things with the India contract were still precarious, but unless something more had gone wrong overnight, he should be back before too long. Meantime, she had her own plans. She would drive to the furniture store on the edge of town and see what they had for children.

Aware that her lips were curved in a smile, Ella wandered round the children's section, looking at little white beds with princess canopies, and miniature desks and chairs. How lovely it was to be planning for a little girl. Rick would have said she was tempting fate, but really, what could go wrong? It was only a matter of time before Soraya joined them. And maybe next year they could start the process again, and complete the family with a little brother for their girl. Ella caught sight of her reflection as she walked through the store, a crazy blonde woman with a grin a mile wide, but oh, she had waited a long time for this. The parent times were beginning.

On the way out she picked up a catalogue, then stopped off at the butcher's to buy steaks for dinner. Rather to her surprise the Peugeot was back in the driveway when she arrived home. So Rick's presence at work wasn't needed today. Good. And there he was, lugging sacks of compost into the shed. A rush of affection spread warmly through Ella, and she walked across the garden and knocked on the shed window.

'Anyone home?'

Rick appeared clutching a red and white basketball basket and a ball, and pulled the door shut. He waved the basket at her. 'Let's get this up, shall we?'

Ella stood by while he marked screw holes on the back wall of the shed, arguing amiably about the height. While he was screwing it on she told him about her visit to the furniture shop.

'Good idea,' he said. 'Now you know what direction to steer her in when it comes to choosing stuff. I suppose we'd take her along to do that?'

'I'd say it would be the best way of all to help her feel she was an important member of the family,' said Ella, happiness shivering through her. This was going to be so good. 'She knows what she likes, too.'

'She does seem to have an opinion about most things, doesn't she? For such a small person. Why don't you drive out to Burnside Centre after lunch? There's a much bigger store there, and a toyshop too.' Whistling, he went back into the shed and closed the door.

Ella went to look at Soraya's shell garden. This was a good idea too, giving her a patch of land of her own. And it was genuinely pretty. They could add some gravel in between the shells, and maybe some rock plants too. It would be up to Soraya.

She returned to the house and heated soup for lunch. Rick was silent as they ate, and Ella groaned inwardly. She hated it when he was so absorbed in his work that their home life suffered, but it had happened before and she knew it would happen again. It might be difficult persuading him to take time off if – when – Soraya joined their family.

Something Liz had told them popped into Ella's head and she leaned towards Rick. 'We could start making a family photo book for Soraya tonight. I suppose she'd get it when the match is officially approved.'

He stared at her. 'Do you think we still have to do that? After all, she knows us; she's been here already. The adoption parties seem to create a different timeline.'

'I don't think it's a must, but it'd help her feel part of the family. We can include photos of our parents, and your sister and her kids.'

Rick was frowning again. 'Whatever you like. Are you going to Burnside?'

'Yes. Are you coming?'

'Not today. I want to work in the garden while it's dry.'

Ella drove the few miles feeling slightly miffed. Would Rick be so distant if it was a little boy they were adopting? Unlikely – it would be all systems go buying boy-toys. Or maybe Rick was afraid of emotional commitment to a child who still wasn't officially their own. Hopefully, that

69

would change very soon.

She arrived back home with more catalogues and a box of board games ranging from Snakes and Ladders to Twister. *The family that plays together, stays together.* She had heard that somewhere and it was probably true.

Rick was in the kitchen when she returned, looking rather white. Could he be sickening for something? Ella dropped her bag on the table and went to hug him.

'Are you all right? You're very pale.'

He fumbled with the glass he was holding. 'Sorry, Ella. It's - ' His eyes met hers for an instant and she saw worry and frustration there. He sipped his water and went on. 'I – I'm not sure how safe my job is, and it's been preying on my mind.'

Ella was astounded. She'd assumed Rick's job was a million per cent safe. Logistics was an area where they never had enough well-qualified people, wasn't it?

'For heaven's sake, why?'

'Just a feeling. If this new contract doesn't come through... The next few weeks'll be critical so I apologise in advance if I'm a bit out of things.'

She kissed him. 'No problem. And I'll be ready any time you want to talk. But absolute worst-case scenario, Rick, even if you lost your job, with your qualifications you'd find another one. Certain sure.'

He shrugged, his face bleak. 'Let's hope it doesn't come to that. Thanks. Why don't I let you organise dinner while I take some stuff to the dump, and then afterwards we'll get on with your photo book for Soraya?' He gave her a thin smile and went outside.

Frustrated, Ella poured a large glass of Merlot, all the

time wanting to scream at him,

'It's not my photo book. It's going to be Soraya's photo book, but for the purposes of this exercise it should be *our* photo book.'

She stood at the sink preparing vegetables, and saw Rick drive off a few minutes later. The dump, her foot. He'd be off back to the factory to see who was in the office and what, if any, progress had been made.

A thought struck her as she was grating carrots for salad. Would they still be allowed to adopt Soraya, if Rick was made redundant? They'd been approved on the basis of Rick in a job...

Trepidation rising, she abandoned the carrots to sit down at the computer, and quickly found what she wanted. Being unemployed didn't exempt you from becoming an adoptive parent, but possibly Rick didn't know this and was worrying needlessly. It might be an idea to mention it casually over dinner. If he lost his job he could be the one at home doing more of the parenting. Ella paused, staring out to where Rick was already pulling up in the driveway. She didn't want to be the breadwinning parent. She wanted to be a hands-on, full-time, stay-at-home mum for a couple of years at least.

But maybe she wouldn't get the chance.

To her surprise, Rick was more cheerful when he came back in. 'I popped into the factory; things seem more stable today,' he said. 'Fingers crossed they stay that way.'

Ella decided not to mention her adoption-related research. Time enough to bring that up if things did go pear-shaped with Rick's job. But *surely*... There had never

71

been the slightest hint the company wasn't doing well. It would just be Rick worrying too much – the prospect of having a family to provide for would be more daunting now they were so close to the end of the process. It was time to do some serious confidence boosting.

# Chapter Ten

Monday 18th May

Gareth's walking tour was to start on Monday morning, one day later than he'd originally planned. Amanda and James had discussed this at length on Saturday – there were pros and cons about both days – but decided that Monday was the better choice. There would be no weekend hikers around, and fewer people meant a smaller risk. Or at least, a less-huge risk.

Amanda shuddered every time she thought about it. They were going to act out Gareth's departure, she and James and Jaden. And how she would manage to stand at Lamorna Cove waving cheerfully as James – playing Gareth – disappeared round the corner, Amanda had no idea.

She woke at ten to six, her head thumping, and lay massaging her temples and watching Jaden sleep. She couldn't face the bed in her own room, and the spare room, where Gareth had lain in his bin bags, was equally impossible. So she'd moved in with Jaden. What she was going through now was completely surreal. She and her baby – both babies – were stuck in the middle of the biggest horror trip imaginable and she would have to live with what she was doing for the rest of her life. She should have phoned for an ambulance. The police wouldn't have arrested her, would they? Nobody could say she'd murdered Gareth. All she'd done was push him to stop him crashing into her and her unborn child. Doing things James' way had turned her into an undercover criminal, and how sick was that? If only she could turn the clock back; if only she had never met him.

Thinking about James drove new shafts of pain through her head. She knew so little about him. They'd never talked in depth about their upbringing, plans for the future, friends. Those other girlfriends, for instance. She'd never seen any indication of them in his flat, but that didn't mean they didn't exist. Thinking about the flat caused a fresh wave of misery to break over her. It was so bare... Few knick-knacks, no piles of books or old photos. She couldn't begin to imagine what that might mean. Or she could, but she didn't want to.

*It's not his home*, whispered a mean little voice in her head. *Fool that you are. It's his pad, his love-nest. What normal person his age lives in a studio flat with no personal bits and pieces?*

And then there was the baby. James hadn't even mentioned it when they'd made their plans. Would he still stick by her? And the most terrifying thought of all – what if James wasn't the father? Suppose he insisted on a paternity test when the baby was born – and suppose it was negative?

The nausea that accompanied her through most days pulled at her gut, and Amanda crept from the room.

Jaden should sleep for another half hour. That would give her time to get her stomach under control.


James arrived on foot at seven o'clock. They were using her car – it was no longer hers and Gareth's, was it? – so that she could pick him up at Mousehole after his walk, compare notes, then leave him in Penzance to catch a train home, safely separate from her and Jaden. James changed into Gareth's jacket and distinctive red woolly hat and turned to Amanda, spreading his arms, waiting for her comment. For a moment she couldn't speak. With his hair – slightly shorter than Gareth's – covered, the only major difference between the two men was the eye colour. How she wished Gareth's grey eyes were looking at her from under his red hat. But they weren't.

She nodded, noticing James' pallor. He was finding this hard too. Amanda tried to breathe her nausea away. She swallowed one of the anti-morning sickness pills left over from her first pregnancy, and got on with the preparations for their trip. Her hands packing the nappy bag were freezing and unsteady; she had never been this unhappy. She was living in her worst nightmare.

'Okay,' said James, when they were ready to go. 'I'll run round into the car, and if anyone sees me we'll have to hope they think I'm Gareth.' He picked up Gareth's blue rucksack, packed with James' own clothes. 'You drive, and I'll hide behind a map till we're out of town.'

Amanda opened her mouth to say Gareth would never have done this, then closed it again. Nobody who might see them knew that either. 'Have you got his phone?'

James patted the rucksack. 'That's all, isn't it?' he said, frowning. 'There's nothing we haven't thought of?'

Amanda was past caring. If a policeman popped up in front of her now she'd have said, 'Excuse me please, can you help? I killed my husband by mistake.' She pushed Jaden into his jacket and handed James the car key.

'Let's do this,' he said grimly. He opened the front door and ten seconds later was sitting in the front passenger seat.

Amanda locked up, and glanced up and down the street. As far as she could see no one was watching. Good. She belted Jaden into his car seat, hoping he would fall asleep for a while.

It was a pretty drive to Lamorna but Amanda was oblivious to the scenery. Her mind was buzzing. What if they were found out? Jaden, poor sweetie – what would happen to him? She stopped to let an elderly woman pushing a rollator cross the road, the panic surging inside her making it impossible to keep a steady hand – or foot. The car kangarooed away from the zebra crossing and Jaden gurgled in the back. James was slumped in the passenger seat, fiddling with his phone.

'Was it okay for you to take the day off work?' said Amanda, when they were about halfway there and the silence had become unnerving.

He started, then glared at her as if she was an errant child. 'It had to be, didn't it?' He went back to his phone.

If she hadn't been driving Amanda would have burst into tears. Was it really too late to stop all this? She could drive to a police station and lay out the whole sorry tale. And be on the front page of all the red tops tomorrow.

And have Jaden taken away – they would give him to Susie to take care of. In Scotland. Amanda bit her lip, blinking hard. They had started this, and they had to continue.

'What did you do with Gareth?' she blurted out, and he glared again.

'Keep your cool, Amanda. We've made our plan and we're going to stick to it.'

Nothing more was said until they reached Lamorna Cove, the starting point of Gareth's walk. Amanda buckled Jaden into his buggy and stared around. There were no cliffs as such here; the land sloped down to the sea, green, grey and brown alternating as grass and scrubland gave way to rocks and the ocean. The coastal path towards Mousehole began here, and Gareth should have done all this yesterday. The place wasn't as deserted as she'd imagined; several hiker-types were stamping around as well as some locals, going about their business, cheerful in the warm spring sunshine. Amanda closed her eyes against the beauty around her.

James reached out and pulled her towards him. For a second she wondered what on earth he was doing and then she realised all he wanted was a word in her ear – literally.

'Happy family, huh? We'll go into the café first and make ourselves conspicuous. Nice and chatty,' he murmured, taking Jaden's buggy and striding towards the white building at the top of the cove. Once inside, he pushed the buggy over to a corner table, leaving Amanda to go to the counter to order.

'Two coffees, please, and, ah... two fruit scones,' Amanda said to the girl, forcing a smile. 'It's a lovely day, isn't it? We're seeing my husband off on the first leg of his walk. Wish I could go too, but the baby's a bit young.'

She gestured across the room to where James was sitting with his back to them, playing a clapping game with Jaden. Infectious baby giggles filled the café and several people chuckled.

The girl nodded sympathetically. 'You're quite right. Some people do take kiddies with them, but if you ask me it isn't worth the hassle and in some parts it's plain dangerous. Going far, is he?'

Amanda moved along the counter as she was joined by two middle-aged women. Now that she had started, the lies came almost automatically, because of course they weren't real lies. If it had been Gareth over there with Jaden, everything she was saying would have been true.

'He's aiming for Plymouth, but we'll see how far he gets by Friday. We live in St Ives so I can pick him up anywhere.'

She paid for the coffee and took the tray across to the table. This was the bad bit. She had to sit here and drink bloody coffee and act all normal and cosy.

They spent most of the time chatting to Jaden, who was in good form, waving to the women at the counter. It was all Amanda could do to force down her scone. She should never have ordered anything so complicated – slapping butter on a fruit scone was the last thing she felt like doing.

Twenty minutes later they left the café, Jaden still waving to all and sundry and James blowing his nose, covering his face with a large hanky. Outside, the show continued, with Amanda buying a paper at the kiosk and James pointing out various landmarks before hugging both Jaden and Amanda fondly and setting off along the coastal path. Jaden played his part magnificently, waving and shouting, 'Bye-bye-bye!'

Tears running down her cheeks, Amanda waved too as James disappeared round the corner – how crap this was. She was crying because her life had turned into a horrible mess, but an observer would think the tears were for her husband away on his tour. And now she had to hang around for hours, her and her guilty conscience. The plan was to pick James up at Mousehole, the next village along the path. This time he'd be wearing his own clothes and Gareth would be gone. They would slink in and out of the place as unobtrusively as possible.

At one o'clock James was safely back in the car. Relief made Amanda positively light-headed. The plan had worked; they could go home. She drove towards the anonymity of Penzance, glancing across at James, slumped in the passenger seat. 'Did you remember the phone?'

He slugged water from his bottle. 'In the Atlantic, with the rucksack. And the hat's about three yards away from the edge of a steep drop into the sea. Thank Christ that's over. Bits of that path are bloody murder, you know. I don't know why more people don't go over the edge. It's up to you now, Amanda. We shouldn't see each other in the next week or two. Get rid of your mobile in case you don't manage to delete all traces of me from it. I'll do the same. We can both get prepaids and use them to contact each other. I'll send you an old-fashioned letter with my number, then you can call me.'

'What about the baby?' said Amanda, fear churning in her gut. She would be on her own for weeks, her and her guilt – and the ghost of Gareth haunting her every time she closed her eyes.

'Well, that's sort of up to you too. Not much I can do about it yet. You'll be all right financially, won't you? I mean you'll get a widow's pension of some kind, and I guess he had life insurance too, didn't he?'

That was when the full horror of her situation hit Amanda. She was going to be – no, she *was* – a single mother with two children and nobody to provide for any of them; she would have to get a job. Misery hit her like something solid. Maybe she should move to Glasgow to be near Susie, but would she find work there? Her own parents lived in Spain, maybe she should go to them. But she couldn't support herself in Spain with two babies, either.

Penzance Station loomed up in front and James pointed to an empty space.

'Let me out, and move on immediately,' he said. 'Don't forget to have a chat with someone tonight, a neighbour if possible. You want to sound absolutely normal. In fact -' He gave her a sudden and dreadful grin. 'You could confide that you think you might be pregnant but you're keeping it as a surprise for Gareth when he gets back. You'd never say that if you had anything to do with his disappearance. I'll be in touch.'

As soon as the car was stationary he leapt out and strode across to the station entrance. Tears blurred

Amanda's sight as his back disappeared among a party of pensioners descending from a coach. That would be the last she would see of him for 'a week or two'.

'Bye-bye-bye,' said Jaden.

Amanda pulled back into the traffic. She had to get away from here, this place she wasn't supposed to be anywhere near.

'That's right, darling,' she said to Jaden, hearing her voice shake. 'Daddy's on holiday.'

'Da-dada,' said Jaden, and Amanda swallowed hard. Jaden wouldn't remember Gareth. All her child would have of his father were the photos and videos they'd made. She should get them saved properly for Jaden when he was older.

But first she'd have to wait until Gareth was officially missing and then dead.

What had James done with him?

# CHAPTER ELEVEN

**Thursday 22nd May**

Ella lifted her phone, catching sight of her reflection in the display. She was wearing a permanent grin these days. The adoption had been approved on Tuesday, so all being well Soraya would move into her new home within the next few weeks. Everything was coming right, and today was another huge landmark – her new daughter's first overnight stay. It was excellent timing as this was the half-term week, so there were no school restrictions. The little girl's last visit to St Ives had been cancelled because she had a bad cold, so Ella went to Redruth. She'd sat with a feverish, snuffling Soraya on her lap, reading a story about a dragon and thinking that next time she'd be able to do this in the comfort of her own home. It was happening, it was all coming right – she was to be a mother.

She called Mel to confirm the visit could go ahead, and was told Soraya was packing her bag already. Ella arranged to be there at eleven, and golly, when had she last been so excited? It would have been better if Rick could have taken the day off too, but the India contract was apparently about to hit another wobbly phase, so he was needed at work – bad timing, but there was nothing they could do about it. All Ella could hope was that the current uncertainty wouldn't make Rick nervous around Soraya. That could affect the entire atmosphere, and she wanted the first sleepover to be fun for them all. And now to tell Rick that the visit was definitely on.

As usual first thing in the morning, Rick was outside. He was obsessed with gardening at the moment, going out before work each day to make sure his seedlings in the shed had survived the night, and to lovingly water and fertilise them. It wasn't something he'd bothered about before. Maybe the new enthusiasm was because they'd soon have a child to nurture – Rick could be starting an 'Earth-father' stage in his life. Well, there was nothing wrong with home-grown vegetables.

'Pooh! It's a bit pongy in here,' she said, putting her head round the shed door.

Rick was hunched on a stool beside the tomato plants, staring into space. He leapt to his feet and glared at her. 'Haven't you heard of knocking before you come in?'

Ella's patience deserted her, and for a moment she stood there struggling. Knocking on a garden shed indeed. But if she snapped back, the day might be ruined, and that was the last thing she wanted. She drew a deep breath and instantly regretted it. That fertiliser smelled like nothing on earth.

'It's ten to eight; you'll be late for work if you're not quick. And good news, Soraya's much better this morning so the visit can go ahead.'

'Wonderful. And stop behaving like my mother.'

'There's an answer to that.' Ella stared round the shed. As well as tomato plants, Rick had courgette seedlings and tiny lettuces – but the smell couldn't be down to such miniature veggies. 'Rick, have you got something illegal in here? Because if you have, get rid of it. At least until the adoption's finalised.' She tried to keep her tone light, but privately she was beginning to wonder what was going on. Could he be growing wacky-baccy?

Rick sprayed water over the seedlings and she could see his hand shaking . 'Don't be so stupid. It's the bone meal you're smelling. It's good for the soil. Let's go.'

He chivvied her out of the shed and demonstratively double-locked the door behind them.

'Oh, for heaven's sake,' said Ella.

'There've been a few break-ins recently,' he said, jogging back indoors and lifting his briefcase. 'I'll see you tonight.'

Ella made an effort to put the scene in the shed behind her. This was an important day for them as prospective parents. 'Don't forget you're taking the Smart car today. And if you can get away a little earlier we could take Soraya to look at bedroom furniture.'

'Can't promise, so don't say anything to her. There's plenty of time for that, anyway.'

He left the house without kissing her goodbye, and Ella heaved a sigh of – yes, of relief. It had come to that. Her husband was so grumpy she was glad to see the back of him in the mornings.

With the weight of Rick's bad temper gone, Ella went to make sure everything was ready in Soraya's room, the grin back on her face. She was going to have a lovely time today no matter what.


Soraya was at the window when Ella drove up, still rather red of nose but much livelier than she'd been on Tuesday.

'Auntie Mel says you've got a surprise for me at your house,' she said, the moment Ella walked in the door.

Ella glanced at Mel, who mouthed 'Photo'.

'I certainly have,' said Ella. She had spent most of Sunday making a family album for Soraya, and it was waiting on the little girl's bed. 'Anything you want to do here before we head for home?'

Soraya shook her head, and Ella took her hand. Soraya knew they were to be a 'forever family', but Tuesday, when the child was so poorly, hadn't been the time for an in-depth talk about it. Ella had opened a bottle of Prosecco on Tuesday evening, but Rick was moody and the celebration of parenthood turned into a bit of an anti-climax.

Today would be different. Soraya had chosen the dinner menu – spaghetti bolognese followed by chocolate ice cream – and Ella bought a bottle of fizzy grape and elderflower which she had every intention of serving in her best crystal glasses. Soraya should know how special she was.

Back in St Ives, Ella made toasted cheese for lunch and then sat with Soraya to look through the photo album. The little girl was drooping now, and Ella abandoned her plan to go to the furniture store even if Rick was home in time. Fortunately, Soraya was fascinated by the photos.

'We might visit your gran and grandad in the summer

holidays,' said Ella, after telling Soraya about her parents' Yorkshire home. 'They're on holiday just now but as soon as they're home we'll Skype – they're dying to meet you.'

'What about Rick's parents?' said Soraya.

Ella hesitated. Should she encourage her almost-daughter to say 'Mummy' and 'Daddy'? But maybe that could wait till Soraya moved in. 'I'm afraid they both died when he was small,' she said. 'Look, here they are on their wedding day.'

'Why did they die?'

Soraya's eyes were huge, and Ella thought fast. She didn't want to encourage gloomy thoughts, but it was important to tell the truth.

'His mum had a very rare illness, and his dad had an accident with a tractor,' she replied. 'They were farmers, you see. He has a sister, your Aunt Marianne, but she lives far away in Shetland. Rick'll tell you more about them later.'

At four o'clock Rick breezed in ready to go furniture shopping, and wasn't pleased to hear the outing had been postponed. 'I wish you'd told me. I could have done with another hour at work.'

His tone was nothing but petulant, and Ella shut the kitchen door so that Soraya, watching children's television in the living room, didn't hear them.

'For heaven's sake pull yourself together,' she said bluntly. 'This is a special day for Soraya and she's not feeling a hundred per cent. You know the fuss you make when you have a cold. Why don't you go through and tell her about your side of the family? She's thrilled with her photo book.'

Rick poured a glass of whisky. 'Give me five minutes.'

In spite of Ella's apprehension Rick did pull himself together and dinner passed off very successfully. They toasted each other and the future, and then sat at the kitchen table playing Snakes and Ladders. When Soraya eventually managed to win a game Ella gathered the counters together.

'Let's walk along to the end of the road. The fresh air will help clear your nose, and we'll show you the park we can play in tomorrow. You can have a lovely smelly bubble bath when we get back.'

They were strolling along Cedar Road when Rick grabbed Ella's arm.

'That's Alan and Caro coming – don't mention the India thing, will you? Alan doesn't know all the ramifications. It's a bit complicated so just keep schtum about it.'

Ella could hardly believe her ears. Alan was Rick's boss and not knowing the ramifications didn't sound like him.

The other couple had been visiting Caro's sister, and they stood for a moment chatting about the area and about Soraya coming to stay. The little girl's face was one big beam and Ella hugged her. This was how she had always wanted to live. Out for a walk with her grumpy husband and beautiful daughter. Happiness spread through her like warm jam, sweet and comforting.

Alan clapped Rick on the back as they said goodbye. 'Good job business is booming, isn't it, with your new arrival,' he said, winking at Ella and Soraya. 'Don't worry, ladies, Rick'll be able to keep you in the manner you'd like to become accustomed to.'

Ella smiled automatically. How very odd, she thought,

glancing up at Rick as they all walked on. Alan seemed completely unaware of the India problem and Rick's fears about his job. Home again, she turned to Soraya. 'Bedtime – I'll read you a story, shall I? You go and choose a book, and I'll be up to run your bath in a minute.'

Soraya sped upstairs, and Ella opened the hall cupboard for a box of tissues to go beside the girl's bed. Rick, of course, had vanished into the shed. He'd barely spoken since they'd said goodbye to his boss. It was so strange, that remark of Alan's...

A sudden, shocking thought made Ella's stomach contract with fear. Maybe there was no complication with an India contract. It was the first time Rick had ever mentioned anything to do with an Asian side of the business; his designated area included factories in Memphis and Chicago. Could the India problem be a fabrication – something for Rick to hide behind because he wasn't happy about adopting Soraya? The more she thought about it, the more likely it sounded.

Sick at heart, Ella went upstairs.

# CHAPTER TWELVE

Thursday 22nd – Saturday 24th May

Amanda waited until late afternoon on Thursday before reporting Gareth missing. They were the longest three days of her life, but she'd supposedly seen him on Monday, and a grown man on a walking tour wouldn't necessarily report back home every night. People on mountains were supposed to leave details of where they were going and when they expected to arrive, but the same couldn't be said for hikers on the South West Coast Path, surely. And even if it could, well – Gareth hadn't done that and she hadn't expected him to.

She lifted her mobile, hesitating as she went through the details in her mind. What if they didn't believe her? But then – why on earth shouldn't they? Stomach churning, she punched out the number of the local police station.

'I – can you help me? I'm a bit worried about my husband. He's on a walking tour and he's not answering his phone.'

The policeman on the other end of the line was sympathetic. 'When did you last hear from him, love?'

Amanda gave the details, suddenly grateful to James for organising that Monday trip. She was able to sound completely convincing, because it was all true. Except, of course, for the minor detail that it hadn't been Gareth she'd driven to Lamorna Cove.

'Where was he going to stay on Monday night?'

They had planned this too. 'He was aiming for Marazion, but he hadn't booked anywhere in case he stayed longer in Penzance. He had a bivvy bag with him – he often sleeps outside if the weather's reasonable.'

'Right. Chances are he's just lost his phone, but you could come by the station, love, and report him missing. It would be good if you bring a photo of him too, in case we need it.'

Amanda had anticipated the request for a photo and even managed to find one of Gareth in his walking gear, complete with the red hat. She bundled Jaden into the car feeling completely unreal. Here she was, an ordinary, law-abiding person; she'd never had as much as a parking ticket, yet she had just lied to the police. She jabbed the key into the ignition, pain tightening across her forehead. This was going to be the real point of no return. Staring some police officer in the eye and lying her head off. For a moment Amanda leaned her head on the steering wheel. She'd never felt so bad about herself, not even when she and James started the affair. She wasn't a criminal; she was a mum, and pregnant at that – and now she was behaving like a character in a crime novel. It was as if she was two people – the woman telling all the lies, and the real Amanda, the one who was suffering.

Sergeant Jacobs, the uniformed policeman who

took the details at the station, was grave without being pessimistic. He listened to Amanda's story, asking more questions about Gareth's planned tour and what exactly had happened on Monday morning. Amanda could hear the convincing tremble in her voice as she told her story again, omitting only the detail that she'd swung by Mousehole and Penzance before driving home again. Jaden sat in his buggy staring at the man and sucking his thumb.

'We'll make enquiries along the route,' said Sergeant Jacobs. 'The photo of him in his hiking gear'll help.'

'His hair's very dark,' said Amanda. 'And his eyes are grey. Like my little boy's. You can't see on the photo but they're unusual – someone might remember them. And oh, he's allergic to penicillin. Just in case he's hurt when you find him.' Her voice tailed off. That was good; she'd sounded authentic there.

'But he's a good hiker?'

'Yes, he's very keen. He's done most of the trails, you know, the West Highland Way and the Pennine Way and the like.'

Sergeant Jacobs looked impressed. 'Right. Try not to worry. We'll be in touch.'

Amanda drove home in a dream. All she wanted to do was curl up and cry, but there was Jaden to look after; she should organise him a clean nappy and some food. What he really needed, of course, was his mummy and daddy happy together and looking after him, but she couldn't supply that; would never be able to supply that. Amanda changed him, putting him straight into pyjamas for an easy bedtime later, then made macaroni cheese for dinner. Jaden loved it and his little face was bright as he finger-picked his way through his portion. Amanda couldn't swallow a thing. Gareth and Jaden had shared so much love and the poor baby would never see his Da-dada again. Telling the police what had happened – no, what hadn't happened – made it seem abruptly and horrifyingly real. Gareth was gone.

Thinking of Gareth reminded her she would have to phone Susie and tell her about her son going missing. She should have done that before calling the police, actually. Amanda lifted her mobile, remembering that another thing she should have done was get a new mobile and destroy this one.

She shivered. The worst thing now was the isolation. Apart from these policemen and the neighbour she'd been careful to joke with on Monday evening, she hadn't spoken to another adult since she dropped James at Penzance. He'd made no effort to contact her – he'd said he wouldn't, but she hadn't realised how hard the solitude would be. Hesitantly, Amanda tried his number, but there was no reply. He could have already destroyed his mobile, in fact he probably had. Maybe the postman would bring a letter from him tomorrow. And now for Suze.

Not unnaturally, Susie was distraught to hear that Gareth was missing and Amanda cursed silently. She should have waited until Jaden was asleep to make this call.

'The police think he might have lost his mobile. They're making enquiries along the route, Suze, all we can hope is they'll find him sa – sa – safe and sound.'

Her voice was trembling; she could hardly speak for tears. She was lying to her mother-in-law, and it would go on, and on, until – what? Until the world accepted that Gareth had been washed out to sea, or until she was arrested for her crimes. Amanda closed her eyes, wishing with all her heart that Gareth could phone and tell her about the spectacular views he'd seen today and where he was going to sleep. But the voice in her ear was Susie's.

'Call me the minute you hear anything. If there's no news tomorrow I'll come down and wait with you.'

Susie rang off abruptly and Amanda hefted her phone. If she chucked it into a bowl of water today she'd be isolated from the world until she got another. It might be best to wait until tomorrow. Meanwhile, she would prepare for the inconvenience by listing her contacts. Sometimes it was better just to concentrate on the job in hand.

It was eleven o'clock the next morning before she heard from the police. Sergeant Jacobs arrived with a female officer, and for a macabre moment Amanda wondered if this was because they had bad news. But they couldn't possibly have found Gareth so there couldn't be much news.

They sat down in the living room and Sergeant Jacobs came straight to the point. 'We haven't found your husband yet, Mrs Waters, but there are several people who saw him on Monday morning. The owners of the café where you had coffee remember you all, and so does the chap at the kiosk next door. And that's down to you, young man,' he said to Jaden, who was on Amanda's knee. 'We sent WPC Campbell here along the first segment of the path and she came across this.'

The WPC opened a bag and produced Gareth's red hat, wrapped in plastic and looking soggy and grubby. Amanda clasped her hands to her mouth and gaped at the hat. What should she say, what would the correct response be?

She reached out and took the package, pretending to examine it closely, her brain racing. 'Oh no. It's his. His mum made it for him. Oh no.' Her voice was shaking, good.

'Don't panic.' Sergeant Jacob's voice was kind. 'By itself, this may not mean much. Monday was a mild day, it could be that he took it off and then dropped it. But in view of this we're going to extend the search.'

'What does that mean?' Her voice was afraid, entirely appropriate. He didn't know she was terrified of being sent to prison for pushing her husband to his accidental death. And how scary it was that she didn't even have to act now.

'We'll search the coastline, use boats where possible, co-ordinate with the coastguards. And we'll increase our efforts to find where he might have slept on Monday night.' He stood up. 'Remember there's still no evidence he's come to any harm. Let's wait and see what happens. Someone will come by tomorrow. Is there anybody you could contact to be with you?'

'My mother-in-law's coming down from Glasgow.'

The officers let themselves out, and Amanda grabbed

Jaden and sobbed into his neck. She was allowed to be distraught now, and soon she'd be able to grieve, and thank God for that, because grieving was way too mild a word for the emotion she felt. And now she'd better phone Susie before destroying her mobile.

Susie sounded calm, but Amanda knew she'd be anything but. Gareth's mother was never one to wear her heart on her sleeve.

'I'll come down as soon as I can,' she said. 'If I can't get a flight to Newquay I'll fly to London and get the train out west.'

'Thanks, Suze,' Amanda managed, realising she didn't sound at all grateful – but then under the circumstances she didn't need to. She ended the call and stared at her phone. Time to wreak some destruction, and one thing she'd learned from Monday was that a dress rehearsal made an explanation sound a lot more convincing.

'Jaden, come to Mummy, sweetheart.' She swept him up and carried him upstairs to the bathroom. 'Drop Mummy's phone in the loo, sweetie.'

Jaden didn't need to be told twice. Amanda's mobile plopped into the blue water and sank.


Going into town for a new phone felt reassuringly normal. The man in the shop was sympathetic when she told him what had happened, and told her about his sister who'd dropped hers the previous Sunday while she was leaning over a bridge at the Eden Project. On the way home Amanda went into a supermarket she didn't normally use to stock up for Susie's visit. It was better to avoid her local

95

store where she'd meet half the neighbourhood and have to tell them about Gareth's disappearance. Buying food reminded Amanda she hadn't eaten anything proper for days, and she rubbed her middle uneasily. That wouldn't be good for the baby. She should be more careful.

Back home, she spent the rest of the afternoon getting to know her new phone and texting people with the number. Doing this reminded her of the laptop, and when Jaden was in bed she sat down with it and opened both her own and Gareth's email accounts. Thank goodness she knew his password. A check through their inboxes and various folders revealed nothing incriminating and Amanda sat back, exhausted. She lifted the glossy mag she'd splashed out on the week before, but there was no way she could read inconsequential gossip. Gareth was dead and she was alive... Amanda closed her eyes, fighting to keep control. When she looked down again, she had torn the front of the magazine into shreds. Take the guilt to bed, Amanda.

Tomorrow would be busy. She would have to contact people and tell them Gareth was missing, not least of all her own parents in Barcelona. She should have done that before now. It was so difficult to know what the normal reaction to mislaying your husband might be, but she could make her father's heart condition the excuse for not worrying them sooner. And Susie would arrive, hoping her boy would be found safe. For a long time Amanda lay awake, thinking of the child she had been and the adult she had become. When was all this going to end?

The following morning Amanda stood buttoning a fresh cover on the duvet in her own room, hoping Susie would accept the story that Jaden was sleeping badly and needed his mother's company at night. Suze would arrive that afternoon, and there would be no peace until she went back home again. It would be acting all the time. Amanda heard a car draw up outside – oh hell, the acting wasn't only for Suze. Sergeant Jacob and the same WPC walked up the path, and to Amanda's dismay the sergeant's face was rigid. There was little sign of the comforting presence today.

Heart thumping, Amanda showed them into the living room, where Jaden was playing with his bricks.

'Mrs Baxter, I have some news for you and I'm afraid it's not very good,' said the sergeant, sinking heavily into the sofa.

Amanda was relieved to hear nothing but kindness in his voice. Whatever had happened, they didn't suspect her. She stared, feeling that no response was best.

'We've found a rucksack washed up further round the coast from Lamorna, and in one of the inside pockets there's a discount card for a sports shop in Newquay, in your husband's name. No other contents. The flap was open.'

He paused, and Amanda gaped at him. She'd had no idea about the card but thank goodness it had been there – it had identified the rucksack as Gareth's.

The sergeant continued. 'We've also heard from a hiker who saw a man answering to your husband's description on the coastal path between Lamorna and Mousehole. He wasn't wearing his hat and the witness said he looked a bit hot and bothered, but he's pretty sure it was the man on the photo.'

Amanda breathed out. It was going to work. Thank God James and Gareth were – had been – so similar in appearance. *You should never have started this*, a voice whispered in her head, and it was true – but they had started, and for Jaden's sake she had to carry on with the subterfuge. She forced her attention back to Sergeant Jacobs.

'I'm sorry, Mrs Baxter, but this could mean that he fell into the sea at some point. That section of the walk is challenging. But I'm afraid there's more. A different witness has come forward with a sighting in a gent's toilet at Mousehole.'

He leaned forward. 'This means we have two scenarios to investigate. One is that your husband fell into the sea between Lamorna and Mousehole.'

Amanda's hands were shaking. They were buying Gareth's drowning; James had been right. She swallowed, feeling her heart beating uncomfortably; she could hear the *lub-dub lub-dub* in her ears. She clasped her hands together hard. What the hell was the second scenario?

Sergeant Jacobs face was grim. 'Falling into the sea doesn't fit in with the second sighting at Mousehole, however, because the next stretch of path is relatively easy and it's unlikely he would fall there. But there's another possibility – your husband could have vanished voluntarily. Maybe he wanted to disappear.'

Shock jerked through Amanda and she sat straight. The thought had never entered her head. Who was he to say that Gareth would leave her like that?

'No. That can't be. He would never have – he would never do that.'

'Has he been worried about anything recently?'

'He's had a very stressful time at work but he's finished that job and he's due to start a new one in June.' She could hear the indignation in her voice. In other circumstances this would have been laughable.

'I'm sorry but I have to ask – is your relationship all right?'

Her teeth began to chatter and her fingers fluttered against cold lips. This was a line of enquiry that neither she nor James had anticipated. 'We're fine. I found out last week that I'm pregnant, that's how fine we are!'

Amanda leaned forward, head almost touching her knees, and began to sob completely genuine tears.

# CHAPTER THIRTEEN

Monday 26th – Tuesday 27th May

The first adoption meeting of the week was sobering – Soraya's school teacher was present to give her account of the girl's school life. According to Ms Landon, Soraya was alternately dreamy and disruptive in class, which meant she was behind in every area of her education.

'She has problems concentrating in a classroom environment,' said the teacher. 'She's a lovely kiddie when you get her in the right mood, but there are nineteen other children in the class. Even with an assistant I can't give her as much individual attention as she needs.'

Ella thought of the child who had sat on her knee listening to stories. 'She works well when she does have individual attention though?'

'Yes – she's obviously intelligent, but she needs something we can't give her enough of. I feel an assessment by a medical expert might be a good next step. She may need medication of some kind. It's something for you to keep in mind.'

Privately, Ella thought that medication was a long way down the line. There didn't seem much point medicating a child with concentration problems which weren't in evidence when she had the right kind of attention. Soraya *could* concentrate; what she needed was help to do this in the noisier environment of a classroom.

The following evening's meeting was to discuss the timing of the next few weeks.

'She loves going to Ella and Rick's,' said Mel to the assembled group of social workers and adoption society workers. 'I don't see any reason why she shouldn't move in quite quickly. Maybe a weekend visit first, and then we can look at the permanent move happening at the end of the week after?'

Ella couldn't stop the smile spreading across her face. Her dream was coming true, at last, at last. 'Sounds great. What would I do about school?'

'You can enroll her at your local school as soon as we have a date for the permanent move. I'd keep her at home for a day or two, then send her for the last few weeks of term,' said Liz. 'She'll get to know the other kids and also have an idea what to expect after the holidays.'

Ella nodded. She smiled up at Rick, who was pulling at his collar as if he was too hot. He hadn't said much at either meeting, but Ella hadn't dared ask him more about the supposed Indian contract. It was horrible, not knowing if he was lying about it, but prodding would only antagonise him. And apart from his silence, which no one else knew wasn't typical, nothing about his behaviour tonight was suggesting that he didn't want to adopt Soraya. Ella took a deep breath, trying not to let her uncertainty show. She was being silly; Rick had assured her he was happy to wait for a son. He'd even pointed out there were no guarantees about the sex of your baby when it entered the family in the usual way.

Ella leaned back as Rick drove home through darkening streets. Two meetings in two days had been tough. And it was difficult not to feel daunted about what was in front of them – a change of school for a six-year-old with concentration problems might not be the easiest part of the adoption. It might be an idea to have a quiet word with the new teacher when they enrolled Soraya. Rick pulled up in their driveway, and Ella jumped in surprise. She'd been so engrossed in her thoughts she hadn't noticed they were home.

'Glass of wine? To celebrate our last week as a twosome?' she suggested.

Rick nodded. 'Be with you in a bit.'

He wandered off up the garden, and Ella fought down impatience – yet again. That bloody shed was turning into Rick's sanctuary from whatever he was trying to avoid. Like her – and Soraya.

She opened the bottle of Sauvignon Blanc she'd put in the fridge and poured a large glass, then sank into a kitchen chair, elbows propped on the table, head in hands. If Liz and the others in the adoption team thought Rick wasn't one hundred per cent enthusiastic about Soraya's placement it could slow the whole thing down. Worst case, they wouldn't get her. Fear took the place of Ella's impatience. That mustn't happen. The connection between her and Soraya was very real; nothing should endanger their burgeoning mother-daughter bond.

She managed to swallow her fear when Rick came in five minutes later. Be nice, Ella, be fun, keep him happy. They sat in the kitchen drinking too much wine and planning the next day's outing with Soraya, when they would pick her up after school and take her for pizza. Then there would be the weekend visit when Soraya would stay over both on Friday and Saturday night, and then – it wouldn't be long before she was home full time.

Ella gave herself a shake. She and Rick would have to get things back to normal; secrecy had never been a part of their relationship before they'd begun this process.

'Rick – what's happening with your job?' she said as he emptied the bottle into their glasses. The question came straight from her gut.

His eyes met hers. 'Don't worry. Things'll be critical for a week or two but then we should be on top of it.' He lifted his glass. 'You know, we should knock through this wall and make a big kitchen/dining room, a family room. Then we can keep the living room to be civilised in.'

Ella sipped her wine. He was changing the subject. But least said, soonest mended did work sometimes, and a kitchen conversion wasn't a bad idea. They sat planning till nearly midnight, when Ella went up to bed, expecting Rick to follow. But a few minutes later she heard the kitchen door close. Rick had gone out to the shed.

# CHAPTER FOURTEEN

Wednesday 28th May

When Ella awoke on Wednesday morning – with a headache – Rick had already gone. She sat in the kitchen nursing a coffee and waiting for the paracetamol to work. That would teach her to drink half a bottle of wine the day before an important outing. At least she was only working for a few hours this afternoon, and by the end of the week she'd be a full-time mum. Hallelujah.

She smiled, remembering Soraya's pleasure when they'd suggested going for pizza. 'A celebration, now that you're to be part of the family,' Ella told her new daughter. The little girl's face shone, and Ella's heart melted yet again. If only Rick would share the fun.

Thinking about him was sobering. Last night had been the first time she could remember when they hadn't said goodnight properly. She couldn't imagine why he'd go out to the shed so late, unless it was to avoid her.

She leaned across for her phone on the work surface. It wouldn't hurt to call and touch base. She put the call through, jumping when Rick's mobile trilled upstairs. Ha – his head must be in a similar state to hers. Maybe he'd appreciate it if she dropped his phone off – she'd call his office landline and ask.

Alan answered the phone and chuckled when she asked for Rick. 'You've got your days mixed up – he's not in today. He'll have gone fishing and left his phone at home on purpose.'

Ella's head reeled – not at work? What was going on? Or – was Rick planning some kind of surprise for her? Or for Soraya – a swing set, maybe. But what had Alan meant by…

'Days mixed up?'

His reply shook her entire world. 'It's Wednesday, remember? I suppose he'll go back to working full-time when you get Soraya?'

'Ah – um, not sure. Don't mention I called, will you, Alan? You know what a tease he can be. I'd never hear the end of it.'

Trembling, Ella put the phone down. So Rick was working part-time. The dodgy contract might mean there wasn't enough work for him. But Alan had sounded as if Rick had chosen not to work full time. Why hadn't he talked this over with her – and just where exactly had he been every Wednesday? Was it the only day he had off?

Making a split second decision, Ella pushed her coffee mug away and rummaged in the cutlery drawer for the spare shed key. Two minutes later, she was staring at the tomato plants, which were growing like mad – tomatoes and everything. Surely they must need more light than they had here. She glanced round but there were no books or pamphlets or anything giving information about tomatoes. In fact, she realised, examining the shed more carefully, there was nothing here that explained Rick's fascination with the place. A shelf of plants under one window and a worktable under the other, a blue plastic tub with the larger tools, and an old bookcase with an assortment of miscellaneous items – what on earth did Rick do all the time he spent here? Looking after the plants wouldn't take more than a couple of minutes a day. The place was still smelly, too, the bag of bone meal under the shelf was responsible for that, but otherwise it was nothing more than a dull, boring shed. Ella switched on the radio on the worktable, surprised when a local station boomed into the shed, discussing safety measures on coastal paths. Rick rarely listened to the radio, and when he did it was Radio Four.

She moved away, grabbing the table when the floor wobbled beneath her feet. The wooden slabs were muddy, too, after this week's rain. She reached for the broom, then stopped. It wasn't that the shed was Rick's private place, but he might not like to think she'd been poking round here. And if she'd been expecting to find a marijuana factory she was disappointed. Maybe Rick simply felt the need for a place to potter – a man-thing, perhaps. Keep him sweet, Ella.

When Rick arrived home at five he seemed as usual, kissing her quickly before going upstairs to change. Ella's mood plummeted – why couldn't he have arrived with a swing set or some other reason for taking a day off work? Of course it wasn't just the one day… She clutched her handbag to her middle. She wouldn't say anything yet. That would ruin the evening, and she needed more time to think. Whatever happened, whatever Rick was doing, it mustn't endanger the adoption.

As usual, Soraya was waiting for them at the window. Ella tried to hug the little girl when she opened the door, but Soraya wriggled away, running to fetch her jacket.

'She's a bit jittery,' said Mel. 'That probably won't change until she's moved in with you and feels safe in her forever home. For the moment we'll need to be patient with her.'

Ella nodded. It would take time, but they had that, and Soraya was certainly happy about becoming their daughter. But happiness didn't always equal trust.


'Can I have pizza with pineapple?' Soraya ran to a table by the window.

Ella saw Rick frown. Oh dear, maybe they should have gone for a hamburger or something in a more child-friendly location. Rick had chosen this restaurant, a traditional pizzeria near Chiverton, and there wasn't a single other child in the room.

The waiter swept up. *'Si, si, signorina. Prego.'* He patted Soraya's head and produced a large cushion for her to sit on, pushed Ella's chair underneath her, and went for menus. Ella's apprehension vanished.

Sheer joy spread through her. Here they were, a family of three; the two of them were *out for a meal with their child*. It was intoxicating. She had dreamed of this for so long, and now it was happening.

And it was fun, this being a family – a completely new kind of fun. Soraya's eyes lit up when the waiter brought her a paper place mat and a box of crayons. She sat colouring the beach scene, giving the waiter a gappy smile when he complimented her on her artwork. Ella felt her beam stretch, heavens, she was turning into one of those besotted mothers. Rick raised his eyebrows at her and she patted his hand. Forget the bad stuff, Ella, just for a little while. This was an important first in their lives.

She relaxed too soon, however. Ella's happiness fizzled away when Soraya, pizza eaten, started to wander round the restaurant, only giggling when Rick called her back. The waiter saved the situation by allowing her to help him lay tables, and then brought her a tub of ice cream when Ella and Rick had finished their own meal. Rick's mouth was tense.

'It's okay,' said Ella, putting her hand on his sleeve. 'Nobody's upset. Good choice of restaurant.'

'Rewarding disobedience isn't the best way to deal with it,' he said. 'Let's get the bill and go.'

Ella opened her mouth to tell him not to be so stuffy, then closed it again. A busy restaurant wasn't the best place to discuss parenting – but wasn't it brilliant that they had parenting issues to discuss? Not to mention job issues... Ah well. The glitter was gone, but it had been a lovely evening and it wasn't over yet.

'I want to go to the swings,' said Soraya, standing up.

They'd passed a swing park on the way to the restaurant, and Ella put her hand on the girl's shoulder, thinking wryly that they should agree to requests that didn't cost anything. It would be iPads and the like soon enough.

'Sit right there until we've paid the bill, and then we'll

stop at the swings for fifteen minutes,' she said.

Soraya squinted at her, then sat down and started to colour her place mat again, an angelic expression on her face.

'She'll test us, but we have to be prepared for that,' said Ella later, as they stood watching Soraya on the climbing frame.

Rick shuffled his feet. 'You're better with her. I just get mad.'

'Remember what Liz said last night? Don't take disobedience as a personal insult. She's looking for stability, and we can give her that.'

He shrugged, and Ella bit her lip. Having a child was a huge change in anyone's life. They had to talk about it. This non-communication on Rick's part was baffling.

'Look at me!' Soraya was at the top of the frame now, standing on a platform, arms stretched to the heavens.

'Hold on!' Rick's call echoed Ella's, and she pulled a face at him. Parenting wasn't so easy. They couldn't protect Soraya twenty-four-seven – what a scary thought. Ella stood grappling with the thought that she'd never have true peace of mind unless her girl was beside her on the sofa reading a book.

'Let's go on the roundabout to finish up!' she called, and Soraya clambered down.

Even the roundabout was tricky. Rick had the job of pushing it, and Ella clung to the iron bars while the world circled and her brain went into shock. How many years was it since she'd done this? But maybe she'd get used to it...

'Faster!' shrieked Soraya, and Rick complied.

'Whoa! Time to go, you're too good at this,' said Ella, jumping off.

Soraya wanted another go, and Ella watched the joy on her new daughter's face as Rick pushed her round. On the way back to the car Soraya took a hand of each of them, and Ella hugged the sensation to her heart. This was real. She was a mother.

On the way back to Redruth they all chatted about next Saturday's visit to the beach, and Ella was allowed to hug Soraya goodbye. And roll on the day when she didn't have to return her child for another woman to put to bed.

'We're going to be permanently exhausted until we all settle down together,' she said as they approached St Ives. Last night's wine and late bedtime had taken their toll; all she wanted to do was sleep.

Rick's reply was like a knife in her back. 'You will, maybe. My work does a pretty good job of exhausting me. I shouldn't think I'll notice the difference.'

He pulled up in the driveway, and tonight Ella wasn't surprised when he went straight to the shed.

# Chapter Fifteen

Wednesday 28th – Thursday 29th May

'I suppose I'd better finish packing,' said Susie, lifting her handbag and trailing over to the door where she turned and gave Amanda a look that was unadulterated misery. 'I wish I didn't have to leave you, hen. But I'll be back, don't worry.'

Amanda nodded, searching for words and inwardly blessing the fact that Suze was doing wedding hair-dos for a friend's daughter tomorrow and didn't want to let them down, even with her son missing.

The visit had been difficult to say the least. Amanda's mind screamed in silent horror every time her mother-in-law looked at her with Gareth's slate-coloured eyes, clouded in grief and fear. If only she'd never met James. If only she hadn't been so shallow as to start an affair. If only she'd never got pregnant. But she had done all these things and they were crushing her.

It wasn't that Susie was suspicious. She didn't see the guilt mixed in with Amanda's grief, and when she heard about the expected baby she rose to the occasion with grim determination. The house was spring-cleaned from top to bottom, Jaden was taken shopping and kitted out with more summer clothes than he'd have hot days to wear them on, and the freezer was filled with healthy homemade meals. Susie even sandpapered and revarnished the wardrobe door where the mirror had been, accepting Amanda's explanation that she'd slammed it too hard one day.

Amanda forced herself to reply. 'You've been brilliant, Suze. I can never thank you enough.'

It only made things worse. Susie dropped her bag and came to hug Amanda, her body shaking with sobs. Amanda hugged back. She had done this. She had allowed a load of trivia to come between her and Gareth and he had paid with his life. If she'd remembered what a great guy her husband was – had been – everything would be different now. Longing for the old life swept through Amanda, and for a moment she and Susie sobbed together. And it was so great, having someone to cry with – but if Susie knew what had really happened, she'd be out that door and on her way to the police station to report Amanda and James, and then she'd be back for Jaden. Amanda retched.

'Oh, I'm sorry, hen – this isn't what you need. I'll make you a cup of tea, plenty of time before we have to leave for the airport.'

Amanda leaned back on the sofa, her head thumping. None of this was going to go away. She'd be alone with her guilt for the rest of her days.

'Bye-bye-bye!' Jaden waved as Susie vanished through the doors, and Amanda slumped. Thank God.

'Na-nana,' said Jaden.

Amanda pulled herself together. 'Nana's gone home, sweetheart. We'll watch her plane take off, shall we – and then we'll go home too.'

And oh, she could relax at home without pretending and lying, now. After four days of healthy meals Amanda felt better physically, but her mind was in a very dark place. It was good to be alone again.

Jaden's eyes were glassy as they drove down the A30. Amanda glanced at him in the baby mirror and cursed. This wasn't a good time for a nap. She wanted to get him home, bathed and into bed and asleep by nine. She should stop and let him run around for a bit. At Chiverton, the opportunity arose and Amanda turned into a parking area beside a small swing park, where about a dozen children and a few adults were spending some time.

And – for a moment she couldn't believe her eyes.

It was James.

She sat in the car, her mouth hanging open as he stood talking to a slim, blonde woman while a dark-haired little girl clambered around the climbing frame. The child looked about five or six, and she turned round every so often and waved to James and the woman. What the hell was going on? Amanda thumped the steering wheel. As if it wasn't perfectly clear what was going on. He was married. He must be. The girl's hair was exactly like James'. He was a married man having a sordid little affair and she had been every kind of idiot. Her baby would be nothing but an inconvenience to him. *Shit*. It was so obvious now; this was why the promised letter and phone number had never arrived. He had dumped her. Nice one, James. He had left her alone with her guilt and her children, not knowing where he'd disposed of her husband.

Amanda couldn't tear her eyes from the little family scene playing out in front of her. It was as if she was staring through a tunnel, darkness surrounding the picture in the centre. The woman called the child, who dropped to the ground and ran over to her parents. After a brief chat the woman and the little girl sat on the roundabout, which James set in motion. Briefly, he turned his head in Amanda's direction and she ducked below the steering wheel, but at this distance he was unlikely to notice her in her car. Next time she looked the child was alone on the roundabout, the woman staring at her, happiness shining from her face. And why wouldn't she be happy? She had James, the perfect, good-looking husband, and a lovely little girl. Tears trickled down Amanda's cheeks and she searched through her bag for a tissue, then slid the car into reverse and left.

Jaden gurgled, and Amanda blew him a kiss. Thank goodness for Jaden, with his grey eyes full of happiness and love. Just like Gareth's had been, once upon a time. Amanda gripped the wheel and turned back into the main road. Act on, woman, you've had plenty of practice. You can do this.

They were halfway back to St Ives before she realised that the clever thing would have been to wait in the car park until James and his wife left, and then follow them. Amanda cursed silently. Talk about having a good idea too late. What she could do, though, was go to James' flat in Hayle; they were passing by anyway. But it wouldn't be where he lived... It wasn't home to a small girl, anyway.

Somehow Amanda wasn't surprised to see James' name gone from the bell push outside. She pressed the neighbour's bell and a woman in her early twenties leaned out of a first floor window.

'He's gone to London, I think,' she said, blowing cigarette smoke towards Amanda. 'That's what he said, anyway.' More smoke, and a pitying glance, and the window was banged shut again.

Amanda drove on towards St Ives. James wasn't in London, he was right here in Cornwall, and he had a wife and a little girl. Sickness that had nothing to do with pregnancy rose in Amanda's throat. He had used her. It was all so obvious now. What a fool she was.


She awoke the next morning to the usual nausea, mixed with relief that no pretending to Susie was necessary today. She'd have to get organised. Without a death certificate there would be no life insurance, and presumably no widow's pension. What were they going to live on? She'd be able to get some kind of benefits to tide her over, but that was a very short term solution; she had no intention of living the rest of her life on the social.

Determination filled Amanda as she thought of James, standing there in the play park, a smug, satisfied look on his face – well, maybe not that, but he must be feeling smug about getting rid of her so successfully. But she wouldn't let him beat her. She could take on secretarial work – something she could do at home. She would go to the Citizens' Advice Bureau today. And she would call in at the police station, check that nothing new had come in – which was hardly likely but it would be the normal thing to keep checking, wouldn't it? As soon as she thought this a lump came into her throat. The real Amanda was sometimes very far away; it was disorientating. She didn't know who she was any more and it was all James' fault.

Slowly, she got up, made tea and waited for the nausea to subside. Thankfully, this pregnancy was easier than her first. She should make an appointment at the clinic and get her 12-week scan scheduled. There would be no Daddy by her side this time, oh no, Gareth...

Eleven o'clock saw her pushing Jaden through town, having collected a handful of leaflets about jobseekers and working from home. So far, so good. Now to make them a nice healthy lunch. Amanda went into the baker's for a loaf of crusty bread to go with Susie's vegetable soup, rushing out again when her phone rang. As soon as she saw the caller ID her heart started racing. It was the police.

Sergeant Jacob's voice was calm. 'Amanda, we need you to look at something and see if you can identify it. Can you come here this afternoon – or should I send someone to get you?'

Amanda thought swiftly. If Gareth really had disappeared, the first thing she'd ask would be...

'Have you found him? Where - ?'

'No, no. It's an item of clothing.'

Clothing? Careful, careful. 'Oh no. I'll come this afternoon after Jaden's nap.'

'That will be fine. See you later.'

Amanda's head was reeling as she heated the soup then sat at the table helping Jaden to use a spoon. An item of clothing could be a jacket, or possibly trousers, or a pullover. The sea had a cruel trick of unclothing its victims. James had dumped the jacket into the sea with the rucksack, but what about the rest of his clothes as 'Gareth'? Amanda massaged her head; think, woman. The jeans had been James' own, so these couldn't have been found... His pullover? Had he been wearing one?

She sat there worrying until she realised her mistake and almost laughed at her own stupidity. Gareth hadn't walked along the coastal path and fallen into the sea, so any clothing found, apart from the jacket, couldn't be his. And how scary it was that the scenario she was acting out had become so real...

She was halfway to the police station when a truly horrific thought blasted into her head. What if the item *was* Gareth's? James could have dumped Gareth in the ocean without telling her.

By the time she arrived at the police station Amanda was genuinely distraught. She pushed Jaden inside, hearing her voice tremble when she told the officer at the desk her name and why she had come.

She was expected; that was clear. 'Right, Mrs Waters, follow me.'

He showed her into an interview room and left. Amanda sat down to wait. Jaden was staring in fascination at the LED lamps in the ceiling, sucking his thumb vigorously. She could only hope he didn't understand; poor baby, she was about to talk about what his father had been wearing before he died – no, stupid. Before he disappeared. She must get this right, a mistake could be fatal for them all. She began to tremble.

Sergeant Jacobs took one look at her and sent for tea. 'I know it's hard on you, but there's nothing to say whether Gareth fell into the sea or disappeared voluntarily. It's still early days.'

He sat opposite her, an officer she didn't know beside him. 'Amanda, from the condition of the found item we feel it won't be Gareth's, but it isn't impossible. So to rule it out we want to go over again what Gareth was wearing when you left him.'

Amanda froze. They were trying to trick her. This was a test, and for the life of her she couldn't remember what she'd said about Gareth's clothes.

She managed to burst into tears. 'I can't remember! I've thought and thought and I just don't know any more!'

Her tea arrived and she sipped, her teeth chattering against the thick white porcelain. Sergeant Jacobs pulled out a plastic parcel containing a blue cotton pullover.

'Is this Gareth's?'

Blackness loomed in front of Amanda's eyes. Gareth did have a very similar pullover, as did thousands of others who shopped in chain stores up and down the country.

Her voice came out in a whisper. 'I don't know. He did have one like that.'

As soon as the words were spoken she realised. She'd used the past tense, she'd said 'did'. Was it normal to talk about your missing husband using the past tense? Had they noticed?

Sergeant Jacob's voice was neutral when he spoke. 'We'll drive back with you and have a look at his things, then.'

In a dream, Amanda followed the young WPC, pushing Jaden's buggy back through the police station, Sergeant Jacob following on behind. Jaden clapped when she got into the back of the car with him – did they keep baby seats especially for such eventualities? Neither officer spoke during the short drive back home, and Amanda sat shaking. They would go upstairs and they would see the bedroom, see the wardrobe. Suze had done a brilliant job on it but it was obvious something violent had happened to it recently. Amanda twisted the strap of her bag round her finger. Would she get out of this without incriminating herself? And James, damn him – he was right out of it now.

'What's this?' The discolouration on the wardrobe door attracted Sergeant Jacob's attention the minute he set foot in the bedroom.

'We had a mirror from the DIY shop stuck there, but it was loose so we took it off a couple of weeks ago, in case Jaden...'

Amanda walked across the room and opened the middle drawer where Gareth's pullovers were. The woman officer pulled on gloves and lifted piles of clothing. Amanda choked back a sob. The Aran sweater Suze had knitted Gareth last year, the stupid Rudolph sweatshirt he'd always worn at Christmas, the black polo neck she'd bought him in the January sales... but no blue pullover came to light.

Amanda blinked. She watched as the search continued

through the remainder of the chest of drawers and then shifted to the wardrobe where her own things were... and still no sign of Gareth's chain store pullover. Where the hell was it? The answer hit her like a ton of bricks. He'd been wearing it that day. The blue pullover was *on Gareth*, so she had no idea where it was... How could she have forgotten?

'Don't you – don't you need a search warrant to do this?' she asked as the policewoman closed her underwear drawer. This was unbearable.

Sergeant Jacobs looked at her. 'We've seen enough. You're sure he had a pullover like that?'

Amanda nodded. 'There are photos on Facebook of him wearing it.'

'Right. This does make it seem more likely that Gareth fell into the sea, Amanda. I'm sorry. We'll continue investigating and get back to you in a day or so.'

He still sounded neutral and Amanda saw the glance he exchanged with the WPC.

She did the only thing she could think of. 'This is so horrible!' She clutched both hands to her head and dropped to her knees on the floor, more or less where Gareth had lain. 'Please, please find my husband, oh please... he can't be dead! I need him, he must come home... He – he doesn't even know I'm pregnant!'

Rocking back and forth, she sobbed loudly.

And the look on his face was once again kind and fatherly.

# PART TWO
# THE FAMILY

# CHAPTER ONE

Wednesday 11th June

Rick jogged along the sea front, the late afternoon sun hot on his back, a stark contrast to the stiff breeze he was running against. Thank God he was working full-time again. There was so much else to worry about at the moment – he didn't need financial problems as well.

Frustration welled up inside him. What an unbelievable fool he'd been. Bad enough that he'd had an affair, he had to go and compound his sins by giving up work for a day and a half each week to give him more time to spend with his mistress. Not to mention splashing out way too much of his reduced wage to rent an old mate's holiday flat to give them somewhere to go when Amanda could get away. He'd been infatuated – she was so bright, with a sparky sense of humour and a refreshing, down-to-earth view of the world. Life with Ella had long-since disintegrated into a never-ending round of 'how to be a parent' discussions and activities. But he should never have started anything with Amanda; all it had brought them was grief. And that was before he started thinking about the Gareth situation.

And that was hopeless. Dire. Guilt about not contacting Amanda hit him every night as soon as he closed his eyes, and at regular intervals during the day too. His behaviour was the pits. But that wasn't even the worst part, no, the worst part was the shed. It stood there in the middle of the garden, mocking him, look what a nice big shed I am, a *chalet*, really, you were so pleased to have me and so was Ella. That was in the days when they thought they'd soon have a couple of kiddies running round, playing in the garden chalet. Now it had crumbled into an over-large glory-hole and he hated it because underneath it all was Gareth.

Bile rose in Rick's throat as he forced his legs on. Last week he'd seen a news item about a guy who'd killed someone by accident. He'd been convicted of manslaughter and given a suspended sentence. In a horrible, gut-wrenching way this had made Rick feel both better and worse – he and Amanda had done something wrong, and a man had lost his life – but it had been an accident. The problem was, by panicking and covering it up they had turned an accident into a crime.

In any case, even a manslaughter conviction would mean he and Ella wouldn't be allowed to adopt, and that would have crushed his wife. So although he'd done it for the wrong reason, the subterfuge was necessary. Because he wanted to stay with Ella... didn't he? Tears stung in his eyes. What he wanted was the old Ella back, the one with a sense of humour who'd been ready to have some fun.

Rick came to the traffic lights and turned up the hill for home. This was the tough part of his run, something he looked forward now to with a kind of masochistic determination that hadn't been part of his character before Gareth's death.

The other worst thing was – you could have any number of worst things, he knew that now – he missed Amanda. She had provided everything that was missing in his marriage – light-hearted fun, laughter, and uncomplicated sex, and he hadn't wanted to hurt her.

The hill became steeper and Rick slowed down. Two more minutes and he'd be home. He could do this; he was strong. He passed a woman pushing a pair of tousle-headed toddlers in a twin buggy, and turned into Cedar Road. He *did* want a child. If it hadn't been for all the bad stuff he'd be happy enough about Soraya. She wasn't a boy, but they could get a brother for her next time and she was a nice little thing when she wasn't being bloody minded. He wanted to do this right, he did, he did. But poor Amanda... there was no 'right' about that.

Ella and Soraya were painting a small wooden table on the side grass when he panted through the gate. A lump rose in his throat. Ella had a streak of yellow paint across her forehead and the happiest expression for years on her face. Having a live-in and soon-to-be-formally-adopted daughter agreed with her. How long was it since he'd been able to put an expression like that on her face?

'Good run? When do you want dinner?'

Rick flopped down on the grass. 'Goodish. Let me grab a shower once I've cooled down.'

Ella straightened up and surveyed their work, then took Soraya's paintbrush. 'No problem, it's spag bol. As requested by her ladyship. That looks great, sweetheart

– we'll leave it here to dry before it goes up to your room. You can help me make dinner while Daddy's freshening up.'

Soraya came over to Rick and sniffed. 'Pooh! You pong!'

'So would you if you'd just run ten K!'

He seized the child and tickled her, amazed he was managing to do such a daddy-like thing, feeling like this. Soraya shrieked, twisted from his grasp and ran inside, giggling.

Rick wandered round to the back garden. The shed sneered at him and he glowered at it. He'd been terrified there would be a smell, even after Gareth was safely underground. And even more terrified Ella would notice what he was doing. It hadn't been easy, lifting half the floor, digging a deep enough hole – he was sure the body was in what would be described by the media as 'a shallow grave'. As for manhandling Gareth, stiff and reeking of something other than a man in a plastic bin bag – it had been desperate. He'd scattered a load of lime around the body – it was supposed to get rid of animal smells as well as do whatever it did to the soil. It had worked, and now that he'd chucked out the bone meal, bought especially to create a stink of a different kind, the shed was back to its normal smell-free state. Which didn't stop him having nightmares about it nearly every night.

He stuck his head in to check, then saw a man in the garden next door was trying to attract his attention. Ah – the new neighbour. He'd moved in on Monday with an older woman who Rick assumed was his mother, but beyond a wave and, 'Good morning', they hadn't spoken.

Rick strode over to the fence separating the two plots of land.

'Hi, I'm Owen Fife. Pleased to meet you.'

Rick shook hands. Owen was somewhere between thirty-five and forty, with a shock of dark hair that was greying at the temples. His handshake was firm.

Rick glanced towards the other house. 'Has your mother settled in?'

'In a way. She has her own place in Penzance, but she's staying with me for a few weeks while she's recovering from a broken leg.'

The expression on the other man's face was wry, and Rick grinned. 'Ah well, at least it's a bungalow. Will she be able to live alone again?'

'She will if she has anything to do with it. She's away at one of those health spas this week. Lots of physiotherapy. And free time for me.'

Rick hesitated. He really should ask the guy over for a drink, but he wasn't feeling sociable today. Mind you, having Owen there to talk to might be a good distraction. All this pretending to Ella was another item on his list of worst things.

'Come and have a drink, meet my wife,' he suggested. 'You're very welcome to stay for a meal too, but I should warn you it's spag bol from a jar. My – daughter's choice.'

It was the first time he'd called Soraya his daughter, and the words stuck in his throat as thoughts of another child crashed into his head, a child who wasn't born yet but who was almost certainly his and whose mother he had cold-bloodedly deserted. Was Amanda coping?

Owen's face brightened. 'I'd love to, if you're sure your

wife won't mind?'

'Oh, Ella loves having people round. She'll be interested to hear about your mother, too.'

Ella *was* interested, and Rick left her opening a bottle of Merlot and chatting to Owen in the kitchen. He ran upstairs two at a time for his shower; oh how good the hot water felt, raining on his shoulders and running down his back. He'd never been so tense. There was no getting away from the fear and the guilt – he was constantly checking his back to ensure that Amanda wasn't creeping up on him, as she often did in his dreams.

When he went downstairs Soraya was laying the table in the kitchen and Owen was looking very much at home grating parmesan. Ella handed him a glass of wine, and Rick forced a smile on his face. This was the woman he loved; all he wanted in the world was to put the clock back four months and just not go to the stupid event where he'd met Amanda.

But... Amanda was carrying his child. *His child.* Another thought came and he jumped, sloshing wine on the kitchen floor.

The baby might be a boy. Not an anonymous 'baby'. A son.

The idea was earth-shattering. He'd always wanted a son, and now... Jeez, what had he done? He'd been so busy worrying about Gareth and Ella that he'd lost sight of what was important here. His baby.

'Butterfingers,' said Ella, handing him a wad of kitchen paper to wipe up the wine. 'Owen says he's getting a ramp made up to his mother's front door in Penzance, and I was recommending those plasterers we had when we did up the bathroom.'

'Yes, they were excellent,' said Rick, stammering as something else struck him. His poor brain was having a workout this afternoon and no mistake. But this was a good idea – he could lay a base of concrete under the shed. That would stop any future smells, and more importantly it would prevent the body being found easily. The earth might settle or shift, but a layer of concrete would hold everything together. He felt his smile stretch as he raised his glass to Ella and Owen.

'To good neighbours!'

And to sorting his own mess out as soon as possible, he added silently. He had to make a choice – Ella and Soraya – who wasn't his child – or Amanda and the baby who was his.

Owen and Ella were looking at him and he realised he was frowning.

'The wine's okay, isn't it?' said Ella. 'I'll put the spag on.'

She stepped over to the cooker, closely followed by Soraya, and Rick turned to Owen, searching for something to say.

'Great you were able to take time off work for the removal. What do you do, anyway?'

The other man swirled the ruby liquid in his glass. 'I'm a police officer.'

# CHAPTER TWO

Wednesday 11th – Friday 13th June

Amanda wandered round the second flat of the afternoon. As soon as she'd seen the area she knew it wouldn't be any good, but the letting agent was already singing the flat's praises. They still had another two to view after this one and if neither of those suited her – well, she didn't know what she would do.

This coming Friday would mark four weeks since Gareth and James had fought so disastrously. She'd been a widow for almost a month, but only she – and James – knew this. As far as everyone else was concerned Gareth was missing, presumed drowned. With the pullover considered likely to be his and no positive sightings elsewhere, the police appeared to have given up the idea that he'd run away voluntarily, but of course there was no proof that he was dead, and without legal proof her life would be difficult for some time to come. Four weeks ago she'd been a stupid bored housewife having an affair... and if she'd known then what she knew now she'd have behaved very differently. Amanda closed her eyes for a second and the usual thought tortured its way through her head. *Your fault, all your fault...*

'...and you don't often see a place with this much cupboard space, do you?' The agent talked himself to a standstill and simpered expectantly.

Amanda ran her hand over the gleaming kitchen units and sighed. It was a lovely flat, and it was in her price range, but...

'It's great, but I need a place nearer public transport links,' she said.

The agent's shoulders sagged. Obviously, she hadn't been supposed to notice the lack of bus stops in the vicinity.

'Okay. But keep it in mind, huh? You have a car, don't you?'

'I'm planning to give it up. I'll be working from home for the foreseeable future, so I need a place within walking distance of a supermarket and close to a bus stop.' All of which she'd told him already.

The agent brightened. 'Well, the next place ticks both those boxes. Let's go.'

Amanda followed him down to his car, listening as he began yet another song of praise. They'd have to hurry if she was to pick Jaden up at five. She'd left him with her friend Eva to give herself the luxury of an afternoon's flat-viewing without a rampaging toddler in tow.

A smaller place to live was the first part of her strategy. The three-bed semi she and Gareth had been so pleased to find was much too big for her and two little ones. They didn't need a dining room, and the large garden was an inconvenience now.

But in spite of the problems, things were improving;

she was taking control of her life. Thanks to benefits and her parents, her finances were okay for the time being, but in a macabre way this only added to her guilt. She and James and their behaviour had killed Gareth, and she would have to live with that for the rest of her life. What would she tell Jaden when he was old enough to ask?

The next flat was up the hill, in a block with five others, with a lovely view over the ocean. Further up the road Amanda saw larger houses with gardens, and there were two small supermarkets within walking distance too. The location was ideal, and Amanda crossed her fingers as she followed the agent inside.

The rooms were small, but large enough, and the kitchen was separate, which she liked. The downside was she would need to carry everything up and down two flights of stairs, but that would keep her fit without a gym membership.

'A serious contender,' she told the agent, looking pointedly at her watch. 'Let's have a quick look at the last one and unless it's better, I'll take this one.'

He glanced at his own watch and hurried towards the stairs, Amanda following on, grinning in spite of herself. Things went faster when you were nearly at knocking-off time.

They were standing beside the car, the agent fumbling for the key, when a little group of schoolchildren approached, accompanied by a couple of mothers. Amanda watched idly as they passed. That could be her in a few years. The tail end of the group went past and Amanda stared at a dark-haired girl holding the hand of the tall blonde woman who was pulling her along. All at once it was difficult to breathe.

This was the woman and child James had been with in the swing park. The shock had imprinted their faces on Amanda's memory. The pair were walking towards the larger houses, the woman talking and laughing and the little girl giggling up at her. James' wife and daughter.

Amanda gripped her bag to stop her hands trembling, and made an instant decision. 'Wait – I'll take this one.'

The agent didn't need to be told twice. 'Excellent choice. Shall we go back in and I'll run over the contract with you? As you saw it's available straightaway...'

That night Amanda bathed Jaden, letting him play for longer than usual. The new flat was a real weight off her mind, for more reasons than one.

'We're going to a lovely new place, sweetie,' she told him. 'Nice and near the beach. And near James too, I hope.' She muttered the last part, but Jaden heard.

'Jay-jayjay.' It was what he called himself too, and Amanda kissed him. If only it was Da-dada she had found. Two tears dripped from her chin into the bathwater.

She put Jaden into his pyjamas and took him downstairs to play for a while before bedtime. He sat on her lap with one of those games where you hit a button according to the animal on the screen; Jaden couldn't do it properly but he loved the rude noise it made when he hit a wrong combination so it didn't matter. Amanda cuddled him – poor baby, he wouldn't remember this house any more than he'd remember his daddy. She could only hope his two remaining grandmothers and his grandad would stick around long enough to make memories for him. Susie was due to visit this weekend, so she'd better have a bit of a tidy. And maybe she'd have found James by that time.

Amanda sat planning, stroking her tummy where the bump would be. What would she do, when she found him? Ask for money? That would be undignified, and it wasn't money she wanted as much as... help. A father for her babies. It might be best to play the whole thing fairly quietly until she could get a paternity test done. It would almost certainly be positive, and that would be the time to push James, the man who'd been happy to lie in Gareth's bed and then disposed of his body. Heck. Did she really want a man like that in her life? But what choice did she have? She had two children to support.

And the body, that was the important thing. She'd have no peace of mind until she knew where Gareth was. She would make James tell her.

But first she had to find him.


At ten to four the following day Amanda was stationed outside her flat-to-be, Jaden in his buggy, waiting for the schoolchildren on their homeward journey. She felt alive as seldom before. The chances were excellent that one day, if not today, she would see the same woman and little girl. And then she'd have found James. How dare he dump her like that?

The children were just round the corner; she could hear them. A chattering group passed by, older children who walked themselves home from school. Amanda stared down the street. Another older group was approaching but there were no younger ones in sight today. She waited another quarter of an hour, then started the long walk home, disappointment making her more determined. The younger ones must have finished school at a different time today. Ah well, there was always tomorrow.

Friday was rainy and cool, and Amanda huddled under an umbrella, thinking savagely that this time four weeks ago, she'd been stuffing duvets into black bags in preparation for James taking Gareth away. And this was Friday the thirteenth, an omen if ever there was one. She was so deep in thought she didn't notice the children until they were passing right by. Kids of all sizes today... and a few mothers... and yes. Yes. They were here, James' wife and daughter. Both were clutching umbrellas so Amanda had little more than a glimpse of them, but it was enough. She waited till the group had passed then followed on, pushing the buggy with a sleepy Jaden. Up the hill went the pair she was following... round a corner... across the road... and through a garden gate.

Amanda walked past on the other side of the road. It was a nice house, detached with a big garden, posher than hers, and it would be their own place and not rented. At the next junction she crossed over and walked back, passing James' house once more. Yes, very nice. Lucky James.

It was time for some serious planning.

# CHAPTER THREE

Saturday 14th – Sunday 15th June

'Can we go to the beach today?'

Soraya peeked at her across the breakfast table, and Ella's heart contracted. It was lovely having her child here. This was Soraya's second week with them and it was so far, so very good. Of course they were still in a honeymoon phase where they were all on their best behaviour and everything was rose-tinted and special – but what the heck, she had waited years to have a child to love and she was going to enjoy every minute. And best of all, Soraya was beginning to realise she was loved – the little girl skipped around the house, often with a happy smile that won Ella's heart every time. It was like watching a butterfly emerging from the drabness of its chrysalis, fluttering its wings, preparing to fly into sunlight. Oh, life wasn't all pink and fluffy; their new daughter had a mind of her own and wasn't afraid to speak it – but it was an excellent beginning.

'How about a picnic lunch on Porthmeor Beach,' Ella suggested. 'You haven't been there yet and it's a good beach for children. We might see some surfers, too, if the tide's right.'

'Yay!' Soraya descended into her cereal.

Rick came in with his Saturday luxury, a real newspaper, and settled down at the other end of the table with a cup of coffee.

'Are we furniture-shopping today?' he asked, turning to the sports section.

'Tomorrow,' said Ella. 'Burnside Centre's having a summer sale; I thought we could try there. Picnic on the beach today.'

Rick winked at Soraya. 'Got your bucket and spade ready? Bet we can make the best sandcastle ever.'

Soraya immediately abandoned her breakfast and ran upstairs.

'Oops,' said Rick.

'Right remark, wrong time,' said Ella ruefully.

They had learned that to think was to act with Soraya. She rarely sat still for longer than it took to finish her food; even watching television she would jump up and down, checking that Ella was still in the kitchen, or dancing around in front of the set.

'She'll calm down,' Liz told them. 'She needs continuity and she needs to learn to trust you, and that takes time.'

Ella topped up both their mugs. They all needed time. Rick still had spells of staring into space with a vacant expression on his face, which come to think of it was permanently pale these days, but he was much better with Soraya than she'd expected. Maybe the grumpiness *had* been down to his job, and not the adoption. She still didn't know what was going on in Rick's office. He assured her the Indian contract was safe now, and as far as she could tell he went to work every day… but it was difficult to judge, and she didn't want to ask too many leading questions.

Ella's gut twisted in fear. What had he been doing, those days he hadn't gone to work? Another thing she didn't know was how long it had gone on for – a couple of weeks might mean he'd simply needed time to digest the fact that he'd soon be a father. It couldn't have been longer – could it? The only way to find out was to ask him, but that might disturb the balance of their new family life. In a few weeks the adoption would be finalised – she could start sorting out her marriage then.

And at least he'd given up visiting the shed ten times a day. The tomato plants were here in the kitchen and the veggies were in the garden. Things *were* improving, thought Ella, grinning as Soraya thundered downstairs. She rose to her feet to pack the beach bag.

'Are we going in the car?' said Soraya, leading the way out the front door.

'It'll be murder – um, much too busy in the car park today,' said Ella. 'It's not far to walk, and if we're tired afterwards we can get the bus back.'

Rick was locking the front door, his mouth a tight slash. What was wrong now? Ella gave his arm a shake. 'Come on, Mister Grumpy. When was the last time we had a day on the beach?'

'A decade or so ago?' His voice was quieter than usual.

'At least,' said Ella. So maybe this wasn't what Rick would have chosen for his Saturday – hopefully he wasn't going to be boring about family outings. She was still searching around for something encouraging to say when Soraya squeezed between them, taking a hand of each. Ella pushed the awkward feeling away.

She gazed through the houses to the ocean, deep blue in the middle distance. This was such a great place to bring up kids. The beach would be mobbed, of course, but that didn't matter because at last, at last she could be with families having fun without thinking, *oh, I want one too, why can't I have one too?* The waiting and wanting were over; now they could grow as a family and give their child the love she so obviously craved. Surely Rick must see it that way too.

'Waah!' shrieked Soraya.

Ella stopped. Rick had slowed right down and Soraya was strung between them, arms stretched sideways. He was staring at a metallic grey Ford parked on the other side of the road, a peculiar little frown on his face.

'Come on, Daddy,' said Ella.

'Ah – right,' he said, his eyes still on the car. 'Coming.'

'Someone you know?'

'No... I don't think it is.' He strode on downhill. 'Let's get to this beach. I can smell the sea!'

When they stopped at the red man he turned and stared at the car again, but he said nothing and Ella fumed inwardly. It was infuriating when he did odd things like that, leaving her not knowing what he was thinking and afraid to ask. This wasn't how she'd imagined their first weeks as parents – she'd been prepared for problems with Soraya, not with Rick.

But oh, it was fun at the beach, collecting shells and making a sandcastle and paddling in the sea – and once even shivering in up to her waist to jump through the waves with Soraya. Watching the tide reduce the sandcastle to a heap of wet sand had the little girl giggling in a way that went straight to Ella's soul. Rick played his part in the sand games and Ella began to wonder if she was imagining his preoccupation. It was a period of adjustment for them all. Real life wasn't like one of those sunshiny soap powder commercials.

'Let's go. There isn't enough beach left for all these people on it,' she said when the castle was gone. 'You can have a pony ride if you want to, Soraya, and then we'll buy huge ice creams before we go home. How's that?'

Soraya shrieked approval, and Ella laughed, glad to see Rick was smiling too. It was so lovely, doing things with their child... who wasn't their child yet. The thought always sobered her. The adoption wouldn't be finalised for another two months, and even after that there would still be meetings and support groups to attend. Was an adopted child ever your own child? No, Ella realised suddenly. An adopted child became your own adopted child. What mattered was those two words 'your own'. It was different, that was all. Soraya knew they weren't her birth parents. Ella hugged the little girl when she returned from her pony ride, and for half a second Soraya let her. Then –

'Ice cream!'

Other families were doing the same thing, and the streets were busy. Ella kept a tight hold of Soraya's hand. They strolled along, stopping occasionally to look at a shop window or a gallery display, and Ella's heart sank when she saw Rick staring at other families as they passed. Families with smaller children... little boys, in buggies. For a moment she was racked with guilt. He had wanted a boy, but she'd bulldozed that idea almost as soon as she set eyes on Soraya. On the other hand, Rick had agreed to the adoption and his behaviour now was bordering on disgraceful. A small boy in a buggy was waiting outside the newsagent's, accompanied by an older child, and Rick actually stopped to peer under the buggy's sunshade.

Tight-lipped, Ella prodded his arm. 'You'll be arrested for voyeurism if you go on like that.' She pulled him away, and he glared at her. Ella shook her head. What was going on in his mind? If he was trying to guilt-trip her because she wanted Soraya, it was the most unfair thing he'd done yet.

Home again, Ella was glad when Rick decided to go to the DIY store to buy paint for Soraya's bedroom. Half an hour apart would give her some breathing space. Still feeling annoyed, she waved as the car disappeared down the road, then took the beach things outside to shake the sand off.

Soraya was shooting balls into the basket. 'Come and play too.'

'Be with you in a minute. I'll put this lot in the machine first.'

It was more than a minute, however, as the bottle of fabric softener was empty and she had to search around for the new one. Who invented these caps, she thought, tearing a nail on her first attempt to open the bottle. Must have been a man. Or maybe she was letting her annoyance at Rick colour her thoughts here. Grinning, she twisted until the cap gave way. Come on, supermum.

Outside, at first glance the garden was deserted. Had Soraya gone next door without saying anything? Owen's mother was back now and had given the little girl a standing invitation. But no – there was Soraya at the front end of the garden, leaning over the fence and staring down the street.

'I was talking to a nice lady,' she said happily. 'She has a new flat here and she had a little boy in a buggy and she thinks she'll get him a basketball set too, when he's bigger. She said I'm the best basketballer she's seen for a long time.'

Ella hesitated. Stranger Danger was something she hadn't yet spoken about with Soraya. They should do that, but this settling-in period didn't seem the right time. She didn't want to make the child afraid of every new person she met.

'Maybe you can teach the little boy, when he's bigger,' she said cheerfully. 'Next time you see them, come and get me straightaway and we can all chat.'

The idea appealed to Soraya and she told Rick all about the encounter over roast chicken salad at dinner time. To Ella's dismay the closed expression was back on Rick's face and his answers were monosyllabic. A little boy in a buggy, of course, was exactly the child he had wanted to adopt.

'She shouldn't be talking to strangers,' said Rick, as soon as Soraya ran upstairs.

'I know. This was just a new neighbour, though. We'll do the Stranger Danger talk soon.'

The following day, Rick started painting the bedroom while Ella and Soraya added the previous day's collection to the shell garden. Ella sat on the grass while Soraya arranged the shells, a serious expression on her face – it was wonderful to see the little girl so engrossed. Her eyes were shining as she added some of the ornamental blue stones they'd found in the craft shop. Unable to concentrate my foot, thought Ella. Mind you, Soraya's new teacher hadn't uttered a negative word about the child yet.

'If we gather any more we'll need to extend this,' said Ella, when the shells were arranged.

'Yes!' Soraya jumped up and down. 'We can – oh! There's my lady!'

She ran towards the street, where a young woman was pushing a buggy containing a toddler, fast asleep. The woman put a finger to her lips as Soraya approached the fence.

'I've just got him off – he's teething, he's been crabby all day,' she said, then turned to Ella. 'Hi. I had a chat with your daughter yesterday. We have a new flat down in the block – haven't moved in yet but we're getting it ready. Not so easy with a teething toddler attached to your hip.'

Be happy you have a teething toddler, thought Ella – but that wasn't fair. This woman didn't know their situation. She leaned on the fence. 'I can imagine. You'll find this is a good area for kids. Plenty about for play dates, and there's a toddler group at the library; your little boy might like that. What's his name?'

'Jaden. And I'm Amanda.'

Ella introduced herself and Soraya, and they stood

for a few minutes chatting about St Ives before Amanda walked on downhill. Soraya ran back to her shells, and Ella followed. The little girl had barely taken her eyes off Jaden. It might be a good idea to team up with some mothers who had younger children. Her peers were still overwhelming to Soraya, who had yet to agree to a play date with any of the children in her class. Thank goodness it was almost the summer holidays. Amanda and her son might be a big part of the settling-in process for Soraya – and Ella could help them settle into the area too, so it would be a two-way thing. She heaved a sigh of pleasure. It was going to be a good summer, she could tell.

# CHAPTER FOUR

Wednesday 18th – Thursday 19th June

'Bye-bye, house,' said Amanda, waiting to pull out behind the removal van and glancing round at Jaden in the back. He was clutching his teddy, unaware that he'd never come back to the only home he'd ever known.

'Bye-bye-bye,' he echoed, waving at nothing in particular.

Amanda grimaced. It was nap time, except there probably wouldn't be a nap today. She'd arranged to leave him with Eva for the duration of the removal, but her friend had called that morning to say her three-year-old had been up sick all night. So Jaden had witnessed the breaking up of his home. Not that he seemed distressed in any way, thought Amanda. He didn't understand, of course, and he shared none of her own feelings about leaving the house. All this was far, far away from where she'd been a few short months ago.

Amanda turned out of the driveway, looking back one last time. Regret was a heavy emotion. It lamed you, and it changed you, too. She wasn't the same person anymore and she never would be, but her job was to take care of her son – and the baby.

They stopped at the end of the road to let the bin lorry past.

'Bin,' said Jaden, and Amanda blew him a kiss in the baby mirror.

He was growing up so fast. She would have to be careful now he was beginning to talk and understand more. Jaden had loved Gareth so much; he must never know what happened to his daddy. Oh God – what *had* James done with Gareth?

For an instant, disbelief almost overpowered Amanda. Gareth was dead and she was involved in a criminal cover-up; life didn't get any more complicated. But it was much too late to tell the truth. She thrust her chin in the air. Her boy had already lost his father, he couldn't lose his mother to the prison system. It wasn't as if she was a bad person; this nightmare was down to bad luck alone. And bad judgement. She should never have taken up with James.

But at least she had found him again, James and his perfect family, and this time she wasn't going to let him disappear. She would stay – not in the background, because she was planning to make him very aware of her presence in the next street, but more – in the middle ground. When the baby was born she would have a paternity test done and take things from there. Did she want James back? That was a decision for later.

It took the rest of that day and all the next, and the help of a team of friends, but by Thursday evening Amanda stood holding Jaden in a comfortably organised flat. Her flat. And oh, how very little of Gareth there was here. She'd given his clothes to a local charity shop, then wondered too late if this would look suspicious. But Sergeant Jacobs had said the sea was by far the most probable place for Gareth to be. Only she and James knew Gareth wasn't in those green and blue depths she could see from her new kitchen window. Or – *had* James dumped the body in the ocean?

And here she was, back to being a single person in a flat. A single mother. But she wasn't really alone.

'Couldn't have managed without you guys,' she said as her friends left.

She waved from the living room window as they piled into cars and drove off. They were all so sorry for her and it was touching in one way but terrifying in another. They had no idea what she'd done.

Jaden was toddling from one piece of furniture to the next, patting them as if to say, it's okay, this is home now. Amanda swept him into her arms and kissed him, inhaling his baby smell and revelling in the way he snuggled against her.

'Come on, lovey. Let's have a nice walk before bedtime. We can see if Soraya's out in her garden.'

With Jaden on one hip and the buggy in the other hand she negotiated the stairs, reflecting grimly that this wouldn't be so easy in a few months' time.

It was a grey evening, cool for the time of year but pleasant enough for children to be outside playing. Amanda stopped to chat to people as she passed, and carried on up the hill feeling better about the move. The awkward part would be telling her new acquaintances about Gareth; it was a real conversation stopper but it would have to be done. Tonight, however, she was content to chat about the weather and the children and then pass on.

Soraya *was* in their garden. Amanda heard her voice as soon as she pushed the buggy round the corner. Her footsteps slowed as she watched the little girl run back and forward. The house was about twenty yards away on the other side of the road, and it looked like a spot of basketball practice was going on.

Amanda glanced down at Jaden. She had left this too late; his eyelids were drooping. If he went to sleep now he'd waken when she lifted him from the buggy; he always did. Then he'd still be running around at midnight, and after the busy day she needed some peace. She would just walk past on the other side of the road and continue round the block and get Jaden to bed. There would be plenty of time to talk to Soraya – and her parents – another day.

Drawing level with the house, she glanced across the road. Soraya was nowhere to be seen now, but oh – James was right there in the garden talking to Ella. Should she go across after all? No – she should work out in her head what she wanted to say to him. It might be better if the first meeting happened when Ella wasn't around.

Ella had seen her, however, and waved. Amanda waved back, then gesticulated towards Jaden and then further along the road. James was standing motionless, his eyes wide and staring right at her. Hadn't Soraya and Ella mentioned her by name? Or maybe he'd thought she didn't know he was the daddy of the family. She'd spooked him well and truly now, anyway. Nice one,

Amanda. Grinning, she continued down the road and round the corner.

'That's given our James something to think about,' she said to Jaden. 'Don't go to sleep, lovey. Did you see James?'

'Jay-jayjay,' said Jaden, then, obligingly, 'Da-dada!'

'That's right,' said Amanda. And maybe one day it would be. As soon as the thought crossed her mind she laughed at her own stupidity. Did she really think James was going to give up his wife and daughter, not to mention his lovely home and lifestyle, to be with her and one child who wasn't his and another who only might be? Dream on, woman. If she managed to organise financial help from James that in itself would be a success.

Home again, Amanda put Jaden to bed and went through to her own room, where a couple of boxes of knickknacks were still waiting to be unpacked. Her jewellery box caught her eye and she lifted it from the removal carton. She would have a sort through this, most of it was old family stuff from her grandmother.

A mug of tea by her side, Amanda settled down on the sofa. Here was her grandmother's wedding ring, red gold, unusual nowadays. And the string of pearls Mum gave her for her eighteenth, expensive no doubt but they'd been Amanda's least-appreciated present. Pearls were for older women with blue rinses and twinsets, not teenagers with pink streaks and piercings. And Aunt Carla's ruby brooch. And -

Amanda lifted a thin gold chain with a St Christopher medallion. James' St Christopher. How had it got into her jewellery box? She stared at the medallion. James had been wearing it that awful day; she could remember feeling it hard against her chest as they lay in bed. It must have come off in the tussle afterwards, yes, look, the catch was broken. But that didn't explain how it got into her jewellery box.

Amanda sat still, her brain working furiously. The medallion must have been lying around in her bedroom at the house, but it was odd she hadn't found it when she was cleaning after James had moved Gareth. Unless – of course. James could have lost it while he was wrapping Gareth up in the spare room. Amanda shuddered. She'd hardly been in there since. Suze must have found the medallion on one of her mammoth cleaning fits and put it in the jewellery box. It was the only way.

Amanda leaned back. She couldn't ask Suze about it – that would look odd, and no way did she want to draw attention to James' medallion. Hadn't he noticed he'd lost it?

Thinking about James, standing there in his garden so completely flabbergasted, Amanda smiled grimly. Maybe she should pop the St Christopher in an envelope and put it through the letter box for him. But no, he didn't deserve such leniency. She would get into conversation with him over the garden fence one day, hand it over in person and watch him squirm. That was when she would do some plain talking, too. An early-evening stroll was going to be part of Jaden's new bedtime routine, and one day James would be in the garden alone.

# CHAPTER FIVE

Saturday 21st June

Helplessness and defeat heavy in his gut, Rick jogged up the hill and turned into Cedar Road. Instead of his usual run he'd wound his way round the local streets today, looking for Amanda's car, but it was nowhere to be seen. Had it been stupid to think he'd be able to avoid her in a town like St Ives? He didn't even know if he wanted to avoid her, and the baby that was more than likely his. The fact was, he'd taken the easy way out, telling himself – no, deluding himself that the new little family with Ella and Soraya was his top priority. In reality he was avoiding the Amanda situation, because he wanted to forget Gareth was under the shed. Some days he did forget for an hour or two, but now Amanda had caught up with him and unless he was very careful his new family life was going to be ruined. What was she planning? He could understand she'd moved out of her semi, but – was it coincidence that she'd come to this part of town?

The house was deserted when he arrived home and the car was gone too, so Ella and Soraya must have got fed up waiting for him and gone to do the weekend shop alone. Which, as they only had one car now, meant he couldn't go to the garden centre for concrete mix until they returned. Rick pulled a carton of orange juice from the fridge and poured a generous glassful before stomping upstairs for his shower. This wasn't a great start to the weekend.

He was towelling his hair when he heard the car pull up outside, and his mood lightened. With any luck he'd be able to start the shed floor before lunch after all. Last night he'd lifted the wood over Gareth's grave to check there was nothing suspicious to be seen or smelled, in case Soraya insisted on helping with the concrete. He glanced outside – it was windy and warm, a good day for laying concrete. It would dry quickly and the horror beneath the shed would be inaccessible. Gone forever. A picture of Gareth's face flashed into Rick's head – empty, slate-coloured eyes staring, but seeing nothing. What would they look like now, those eyes? Rick swallowed. He must *not* think like this or he'd go mad. It was an accident. End of and get going, Rick, back into Saturday.

Deliberately whistling to erase the ghost of Gareth from his mind, Rick pulled on shorts and was halfway into his t-shirt when a child's voice floated up the stairs. Rick froze. A small child was crying down there, and hadn't he heard that throaty, high-pitched wail before?

'Ma-Mama!'

Jaden. It was. What the hell was Jaden doing here? Nausea rose in Rick's gut. He was not going to confront Amanda with Ella and Soraya looking on. No way.

He crept downstairs and was sneaking towards the front door when he heard Ella telling Jaden that Mummy would be back soon. Cautiously, Rick put his head into the kitchen. Amanda was nowhere to be seen, but Jaden was vociferous enough for them both. Ella had him clutched on one hip, and Soraya was jumping up and down beside them, trying to attract Jaden's attention. But the little boy was having none of it. Howls filled the air.

Ella pulled a face at him. 'This is our new neighbour's little boy – she was taken ill outside, so I drove her home. I said we'd look after Jaden for a bit but he's not too happy about it, poor baby.'

'Taken ill? How?' Suspicion swirled round Rick's head. Was this the start of some kind of payback by Amanda?

'She was sick,' said Soraya. 'Into the drain outside and again in the toilet when she was back in her house. It was yuk.'

'Dodgy curry last night, apparently. She thought she'd got over it but she hadn't, poor soul.' Ella turned so that Jaden's face was visible. 'Say hello to Rick, Jaden.'

To Rick's horror Jaden recognised him immediately and held out frantic arms.

'Well! How does it feel to be Mr Popularity?' said Ella, handing the child over and staring as Jaden snuggled into Rick's chest.

'I guess I look like someone he knows,' said Rick weakly. 'Hello, Jaden. So she really was ill, this woman?'

Ella gaped at him. 'What an odd thing to ask. She was sick and she was burning up, too. And as it looks like you're chief babysitter I'll get off to the supermarket, shall I?'

'I want to stay with Jaden,' said Soraya.

Rick forced a grin. 'Excellent idea. Why don't you take

some toys into the living room and we'll see if he wants to play?'

Jaden on his knee, he perched on the edge of the sofa as Soraya spread a selection of toys on the floor. The situation was farcical. Here he was, clutching his (probable) expected child's older half-brother and encouraging him to interact with the child he'd adopted almost by accident. Or was adopting, anyway. The thought that the adoption was in no way final did nothing for Rick's sense of well-being. He would have to get out of this mess.

Jaden was calm now, watching from the safety of Rick's knee as Soraya play-acted with a couple of soft toys.

'Come down on the floor, Jaden,' she wheedled, patting the rug by her side.

Rick tried to sit the little boy beside her, but Jaden screamed.

'Jay-jayjay!' He scrambled back into Rick's arms as Soraya shrieked with laughter.

'Isn't he funny! It's Ja – den. Can you say that? Ja – den.'

Jaden was gripping Rick's t-shirt with plump fists, his small body shaking.

Rick turned on Soraya, fury and frustration hardening his voice. 'For heaven's sake, Soraya, don't be so noisy! You're frightening him!'

Soraya's face fell a mile and a half and she rose stiffly and went out to the kitchen. Rick could have kicked himself. Noisy or not, Soraya was the best distraction he had for Jaden.

'Bring some biscuits, sweetheart,' he called. 'Maybe

Jaden's hungry.'

Fortunately this appealed to Soraya and a few minutes later both children were sitting on the living room floor clutching custard creams. A biscuit, it seemed, made all the difference. Rick sat watching as Soraya showed Jaden her toys, feeling as if he'd run a marathon that morning and not 5K. All this stress wasn't good for him, and now Ella had started a baby-sitting service for Amanda... He needed to plan what to do when the inevitable happened and he and Amanda came face to face. And what had she told Ella, anyway?

Thinking time, that was what he needed. Alone. He would either start concreting in the shed, or get right away for the afternoon, depending on what arrangement Ella had made to return Jaden. But whatever happened, he wasn't going to allow Amanda to confront him today.

It was after eleven before Ella reappeared, by which time the two children were new best friends and Rick was dancing with impatience. He seized the bag of freezer food and started to transfer the contents.

'What are we doing about Jaden?' he said, moving to let Ella into the grocery cupboard.

'I said I'd give him lunch and take him home for his nap. Apparently he sleeps till after two. But I'll call Amanda first and check she's up for it.'

'Look! He likes me! And he can say his name, can't you, Jay-jayjay?' Soraya was standing in the doorway, Jaden by her side.

The little boy toddled over to Rick and held up his arms. 'Jay-jayjay!'

Soraya shrieked with laughter again and Rick snapped.

'I *told* you to be quieter around him!'

Ella glared and Rick closed his eyes. How had this turned into his fault? 'Sorry, Soraya. It's okay.'

Ella hugged Soraya. 'Would you like to make lunch for Jaden while I phone Amanda?'

Rick stood helplessly as Ella put water on for pasta and gave Soraya a lump of cheese to grate. So the two women had exchanged phone numbers. This was exactly what he didn't need. Ella raised her eyebrows, indicating that he should oversee proceedings in the kitchen, and moved into the hallway with her phone. Rick leaned on the door frame and listened to her side of the conversation.

'Hi, how are you?... Good... He's fine, very attached to my husband... Are you sure?... Okay, be with you in half an hour.'

'She's feeling better. I'll take him home after he's eaten,' said Ella, coming back into the kitchen.

'Can I come too?'

Soraya was jumping up and down again and Rick felt impotence wash through him. How had they ended up Amanda's best friends in the neighbourhood? It was either a horrible coincidence, or Amanda had orchestrated the entire thing – though the sickness had apparently been genuine. But at least he wouldn't have to see her today.

And here he was, Jaden on his knee, eating pasta penne as if nothing was wrong.

'You're so good with him,' said Ella, when the meal was over. 'Maybe next year you'll be having lunch with our own little boy on your knee.'

Rick managed to smile back – she was trying to make peace. The car containing Ella and the two children drove off, and he paced up and down, unable to concentrate on anything but dread of what his wife might soon be hearing.

It was half an hour before they returned, and Rick could tell by the way she slammed the car door that Ella was upset. He grasped the back of a kitchen chair, bracing for the storm, and was astounded when she walked straight in and hugged him.

'Oh Rick, the most horrible thing. Remember a few weeks ago a guy disappeared on a walking tour on the south coast? That was Amanda's husband. Poor soul, she doesn't have a clue where he is. The police think he drowned, but there's no proof he didn't disappear voluntarily, so she has a load of hassle with the authorities. It's holding up her pension and everything. And she's pregnant, and he didn't even know about the baby. It's awful for her – we'll need to help as much as we can.'

Rick patted her back, dismay filling his head. Hassle with the authorities was something he hadn't reckoned with. He'd been imagining Amanda secure with a widow's pension and lots of insurance money, but it didn't sound as if that was the case. This would be why she had tracked him down. She wanted money, and all she had to do to get it was announce the fact that the coming baby was his. That would ruin his marriage, and their chances of adopting Soraya. And if it ever came to light that Gareth was under the garden shed…

But that was something he really didn't want to think about.

# CHAPTER SIX

Sunday 22nd – Monday 23rd June

'You've got your hands full today!'

Ella rose from the cushion she was kneeling on to weed the vegetable patch, and rubbed her back, smiling ruefully at Owen on the other side of the fence. Soraya and Jaden were running around with a ball, and Rick had shut himself in the shed with a wheelbarrow full of concrete. It couldn't be easy working in such cramped conditions, she thought, joining Owen at the fence. She'd suggested leaving the concrete, but Rick had nearly snapped her head off. He'd been in a funny mood all weekend, and she could understand why. All he'd wanted was to adopt a little boy, and here they were looking after what must surely be her husband's dream child. Rick and Jaden had an amazing rapport, when you considered they'd met for the first time yesterday. Having Jaden here was tough on Rick, but what else could she have done? She'd phoned Amanda that morning to check that everything was all right, only to hear that the other woman had been up most of the night with nausea. Amanda leapt at Ella's offer to baby-sit for a few hours.

'He lives down the road; his mum's not too well,' she said to Owen.

Soraya ran over, her fringe damp with sweat, and jigged about in front of the fence.

'And his dad went for a walk and he never came home again,' she said, then turned to Ella, her face full of anguish. 'Why didn't he? Didn't he want to be with Jaden?'

Ella put her hand on Soraya's hot cheek. 'Oh sweetheart, I'm sure he did. It's something that almost never happens and it's so sad for Jaden and Amanda. We have to hope hard he's all right.'

But Amanda was hoping no such thing; Ella had seen it in the younger woman's eyes. Amanda was convinced her husband was dead. It was a bad situation and Soraya was finding it difficult to deal with. She scowled at Ella now, but Jaden called and she ran off immediately, her face clearing.

'Not so easy,' said Owen, and Ella had to fight to keep the tears back. What with Rick's oddness and Soraya's neediness, she felt as if no one in the world was in her corner.

'Sorry,' she said, fishing in her shorts for a tissue. 'I'm a bit emotional – having Soraya here's a dream come true, and now this poor woman...'

She told Owen all about it – the relief to have another adult to talk to was incredible. It was weeks since she'd discussed the adoption with anyone other than Rick and Liz.

'Maybe you can find someone else to help Amanda too?' suggested Owen. 'I'm not saying you should abandon her, especially as Soraya and Jaden get on so well, but I think you're taking on a lot here.'

He was right, thought Ella, feeling the stress slide off her shoulders as they talked. She should see if one of the other neighbours could lend Amanda a hand; helping Soraya adjust was using up all her own energy. Come to think of it, she hadn't seen her friends for ages either. She shouldn't be giving up her social life for Soraya, that would do no one any good.

Owen hadn't known that Soraya was adopted, and asked several questions. He was divorced, she learned, and his wife had kept their flat near Newquay, where his job was still based. And as one of his previous police jobs had involved working with deprived youngsters, he was aware of problems that parents and children face in difficult situations. 'Why don't you and Caroline come for dinner one night next week?' Ella suggested. 'It would be lovely to have time for a proper chat.'

'I'm sure Mum would love that,' said Owen, staring at Rick who had emerged from the shed with a red face and was yelling at Soraya. 'I'll get back to you, will I?'

'Yes, I'll – sorry.' Ella loped across the garden, sweeping up a howling Jaden as she went. 'What in the name of all that's sensible is going on?' she snapped as Rick paused to draw breath.

Soraya was standing mutely, her posture stiff with fear, and Ella gripped the child's shoulder, conscious that for once Jaden was cuddling into her neck and not agitating to go to Rick. Thank goodness Owen'd had the tact to go inside, an audience was the last thing she needed here.

'That bloody ball's shaking the whole bloody shed - '

Ella felt her own temper explode. 'Please don't swear. And that's no reason to shout – if the ball was disturbing you why on earth didn't you tell Soraya to play somewhere else?'

He glared at her. 'I asked her repeatedly but she ignored me. And all the shrieking she does, that's hardly normal, is it? I think you should do what that teacher suggested and get her on some kind of medication. I can't take any more of this.' He strode towards the house.

Ella stood trembling. Was she supposed to pick up the pieces now? And how horrible, she couldn't even comfort Soraya properly because she was holding another woman's child. Her knees were shaking but she bent and pulled the little girl towards her.

'Daddy's upset. He shouldn't have shouted, and you shouldn't have banged the ball on the shed after he'd asked you not to,' she said, trying to meet Soraya's eye and failing. 'You were both wrong and when you've calmed down you can both say sorry and make up. You play quietly with Jaden while I put my stuff away and then we'll go inside. You can help me make dinner.'

Feeling as if she'd run to Land's End and back, Ella collected her tools and took them to the shed. For a moment she stood motionless, staring at the chaos inside. Rick had insisted he was fully capable of 'slapping down some concrete'. But the grey mass covering half the floor was uneven and patchy, and there were lumps everywhere. But this maybe wasn't the best time to complain about the shed floor.

Ella closed the door on the mess and reached for a hand of each child. She led them at Jaden's speed towards the house, only just managing to control her anger. Look at poor Soraya's face, dejected didn't come into it. Rick's behaviour was intolerable, but somehow she'd have to calm things down for them to arrive at some kind of peace before bedtime. The first thing was to get Jaden, who was probably the innocent cause of Rick's outburst, out of the equation. Ella reached for her phone to tell Amanda they were on their way.

The walk downhill with Soraya, who was still silent, and a sleepy Jaden – thank heavens he was too young to tell his mother about the scene he'd witnessed – gave Ella some much-needed thinking time. She mustn't make this more important than it was – Soraya had been disobedient and Rick had lost his temper, that was all. His remark about medication had been a bit over the top, but hopefully Soraya hadn't understood. Ella glanced down at the little girl, who was walking beside the buggy, no sign of her usual exuberance, and cursed Rick. All this aggro over a ball... or was he worried about something else, too? She still didn't know what was going on at his work. Perhaps her idea of smoothing things down until the adoption was finalised wasn't such a good one after all. They would have to talk tonight.

Amanda was waiting at the street door when they arrived, still pale but looking more cheerful. 'Thanks a million. Was he good?'

'An angel,' said Ella, managing to smile as she jerked her head towards Soraya, who was a few feet away, staring towards the sea. 'Unlike some. I hope you have a better night.'

Soraya remained silent on the way home. At the gate

Ella kissed the child's head. 'It's all right, sweetie. Families have fights, it happens. The important thing is to make up afterwards.'

'Uncle Ben never shouted at me.'

Ella tried to sound positive and uplifting. 'Auntie Mel and Uncle Ben are foster parents. It's their job to be good at looking after children. You and me and Daddy are just normal people, so we make mistakes sometimes. It's not a big deal, okay? You can say sorry to Daddy now and he'll do the same.' I hope, she added inwardly.

Rick was sitting at the kitchen table with yesterday's paper and a large whisky. His expression was both hostile and embarrassed.

'Soraya has something to say and then you can reciprocate, please,' said Ella, her heart thudding uncomfortably in her throat. She gave Soraya's hand an encouraging squeeze.

'Sorry,' mumbled Soraya, kicking the table leg.

Ella swallowed a smile as Rick's face became almost as sheepish as his daughter's. She raised her eyebrows at him.

'I'm sorry too. I shouldn't have shouted,' said Rick, after a pause that was long enough for Ella to wonder what on earth she would say if he didn't apologise.

'Good! Let's make chicken and chips for tea. I think we could all do with a treat,' said Ella, and Soraya brightened immediately.

In spite of Ella's efforts the atmosphere at the table was strained, and by the time Soraya was safely in bed Ella felt as if she'd been trampled by a herd of elephants. She read the little girl a bedtime story and went downstairs to find Rick in the middle of another very large whisky.

'You'll regret that in the morning,' she said lightly, stopping to give his shoulders a rub before pouring herself some wine. She sank into an armchair and raised her glass to Rick. He gave her the most ironic look in the world before raising his own.

'Let it go, Ella,' he said, taking a large swallow. 'It's done, forget it. We don't need to sit discussing my lack of parenting skills all evening.'

'No problem,' said Ella. 'It's a stressful time for us all. I noticed you'd had problems with the concrete – shall we get someone in to finish it off? That would take some of the strain away from you.'

Rick leapt to his feet. 'Will you stop nagging! It's intolerable. As if it's important how the shed floor looks.'

Astounded, Ella tried to speak calmly. 'It's not important, but someone might trip on an uneven bit and fall. We have to get it fixed. I'll call the plasterers, shall I?'

'No, you damn well won't. And I mean that, Ella. The wood'll go back down on top of the concrete. Keep your nose out of it.' He gave a sudden hysterical guffaw, then strode through to the kitchen.

Ella heard the *glug glug glug* as he poured another whisky.

Standing at the school gate the next morning, watching Soraya run across the playground to a little group of children, Ella felt the tightness in her jaw relax. Woo hoo, she had six lovely solitary hours. That should be time to recover her sense of self after Rick's attack yesterday.

She'd wondered about keeping Soraya off school to make sure the girl was back to normal after the first big squabble of the adoption, but decided against it. If Soraya looked for a day off school every time they disagreed about something, they'd end up in big trouble.

A visit to the sauna and a salad lunch with her friend Lindsay left Ella feeling like a new woman and vowing to do this feel-good stuff more often. She should make the most of her child-free hours; the school hols started in three weeks. And here she was, thinking like a mother who hadn't had half a minute to herself for years – how things changed. Grinning, Ella scrabbled for her phone as it rang. It was Amanda.

'Hey, Ella. Why don't you and Soraya come in for a coffee on your way home from school this afternoon? Jaden would love that too.'

Ella agreed, hoping that Soraya would have found her usual sunshiny self by that time.

Later that afternoon she joined the group of waiting mothers at the school gates, trepidation making her gut twist. Maybe she should have told Soraya's teacher about the upset. But it was only a row... and hallelujah, here was her daughter with a beam stretching from New York to Moscow.

'Mummy, look! I got a gold star for my nature drawing!' She thrust a worksheet covered in gaudy turquoise and orange butterflies under Ella's nose.

Tears of joy welled up in Ella's eyes. This was the first time Soraya had called her 'Mummy'. The little girl had dropped 'Ella' and 'Rick', but she had never used the word Ella had been dying to hear. Until now.

'Wow, clever you! Just like the ones in the garden, huh?'

Amanda had posh baker's shop Florentines waiting for the grown-ups, and banana yoghurt for the children. Ella sipped her coffee, wondering if she should ask more about Amanda's husband, but with Soraya there she didn't like to. Amanda kept the conversation very general all the time they were there, and Ella gave up on the idea of a more personal talk. At the end of the visit Amanda accompanied them down to the street, Jaden on one hip.

'I'm so grateful you could take him while I was ill,' she said. 'I'll keep Soraya for you sometime too. You'd like to visit Jaden sometime, wouldn't you, sweetie?'

'Oh yes!' Soraya danced up the road, turning to wave to Jaden before tearing round the corner.

Ella pulled a face at Amanda. 'She's as good as a gym membership,' she said, sliding into a slow jog uphill. It wasn't until she was almost home that an odd thought crossed Ella's mind. Did Amanda know about the adoption? No, she decided. They'd never spoken about it. Apart from the time Amanda told them about her husband, the conversation had always been superficial, like this afternoon. Which seemed a little... unusual. But then Amanda had a lot to cope with at the moment.

And there was enough to worry about at home, anyway, because quite possibly Rick's bad temper now was because they were adopting a little girl and not a baby boy... Ella felt her shoulders slump. Looked at like that, Rick's moodiness was all her fault.

# Chapter Seven

Wednesday 25th June

Rick drove home through rain-spattered streets, the bleakness of the weather matching his mood. Everything, but everything that could possibly go wrong, was doing exactly that. What could he do to get his life back to normal? Not that 'normal' existed any more. The arrival of Soraya had changed things to 'new normal', and that had been all right, as long as the Amanda situation was under control. But with Amanda two minutes down the road and best girlfriends with Ella, and Soraya yakking on and on about how cute Jaden was, Rick felt as if Gareth's wife was taking over his life. What the hell was she up to? The way he'd treated her, she might be getting ready to blackmail him for every penny he had. He'd have to talk to her, but supposing he lost his temper? That would show her clearly she had the power – and she did have the power. He should have stuck by her... But if he'd done that he'd have endangered the adoption and it would be Ella after his blood now. He couldn't win. But then, why he should win? His behaviour had put Gareth under the shed.

Rick pulled into the driveway, his mood darkening further at the thought of sitting through another evening with Ella trying to have a meaningful talk. She was suspicious about his job, he could tell, so many remarks recently had been loaded – ironic because work was the one area which was completely normal. There it was again, 'normal'. Pity he couldn't organise a business trip, get right away from all the hassle. Being at home was like walking on ice, and the fear in Ella's eyes as she gaped at him was infuriating.

The cinema, he thought, running the few steps to the front door. He would suggest a family outing to the cinema, a nice fun place where you didn't need to talk much. Then afterwards he could have a headache and go to bed early.

'Yes!' cried Soraya, when he mentioned it. 'Rosie in my class went to see The Muppets, can we go there, Mummy?'

'Great idea, but let's go on Friday. Then you'll be able to stay up late because there's no school the next day,' said Ella, and Rick winced. His wife had turned into supermum. Of course Soraya took the bribe immediately; he didn't even have an ally now.

'Right. Let's play – Monopoly after tea, then,' he said, forcing a grin for Soraya, who ran for the games box. Monopoly, of course, wasn't there – how was he supposed to know what games were suitable for six-year-old girls?

'You two choose a game. Dinner's in the oven. I'm going for a quick shower,' said Ella, and Rick was left with his almost-daughter. Which was actually okay because she was busy choosing games so he didn't have to talk to her. Maybe if he buttered Ella up enough with family games and fun-Daddy, they *could* have a chat after Soraya was in bed. He could tell her the department had problems they were trying to hide from Alan... yes, that was good. And he could mention Amanda reminded him of an old girlfriend and please keep her away from him. And Soraya was the best thing ever. Then 'all' he'd need to do was sort things out with Amanda. It was worth a try, anyway. And some flowers would put Ella in a good mood right at the start...

He tapped Soraya's shoulder. 'Let's pop down to the shops and buy Mummy a surprise.'

He scribbled 'Gone for petrol with S' on the shopping pad and left it on the table, and followed Soraya to the car. The rain had slackened off, and Rick drove on automatic pilot, down towards the town centre and on along the main road. Soraya was quiet in the back, staring between houses to the sea, grey and surging today.

'Where are we going?' she asked after a while, and Rick jumped. He glared out of the window. They were passing the road down to Carbis Bay station, right out of St Ives. Where *were* they going?

'There's, um, a good shop further along here,' he said. They came to the A30 and Rick put his foot down.

'Oooh!' cried Soraya. 'Go faster!'

'Be quiet, please. I have to concentrate to, um, find the place,' said Rick.

What was he doing here? He was running away, that was what, he was running away from an intolerable situation, taking with him one of the people who was making it intolerable... and he knew no matter fast he went, he'd never get away. There was no escaping the shed and what lay beneath it.

Gareth's dead face flashed in front of Rick's eyes. It had done that a lot this week; ever since he'd made such a pig's ear of laying the stupid concrete. On Monday evening he'd tried – and failed – to remove it. Unless he got someone with a heavy machine in to dig the grey rectangle out again, the concrete was there for keeps.

As was he. He'd lain awake every night that week trying to plan, but it always came back to the same thing. He was stuck with the shed forever; doomed to living the rest of his life with Gareth and his terrible eyes mouldering in the garden. He could never sell the house... But would he and Ella be able to mend their marriage, the marriage that was now so wrecked he didn't know – let's be honest here – he didn't know if he wanted to mend it? He didn't know if he wanted Amanda either, and even if he did they could hardly live in a house with Gareth under the shed. But if he and Ella split up, he would *need* to sell the house. There was no way out that he could see.

His mobile buzzed in his pocket. No prizes for guessing who that would be. Dinner was in the oven and neither he nor Soraya were there to eat it. Rick counted rings until they stopped. Ella would be leaving a message now; it would be interesting to hear what tone she took. Aggrieved, concerned, afraid? But any fear would be for Soraya. They should never have started this adoption.

Bugger, they were coming to a tailback. This was the wrong time of day to practise the great escape. Rick slowed down and glanced at the child in the back.

'Are we nearly there?' Her lower lip was trembling.

Abruptly, Rick came to his senses. Christ. He'd yelled at her on Sunday and today he was kidnapping her. Whatever he had to do to make things right, it wasn't this. He would turn at the roundabout and go back.

'Two more minutes. There's a petrol station and a nice shop. You can choose something for Mummy while I answer my phone,' he said, hearing her sigh of relief.

Soraya was happy wandering round the collection of filling-station tat, and Rick stood in the doorway and listened to Ella's message. It was very short; her voice surprised in a 'what are you doing, you silly boy' tone. With an effort, Rick swallowed his ire and pulled up Ella's number.

'Sorry, love – we had a good idea for a surprise for you but it's been a bit tricky finding exactly what Soraya wanted,' he said, making his voice warm and amused. 'I hope dinner isn't completely ruined?'

Rick heard the disguised annoyance in her voice when she assured him that dinner wasn't a problem, as long as they were both all right. He rang off to find Soraya had chosen a weather house in the shape of a lighthouse. The little girl was one big beam, and unexpected tears shot into Rick's eyes. Poor kiddie – so happy to have found a lovely present for her mum... and Ella would be happy too. If only he felt the same way.

He drove home as quickly as he could, Soraya silent in the back. Maybe she sensed this outing of theirs wasn't quite right, that he had used it – and her – to do something odd. But if he was lucky, and careful for the rest of the evening, he might yet be able to turn it to his advantage. He needed Ella on his side.

Soraya ran into the kitchen with the weather house and presented it to Ella, her face shining. Rick met Ella's eyes over the little girl's head and mouthed 'Sorry,' then said, 'Hope you like it, Mummy, we had to go a long way to find it, didn't we, honey?'

Soraya didn't notice this remark was meant for her, so intent was she on showing Ella how the little man came out when it was raining and the lady when the sun shone. Rick saw tears in Ella's eyes when she kissed Soraya and put the weather house on the shelf by the door. So far, so good.

He was careful to chat about this and that during the meal, after which they all played Mousetrap, which in Rick's opinion hadn't improved in the twenty-odd years since his last game. In spite of his sombre mood he managed to play the part of devoted daddy; well done, Rick, he thought, you've turned a very rocky start into something halfway successful. Hopefully the talk with Ella would go equally well.

But of course, it didn't. Ella was still furious that he'd upped and offed with Soraya – or at least she was furious he'd turned the supposed petrol purchase into a longer outing *without telling her.* She was treating him like a schoolboy. Rick could see the worry in her head and it was all for this child she had chosen, but – he needed to be loved too. With Gareth under the shed he needed someone there for him. He gaped at her wordlessly, which only infuriated her more.

'Rick, with Soraya involved we have to communicate stuff like that a whole lot better. Promise me.'

'I'm sorry. It was a spontaneous thing,' he said, trying to look wretched. If she felt sorry for him it might make things easier.

She sniffed. 'All I want is for us to grow together as a family. I know this isn't what you planned at first, but Soraya's a lovely child and we need to do our best for her. And Rick, I don't know what's happening in your job, but it feels like you're hiding something big.'

He sat twirling his whisky glass, watching the oily, amber liquid swirl round, wishing he was a million miles away from the accusations, and unable to get out of his chair. Just get her back on side, Rick.

'The job thing's – complicated, but I promise it'll be okay. And you have to admit things haven't been easy with the adoption. We all need time to adjust.'

'But what's been so difficult? Of course we need time but we have it. At the weekend – I – I saw you looking at Jaden as if you were wishing he was yours and not Soraya.'

Rick balked. She was putting words into his mouth now. And she was wrong because he didn't wish he was Jaden's father – or Soraya's for that matter.

The words came tumbling out. 'Oh, forget it, I know whose kid Jaden is. What I don't know is if I can ever feel like family with Soraya. She's so – awkward. I know I said I was happy to have her but that was - '

That was because he'd been so bloody guilty about having an affair.

'That was before I realised I don't want her, Ella. I don't want her.' The whisky glass slid through his fingers and cracked on the wooden floor. Glenmorangie oozed between the boards, glinting on shards of Edinburgh crystal.

The sound of feet scampering upstairs broke the silence that followed. Ella's eyes were appalled as she stared at Rick, but all he felt now was fury that his life was so totally out of control. He had fucked up and no mistake.

And Soraya had heard every word.

# CHAPTER EIGHT

Saturday 28th June

'Me and Mummy went to the cinema last night. We had a huge bag of popcorn and chocolate cornets too.'

'Lovely. What film was it?'

Amanda listened as Soraya chattered on. They were in her kitchen, where she was making macaroni cheese and the children were sitting at the table with crayons and paper. Amanda's heart melted when she glanced up from grating cheese. Jaden's little face was beaming; he loved having Soraya here.

'Daddy didn't come because he was working but I think he was just cross,' said Soraya, coming to hover at Amanda's elbow.

Left alone, Jaden screamed in his highchair, and Amanda lifted him to the floor. 'Why don't you two go through to the living room while I get this in the oven, and then we'll play together.'

The children ran off, Jaden clutching Soraya's hand, and silence fell in the kitchen. Amanda smiled. Her plan to get involved with James' – Rick's – family was coming along very nicely. Ella'd called at lunchtime yesterday, saying she and Rick could use some quality time, and asking if Amanda could take Soraya for an hour or two on Saturday evening. The vision of Ella informing Rick that his ex-mistress would be looking after his daughter was a satisfying one. How did you react to that, Mr Disappearing-Act? she wondered. I hope you're enjoying your date night. Needing quality time sounded as if there was trouble in Rick's marriage, and serve him right too. And best of all, according to Ella they would pick Soraya up on their way home. Both of them. That was a situation waiting for a good idea Amanda hadn't had yet. She slid her dish into the oven and closed the door with a satisfying bang. What was Rick doing now, out with his wife in a nice restaurant? Depressed, Amanda sank down on the chair Soraya had vacated.

They'd destroyed each other, she and James – Rick. She had to get used to thinking about him with his real name; using a stupid alias made it feel like play-acting, and they'd done enough of that. Remembering the lies she'd told the police still made Amanda feel queasy. The affair had doomed her already shaky marriage, and now it seemed Rick's was in trouble too. Serve him right.

Amanda stirred uncomfortably. Three children as well as three adults were involved here, and they were all going to get hurt unless she planned something very, very clever. Or rather, some of them were going to get hurt no matter what happened. All she could do was make sure her own kids stayed safe.

The macaroni cheese went down well with both children, and Amanda allowed Soraya to help bath Jaden, which ended up being a lot messier than usual but a lot more fun too. She parked the little girl in front of the television while she put Jaden down – he fell asleep in minutes, tired out by his visit. Soraya should come more often, thought Amanda, closing the bedroom door.

'What can we do now? I don't want to watch TV,' said Soraya, bouncing up and down on the sofa.

Amanda gazed round for inspiration. All she wanted to do was blob. Heaven help her if her own two were as exhausting as Jaden and Soraya. Her jewellery box was still on the bookshelf, and she lifted it and plumped down beside the little girl. Soraya was intrigued, and they spent a pleasant half hour trying on bracelets and chains. Amanda found herself hoping the baby would be a girl. This was fun, a nice girly time.

Soraya lifted the lid from the bottom section and too late Amanda saw Rick's St Christopher still lying there. She'd forgotten all about that. Would Soraya...?

'Daddy's got one like that. He was wearing it at the party. Is this yours?' Soraya lifted the chain and swung the medallion round. Amanda grabbed it before it hit her in the face. Time to talk about something completely different.

'It was my husband's. A lot of men have one. Look, try this bracelet. My godmother gave it to me when I was eighteen.'

Soraya wasn't to be distracted. 'Mummy said it was a St. Christ or something.'

'St Christopher. He's the patron saint of travellers.'

Soraya bent over the gold disc. 'Pro – te – ctus. What's that?'

'Protect us. It means when they wear this, people

think St Christopher will keep them safe.'

'Did your husband think that too?'

Amanda swayed on the sofa. But the child hadn't meant to be cruel. 'He – um, yes, he always wore it. That's why I keep it. To remember him. Want to try this bracelet? They're real emeralds.'

Soraya was polishing the medallion on her sleeve. 'There's a mark on it. My daddy's has – emeralds? Are they jewels?'

Amanda sagged in relief as the St Christopher was abandoned in favour of the emeralds.

They were sorting through earrings when Jaden's sleepy voice called out, and Amanda closed the jewellery box. She rushed through to the kitchen for a yoghurt to keep Soraya occupied, and crept back into Jaden's room, where she sat rubbing his back until his eyes closed again. Leaning forwards made her jeans tight round the middle; in a couple of weeks her pregnancy would be obvious – and what did she think about that? People were getting used to her as 'the woman whose husband fell into the ocean' – soon they would be thinking of her as 'the pregnant woman whose husband fell into the ocean'. It wasn't an alluring prospect.

Back in the living room, Soraya was watching cartoons, and Amanda went to clear the kitchen. A few minutes later her mobile buzzed.

'We're walking up towards your building,' said Ella. 'I didn't want to wake Jaden with the doorbell.'

The perfect plan flashed into Amanda's head. She needed to speak to Rick, alone, and there was an easy way to achieve this. Enter the helpless little woman...

'I'll bring Soraya down, shall I? Did you have a nice time?'

'Great, thanks.'

Ella's voice was anything but enthusiastic and Amanda nodded. There was definitely trouble in Paradise, and she was about to add to it as far as Daddy was concerned.

Ella was just outside, but Rick was several yards away on the pavement when Amanda opened the street door. She smiled to herself. His face was thinner than a few weeks ago. For a second she wondered if she was doing the right thing, then Jaden's voice crackled through the baby monitor in her hand.

'Bye, Soraya love, you were a big help to me tonight,' she said, smiling at Ella then raising her voice. 'Rick, can I ask you a favour – I need to change the filter on the air-conditioning but the catch has jammed - ' His face was stiff and Amanda turned back to Ella. 'Can I borrow his strong arm for a minute?'

'Sure. See you at home, Rick.'

Amanda ran back upstairs, the sweat of fear damp on her back. Rick was right behind her – would she be able to carry this through?

'What are you playing at, Amanda?' His voice was higher than usual.

'Hush. Let me see if Jaden'll go back down. Help yourself to a drink.'

Amanda stayed in Jaden's room for several minutes, although the little boy wasn't really awake.

Rick glared when she joined him in the living room. 'Congratulations. You've got your way – I'm here. What do you want?'

Amanda patted her belly. 'To remind you our baby's in here.' She saw him wince. Ah – that had struck a nerve. Maybe he wasn't as indifferent to the baby as he was making out.

'You don't know that.'

'I think I do, *Rick*, and I think I want a whole lot more support than you're giving me, too. And you're going to help me, aren't you? If I mention to the police what happened to Gareth they'd soon make you tell what you did with the body. And it's your word against mine that it was an accident, isn't it?'

He blinked at her, and she noticed his eyes had somehow sunk into the dark circles surrounding them.

'How much?' he said, his voice quite unlike the voice she remembered as James'. It was Amanda's turn to wince. What had happened to her? The start of the affair had been as much her fault as his.

'I don't want money,' she said, stepping towards him.

The kiss was as passionate as any they'd ever shared and oh, being back in his arms was everything she'd ever dreamed of.

After a few moments he broke away and stared at her, eyes wide. 'Do you want to destroy me?'

Amanda's heart was thundering under her ribs – would the baby feel it? 'Of course not. All I want is a life for me and my children and I think that's what you want too.'

He almost ran to the door. 'I don't – I can't – I'll have to think what to do. I'll get some money to you.'

Amanda heard the outside door bang as he left the building. She stood at the kitchen window as he went on up the hill. He wasn't hurrying now, was he, it was clear poor Rick was in no hurry to get home. Next time it would be more than a kiss, she thought. He would come back to her. And she would make him tell her where Gareth was. Satisfied, Amanda poured orange juice and took it back to the sofa.

It was all still there between her and Rick. Poor Ella, and poor Soraya; they were going to lose him.

Idly, she lifted the jewellery box and began to organise her pieces back into their usual places. Soraya wasn't a girly girl in many ways, but she loved pretty things. There. The top was tidy again, and all they'd looked at from the bottom section was –

Amanda lifted the lid of the smallest compartment and the shock made her heart beat as swiftly as when she and Rick had kissed.

The St Christopher was gone.

# Chapter Nine

Saturday 28th – Sunday 29th June

Ella rubbed her eyes, waiting for Soraya to finish her teeth and get into bed. The evening had been a disaster from start to finish. Why had it all gone so wrong? She'd booked a table at a favourite restaurant, one within walking distance so she and Rick could have a couple of glasses of wine. She'd chatted about holidays, old friends, and a load of other fun trivia all through the meal, planning to start the heart-to-heart over coffee, when they'd be feeling full and mellow and the waiter wouldn't be bobbing around all the time. But Rick had seen right through this and interrupted as soon as she started.

'Ella, listen. I don't want to talk about it. Hear that? We've had problems at work but they're nearly fixed, and I know I've been a pain in the bum at home, but talking it over and over isn't going to help. So leave it. Please.'

'But Soraya needs -'

'And maybe I need to think about something other than Soraya all the time. Maybe I need a wife as my partner and not a mummy. I'll have the bill, please.' This last was to the waiter.

And that had been it as far as Ella's frank discussion was concerned. It was all she could do not to howl in exasperation. Her family was falling apart and she didn't know what to do about it.

Soraya jumped into bed, the picture of a good child, and for the millionth time Ella blessed the adoption party. She would never have believed it was possible to love a child so much.

"Night, sweetheart. I'm glad you had a nice time with Jaden and Amanda.'

'I like Amanda better than Daddy.'

Soraya closed her eyes, and Ella perched on the edge of the bed. Should she say something? But a late bedtime wasn't ideal for starting potentially complicated conversations. What had Soraya heard on Wednesday night, and what had she understood? How cruel Rick had been, saying he didn't want the child. Even if it was the whisky talking, it probably had its roots in the truth. That was terrifying. They needed to talk about Soraya as much as they needed to talk about how to get their marriage back on track.

Ella sat stroking the little girl's hair for a few moments. She'd done this on Wednesday too, but Soraya had pretended to be asleep. "Night, 'night, sleep tight, I love you,' she said at last.

Soraya blinked sleepy eyes and gave her a wonderful smile.

Easing out of the room, Ella heard the front door open and close. So Amanda's filter had been quickly dealt with. At least Rick hadn't made it an excuse to stay longer and avoid further confrontation at home. Ella stood on the upstairs landing, undecided. She was in a real lose-lose situation here. If she went downstairs and tried again Rick might be even more infuriated. If she went down and talked about the state of British beaches, he would have won. And he was being ridiculous. They had to talk. Ella marched downstairs.

Rick was in the kitchen, sipping a glass of water. Ella sat at the table.

'Rick. I'm sorry but we have to talk about why you said didn't want Soraya. It was cruel – I'm appalled.'

He didn't look at her. 'I was drunk. Let it go, Ella. It was bad luck she came down right then but she'll have forgotten by now. I didn't mean it.'

Ella's head reeled. Forgotten, her foot. All she wanted to do was shake him and scream about his insensitivity, but... they could *not* have a big bust up. As it was – suppose Soraya said something to Liz?

'So you're happy about the adoption?'

His eyes met hers then swivelled away. 'Yes. But don't push it, Ella. We've said enough tonight.'

She got up, unconvinced. It was horrible, leaving things unsaid, just to keep the peace. But too much said could delay the adoption and that was the last thing any of them needed. The best way to show Soraya she was loved and wanted was to carry on and get things finalised.

Demonstratively, Ella lifted her eBook without looking at Rick.

'I'm going to bed. Have a good think, Rick. That kind of thing can't happen again.'

She lay in bed, reading the same paragraph over

and over and listening as he moved around downstairs and then came up – and went into the spare room. The door clicked shut behind him. Shocked, Ella dropped the eReader on her chest. When was the last time – but there wasn't a last time. None of the arguments they'd had before had resulted in them sleeping apart. And come to think of it, they hadn't had sex since Soraya's arrival. Horror mixed with desperation chilled its way through Ella. Supposing her marriage broke down completely and they took Soraya away?

The little girl was standing in the kitchen when Ella went down the next morning. Ella bent to kiss her but Soraya ducked, an aggrieved look on her face.

'You weren't here.'

'Sorry, sweetie. I was tired. Do you want cornflakes?'

'I want to go to the beach.'

Ella handed over the variety pack she'd bought the day before. 'Look, you can choose your cereal. We'll go to the beach this afternoon, okay?'

Soraya chose Coco-Pops, her expression still sombre.

'You look a bit sad. Want a hug?' said Ella when they were finished, but Soraya ran upstairs.

Give her time, thought Ella. She must have noticed the atmosphere in the house, and if she'd heard Rick on Wednesday... Oh dear, she should talk about it to Soraya too. 'Least said soonest mended' was the coward's way out. When the girl came back down Ella beckoned her into the living room.

'Let's have a chat on the sofa. Sweetie, I know things

have been difficult for a few days. Daddy's had problems at work and it's made him grumpy, but they're almost fixed so everything'll be better very soon. I'm sorry if you felt we didn't want you. We do. You're our Soraya and that will never change.'

Soraya nodded. She took a deep breath and Ella held hers – would the child say what she felt about Rick's behaviour?

'I found something at Amanda's yesterday.'

Ella breathed out slowly, disappointment gnawing at her middle. But if a grown man couldn't talk about his feelings, it was unrealistic to expect a six-year-old to talk about hers. Take this at her pace, Ella.

She tried to look interested and encouraging. 'What was that?'

Soraya ran upstairs and returned clutching something to her chest, then dropped a medallion on a gold chain into Ella's hand. Ella's fingers closed round the chain as she struggled to say the right thing. Didn't Soraya know stealing was wrong?

'Sweetheart, you can't just take things – '

'It's Daddy's. I saw the mark where he drove on it.'

Ella opened her fist and examined the medallion. Dear heavens, it *was* Rick's. There was the blackened little dent on one side of the medallion... Hot confusion swept through Ella. Rick had never been to Amanda's before yesterday – had he? Impossible to know what to think, but Soraya was waiting for an answer.

'You're right. There must have been a misunderstanding sometime – I'll sort it out.' Soraya frowned, and Ella hugged her. 'Sweetheart, I know you weren't stealing this, and I'm glad, because stealing's wrong. People go to prison for it. But thank you for telling me. We'll have a chat about it another time.'

Another time when she'd had the chance to work out what to say... And why was she having to do all the parenting?

The sound of Rick upstairs galvanised Ella into action. No way did she want a confrontation between Rick and Soraya about the St Christopher before she had a chance to find out what was going on. 'Let's go and look at your shell garden. We can collect more this afternoon.'

Next door, Owen was setting up a sprinkler on his lawn. 'Hi, ladies, how're you doing?' He came and leaned on his usual spot on the fence.

'Daddy's cross,' said Soraya, kneeling by her shell garden.

Ella joined Owen. 'He's had problems at work and he's finding it hard to – adjust,' she said, waving vaguely at Soraya.

Owen pulled a face. 'Takes time. He'll get there. Listen, about that dinner we mentioned once – why don't the three of you come to us tonight? I'm still on leave so I've plenty of time to cook, and I do a mean lasagne – if that would be to her ladyship's taste?'

'I like lasagne,' called Soraya, and Ella and Owen laughed.

Ella accepted the invitation and went to join Soraya, but oh, dear, if her poor daughter had heard and understood that remark, the odds were she'd understood Rick's stupid statement last week too. Lots of love and attention for Soraya today, thought Ella, no matter how grumpy the child was.

Soraya wasn't the only one who was grumpy. When Rick appeared he barely gave her a second glance, and Ella's frustration levels rose even further.

'We're invited next door for dinner tonight,' she said, wondering if this really was a good idea.

'Fine. Some intelligent conversation at last,' said Rick. 'I'm going to do the accounts, please don't disturb me.'

He marched into the dining room and closed the door, and Ella looked round for her mobile. Soraya was playing basketball so this was a good opportunity to ask Amanda about the St Christopher. The other woman sounded breezy, and for a few moments they chatted about the weather and Jaden, then Ella grasped her courage.

'Soraya brought home a gold St Christopher last night, it's Rick's and - '

'Oh Lord, yes, I meant to call you about that. Jaden must have lifted it when he was at your place – I found it in the pocket of his overall. Sorry, Ella.'

Ella breathed out slowly. The simplest explanation. Why on earth hadn't she thought of that?

'No problem. Kids are like magpies, aren't they?' She ended the call feeling happier. Now to reassure Soraya. The little girl was sitting in front of the buddleia, eyes shining as multi-coloured butterflies flitted round purple blooms, and Ella crossed the grass, glancing into the shed as she passed. The mess of concrete on one half of the floor didn't look any better now it was dry.

She squatted beside Soraya. 'I've sorted things with Amanda about the St Christopher. Jaden took it from here last week.'

Soraya shook her head. 'She said it was her husband's.'

Ella frowned. 'She must have meant *my* husband's?'

'She meant the lost husband. She said he always wore it.' Soraya turned back to her shells.

Ella wandered back across the garden, her thoughts so confused she couldn't remember who'd said what first. Rick did almost always wear the medallion, but she'd noticed the catch was broken so that would be why he'd left it lying around for Jaden to lift. But...

There was something wrong about the medallion story, but for the life of her she couldn't see what.

# CHAPTER TEN

Sunday 29th June

Rick logged out of his e-banking account and pushed the laptop away. So now the bills for June were paid, bloody brilliant. And his wife was out in the garden with the child that was going to be their own, and probably neither of them were speaking to him. Fear for the future brought tears to his eyes – he hadn't wanted this, not for a moment. He regretted... no, he didn't regret ever setting eyes on Amanda. He regretted the mess they were in.

In fact, the more he thought about it, the more he felt that he and Amanda would be each other's future. His marriage had taken a nose-dive as soon as they'd made the decision to adopt, and there was no way back that he could see. Seeing Ella as supermum had killed the passion. Amanda was different; she managed to be a mother and a lover at the same time. He'd treated her abominably, but that had been down to the stress. She would forgive him, last night's kiss had shown that. And they had a lot going for them – good sex, a similar sense of humour... and a baby.

And the Gareth secret.

Gareth's marble face flashed in front of his eyes and Rick groaned aloud. Amanda's ex was going to bind them together for all eternity, and they needed to organise that eternity, starting with a fool-proof plan for the next few months. It would be a slow kind of plan, because the whole shed thing would only work if Ella co-operated enough to move out of here. For his wife, no plan would be good unless Soraya was in it, which meant the adoption had to be finalised before they separated.

Okay, he had the rest of the day to be a nice daddy, get Ella back on side enough to give him some space – and have dinner with the neighbours, which would be the good bit. Time to grovel.

His positive mood lasted as far as the kitchen.

Ella was extracting the new star-shaped ice cubes from their tray, Soraya bobbing up and down beside her. The child glanced at Rick and he swallowed; her face was nothing but antagonistic – but what could he expect?

'I found your gold chain at Amanda's and then she told a lie,' she said, taking her glass of fizzy orange plus star-shaped ice to the table.

Rick felt his eyes glaze over. The St Christopher... hell, where was it? Sweat broke out on his brow. What was he supposed to say here? Ella was watching him, and he forced a smile.

'I'm sure she wouldn't do that, honey. You must have misunderstood.' He slid a cup under the coffee machine.

'I didn't. And she said it was her husband's but he's gone. And I don't want you either.' Her tone was entirely matter of fact. Rick glared at her before remembering he was trying to be nice.

'I'm sorry I said that, Soraya. I didn't mean - ' He could only watch as she ran from the room. The kitchen door slammed behind her.

Ella was staring at him and there was no friendliness in her eyes. 'I'm not sure what you're trying to do, Rick, but you're not going about it the right way.'

He felt his ribs rise and fall as he prepared his little speech in his head. Now for it. 'Ella, love, I want things to be better again but I'm going to need some time. It's all been too much – work, the adoption, all the changes in our lives - '

'None of that is Soraya's fault. She's the innocent victim here and your behaviour is – abysmal.'

He closed his eyes to hide his impatience. Every single damned thing came back to Soraya. But try again, Rick. You can do this.

'I'm truly sorry. I was thinking... please, can we give each other some space for a week or two? Live life as it comes and not bother each other. I do still need to get the work thing finalised – but I'll soon have that behind me.' He saw the question on her face and hurried on. 'How about planning a big celebration when the adoption's finalised? And we could have a little holiday, the three of us. Visit your parents.'

She stood with her head on one side, and he held his breath. 'Okay. Mum suggested it too, when I called at the weekend. There's a kids' exhibition in York this summer. I'll get Soraya back in and we'll tell her all that. And the most important thing is, Rick, that you don't make any more stupid remarks about not wanting her. She's not a boy, but she's going to be our child.'

Rick stood straighter. Sorted. But Ella knew if their marriage went down the pan the adoption might never be finalised. She would agree to anything he suggested – he should grab this chance while he had it.

Soraya came back inside, and again Rick explained about the family holiday and celebrating the adoption. A tiny smile appeared on the little girl's face, and the tight band Rick hadn't realised was there round his head relaxed. He *would* manage this.

Ella was rinsing glasses. 'By the way, I'll call the builder about the shed floor, shall I? You don't need to feel you have to fix it yourself.'

The biscuit tin Rick was holding clattered to the kitchen floor. 'No – leave that to me, Ella. Some physical work is just what I need to – to distract me.'

It took all the acting power he had, but he managed to bluff his way through the rest of the afternoon, and an early dinner next door. Owen and his mother were good company, and conversation flowed, even Soraya chatting away like a good child. And Ella's expression when she looked at the girl was – besotted, thought Rick. The woman he'd married had turned into a mummy-machine, but that would help him out of the mess. And, as this dinner was proving an effective distraction, he should organise more things like this for them. If Ella was distracted she wouldn't start wondering about things he didn't want her to wonder about.

Back home, Ella chased Soraya towards bed. Rick stopped her as she was following the little girl upstairs.

'I'll pop into the office, check what's come in over the weekend, get ready for next week. Well-prepared is half

– whatever.'

'Half done,' said Ella.

He saw her uncertainty and willingness to believe him, and continued gently. 'Don't wait up, love. Oh, and I'll stay in the spare room for a bit. I've been waking a lot at night, and it's easier if I can put the light on and read. You need your sleep – you have to be rested for Soraya.'

There was no expression at all on her face now.


Amanda was watching television when he arrived. She turned the sound down but didn't switch the set off, which made Rick think he had a bit of buttering up to do here too.

'Cards on the table,' he said, sitting on the armchair and leaning towards the sofa. 'I was the biggest bastard in creation to leave you alone like that. I was terrified if we were seen together someone might have rumbled us-' hell, he was beginning to sound like a bad movie, '-and I panicked. I do want to be with you and Jaden and the baby, and I think that's what you want too. But we need to wait up for now. Let things settle with Gareth and my home situation. Come the autumn, the adoption'll be finalised and we can be together properly.'

Her eyes narrowed. 'What did you do with Gareth?'

He took her hand. 'Amanda, you don't need to know. Don't worry, I'm sure you'd be fine with what I did. But if you know nothing, you can't give anything away. What's happening with the police?'

She removed her hand and went through to the kitchen. He followed and watched as she poured two glasses of grape and elderflower. Rick had to fight to look grateful – what wouldn't he give for a double Glenmorangie in that glass.

'They reckon he's in the sea. The search has been called off. At some point he'll be declared dead and I'll get a widowed parent's allowance.'

She leaned against the sink, somehow looking tough and vulnerable at the same time, and Rick felt his heart start its usual anticipatory dance. It was going to be all right... 'And you're okay for cash?'

'I'm on benefits and I've got some freelance secretarial work. Could do with a new computer, though.'

'I'll get you one. We should -'

'I'm going to Scotland tomorrow,' she interrupted. 'To stay with Gareth's mum. For a week.'

Relief crashed over Rick. An absent Amanda would give him space to sort out Ella and Soraya. 'Excellent. You have a think about what you want to do, and I'll get things organised at home. We're going to Ella's parents when the school holidays start, and after that...'

She set her glass down and came to stand in front of him, putting one hand on his chest and running the other down his side.

'After that,' she said, her lips brushing his chin, 'It'll be our time, won't it?'

He kissed her, feeling her body mould itself to his for a few moments until he pulled her towards the bedroom. Oh yes, it was all still there between them.

# PART THREE
## DOWNSLIDE

# CHAPTER ONE

Thursday 17th – Friday 18th July

'Woo-hoo! Summer holidays!' Soraya raced across the playground, and Ella caught the little girl's hand as she swung to a halt by the gate.

'Yes – and we're going to enjoy them, aren't we?'

Soraya's face was a picture. 'Can we go for ice cream now?'

Warm satisfaction filled Ella. 'Why not? And we'll make a celebration pizza for dinner!'

They wandered along the sea front, Soraya dripping chocolate soft ice all the way down the front of her school sweatshirt, but what the heck. Ella beamed. It was lovely to see the child so happy. It wasn't that Soraya didn't like school, just... Ella sighed. They'd been invited for a 'chat' with Soraya's teacher the week before and while the woman genuinely appeared to like her new pupil, it hadn't been all good news. They were to have Soraya's hearing tested in the holidays, to make sure her concentration problem wasn't at least partially caused by poor hearing. It didn't sound likely to Ella, but who was she to judge?

Another thing that was testing now was her daughter's behaviour at home. The honeymoon phase was over and Soraya was pushing her boundaries all the time. Ella tried to be patient, and actually it wasn't Soraya's cheek that had her fizzing with resentment, it was Rick's calm assumption that she would do all the parenting necessary – anyone watching would think the two of them were playing good cop/bad cop with their daughter. It was boring being bad cop all the time, but in spite of this Soraya seemed to prefer being with Ella.

The little girl stopped to gaze into a shop window full of seaside souvenirs, and Ella smiled at their reflection in the glass. A tall blonde mother and a dark-haired wisp of a child, her child; she could feel it all the way to her soul. The wait to become official parents was nearly over. They had a court date on the 20th of August, and then hallelujah, they'd have made it.

Turning into Cedar Road, Ella was unsurprised to see no sign of the car in their driveway. That would have been too much to expect, she thought resignedly. Rick had always been home early before Soraya came to stay, but nowadays it was more often after seven before he appeared. Ella couldn't get rid of the feeling that he was avoiding spending time with them. Yes, it had turned into 'him' and 'us'. Yet he was more intent than ever on having the adoption finalised. At least, he talked about it regularly, but... Ella bit her lip. His adoption talk – something about it wasn't genuine, but she couldn't put her finger on what was wrong.

At ten past seven the car lurched into the driveway and Rick emerged, switching on a grin as soon as he saw her at the window.

'Hi, honey. Hi, love.' He tossed a packet of crisps to Soraya, and came to kiss Ella's cheek.

It was difficult not to scream at him. What on earth did he think he was doing? A peck on the cheek twice a day was the sum total of their physical relationship now; a symptom of the decay in their marriage. Rick was still sleeping in the spare room, and although she had tried to say they'd never make their marriage work like this, he wouldn't change. Which didn't make her feel great. Had he gone off her completely? Yet she was still 'love' – and he brought flowers too, once a week at least. A guilty conscience? But he couldn't be having an affair, he was home every evening. Nothing about his behaviour added up, but at least he was always nice to Soraya now. Although... Ella joined them, frowning as Rick examined the drawings the girl had brought home from school. Soraya still wasn't relaxed in Rick's company. Trust had been broken, and it would take a long time to rebuild it. Hopefully Liz wouldn't notice, because a postponement of the court date was the last thing they needed. And talking of Liz, the adoption worker was visiting them tomorrow for the last time before the holidays. Had Rick remembered?

As usual, Ella had coffee ready in the kitchen when Liz arrived. The social worker wasn't one for formality.

'Where's Soraya this morning?' Liz helped herself to sugar.

'Getting dressed. First long lie-in of the holidays and

all that.' Ella passed the biscuits, noticing that Rick was shifting around on his chair. He was having to take an hour off work for this meeting, but big deal. He was there until nearly seven in the evening nowadays so it couldn't be a problem – could it?

Feet thundering on the stairs was followed by a thud and a shriek before Soraya burst into the kitchen, clutching her head.

'I banged my head on the banister!'

Rick was nearest and Ella was glad – and surprised, to be honest – to see him reach out to the child, but she swerved away and buried her head in Ella's front. A cuddle and a cold cloth followed by some magic cream did the trick, and Soraya ate her cereal at her usual breakneck speed. When she pushed her bowl away Liz stood up, looking from Ella to Rick.

'Maybe Soraya could show me her shell garden, and afterwards the three of us can have a talk?'

Soraya jumped up and led the way outside.

Ella clasped shaking hands under her chin. Liz had never suggested 'a talk' so specifically before. 'She's noticed something.'

'Like what?'

'Oh for heaven's sake, Rick, stop pretending everything's all right; it's infuriating. Anyone with half a brain can see things are all wrong here.'

A muscle was jumping in the corner of his eye, and she stared at it. Where had that come from?

He turned his head away. 'You're exaggerating. As usual. Don't worry, I'll explain to Liz.'

Ella propped her elbows on the table and leaned her

head on both hands. There was no time to talk tactics; all she could hope was Rick's explanation wouldn't make things worse. And hopefully too Liz wouldn't look in the shed, because the floor was still an embarrassing mess.

Liz appeared at the kitchen door. 'She sure loves those shells, doesn't she?' She sat down and opened her folder, frowning as she shuffled a couple of papers around. 'So, just a few more weeks and then you're finalised. Ella, Rick – is everything all right? I couldn't help feeling a tension in the air. Is there anything I can help with?'

Rick leaned back in his chair. 'You know us too well. I've had work-related problems this summer, and I suppose it's made me grumpy, but it's just a blip. We're going to stay with Ella's parents in Yorkshire tomorrow so we'll be able to do loads of family things there. Did Soraya say anything?'

'It was more what she didn't say. She seems happier in Ella's company. No doubts about the adoption, then?' She was looking straight at Rick, and Ella held her breath.

'It can't come soon enough for me.' The sincerity in his voice was unmistakable, and Liz laughed.

'Won't be much longer now. Summer holidays first, then you'll be official parents.'

Yes, thought Ella, and the problem with summer holidays was they'd be together all day, every day for the next two weeks. It suddenly sounded like a very long time. Was the visit to her parents – where they'd have to share a bedroom – really a good idea? But Mum and Dad would be disappointed if they didn't go.

'I don't know when I'll be home tonight, might be after seven again,' said Rick, when Liz had gone. 'I'll have to leave things in order for the others while I'm away.'

Exhaustion washed over Ella. 'Does it matter? All you do when you are here is avoid talking about the important stuff.'

He patted her shoulder and she cringed. His touch made her cringe.

'Don't worry, Ella. There'll be plenty of time to talk when we're on holiday, and new things to think about too.'

He drove off, and Ella slumped, then turned to the stairs. She would pack a case for each of them, ready for the journey tomorrow. Then she and Soraya would go to the beach. At least she could give her girl a happy day.


It was after five when they returned home, and to Ella's surprise the car was in the driveway. Soraya ran up the garden with the new shells, carefully washed in sea water, and Ella took the swimming things in through the kitchen door. She'd need to use the dryer to have this lot ready to go tomorrow; an afternoon at the beach the day before they left maybe hadn't been such a clever idea. She plonked the beach bag on a chair and pulled out the towels. Rick was on the phone, she could hear his voice in the dining room. Hopefully they wouldn't call him from work every five minutes while they were away. But... was this work calling? Rick's voice sounded odd...

Ella inched towards the dining room and leaned her head on the door frame. It was a long, long time since she'd heard that tone in Rick's voice. Bile rose in her throat.

'Oh, darling, I know, it was such bad luck... it's only another four weeks... I'll call you every day... 'Bye, sweetheart.'

Horror and fury vied for space in her head and Ella shoved the door open, spitting the words out. 'Who the *hell* were you talking to?'

Was she doing the right thing, confronting him? It had been a gut reaction. For her own self-respect, she had to say something.

Rick dropped his phone on the table, his face expressionless. 'I'm sorry you heard that, Ella, but if you do things my way it'll all work out for you and Soraya. Please.'

Ella couldn't stop her temper boiling over. He had another woman – *bloody* hell, who was it? – and what did he mean by 'It'll all work out'? Was that a threat – if she didn't co-operate with his sordid little affair, he would sabotage the adoption?

'Are you blackmailing me?'

His voice was tired. 'Ella, we're going to do this my way. You know it's Soraya you want, not me, so don't pretend to be so indignant.'

'That is so not true. And how stupid – oh, get out of my sight, Rick. Go.'

Hearing Soraya skip into the kitchen, Ella fled upstairs. She couldn't speak to him now with Soraya looking on. Dear God in heaven, what could she do? They couldn't possibly all go on holiday to her parents and pretend everything was all right. What could she do to make this better? And Soraya – her beautiful girl...

Tears dripping from her chin, Ella went into the

bathroom and turned on the shower to drown her sobs. She sat on the stool, face buried in her towel, her body shaking. This was the worst thing, the most awful thing...

The sound of the car driving off calmed her. Thank heavens, he'd gone. She didn't have to go downstairs and look at him. Ella splashed cold water on her cheeks and examined her face in the mirror. She wouldn't win Miss Cornwall, but a six-year-old wouldn't notice that. A slosh of lippie and some powder and she almost looked normal. And – best idea ever – she would call her parents and tell them she and Soraya would be visiting by themselves. A complete break from the situation here was the only way forward.

'How about pasta bake for tea?' she called as she ran downstairs. 'You can chop some ham to put in it – Soraya?'

The house was silent, and Ella went into the garden.

'Soraya?'

Nothing.

Cold sweat broke out on Ella's forehead. No. Oh no. Her breath ragged, she ran back inside. The living room was empty. She stumbled into the dining room and the world spun darkly. The cases... she'd left them by the sideboard, ready for tomorrow's departure.

One case stood there now. Her own.

# CHAPTER TWO

Saturday 19th July

'Can you be a big boy and walk downstairs for Mummy?'

Amanda held out her hand and Jaden gripped it, reaching for the banister with the other plump fist. It was a good thing he enjoyed being independent; there was a lot of him to carry when you had a buggy under the other arm. It took them forever to get to the ground floor this way, but at least it was easy going.

Jaden climbed into his buggy at the bottom and sat prodding the fading rash on his leg. Amanda pulled a face. Talk about bad luck. The rash had flared up yesterday after lunch, and getting it checked out ruined her last day with Rick till after his holiday. She'd wanted to cook dinner for him but by the time she arrived back from the doctor's it was after five and Rick had given up and gone home. Tears flooded Amanda's eyes. She was going to miss their late afternoon dates. He'd taken to coming by three or four times a week after work, for an hour or two. Sometimes she managed to organise Jaden into a nap and she and Rick spent the time in bed, and when that didn't work they had family time. Jaden loved having Rick round.

Halfway up the hill, Amanda paused. It was juvenile, walking past Rick and Ella's to see if she could catch a glimpse of him before they left. Something a teenager would do. But she couldn't help it; she was in love. The fact that he'd left her for so long was forgiven, if not forgotten – she could understand how he might have panicked about someone finding out what happened to Gareth.

The minute the thought entered her head, the usual doubt wormed in after it and Amanda stopped again, her breath catching. What *had* happened to Gareth?

'Up, up!' Jaden bounced in the buggy, then turned to look at her, dark hair flopping into his eyes in exactly the same way Gareth's had. In the two months since Gareth's death, his son had changed from a baby into a little boy. How tragic.

'Up the hill, that's right. And next time you can walk, you heavy lump!'

Ten yards of hard pushing brought them to Cedar Road and Amanda turned left thankfully, disappointment flashing through her when she saw the empty driveway at Rick's house. She was too late – they had gone. A lump swelled in her throat as she pictured the three of them in the car, Rick driving and Ella beside him chatting to Soraya in the back. Oh, how she wanted to do just that with Rick and Jaden.

You will, she told herself as she trudged along the pavement. He'll leave them after the adoption… '- and then it'll be our time, won't it, lovey?' She said the last few words aloud, and Jaden turned again and beamed at her. It was amazing, having a little boy. And soon she'd have two babies.

Amanda glanced at her middle, then frowned. She'd been for her twelve week scan last Friday, and asked the sonographer if she could tell the sex of the baby. Rick wanted a boy, she knew. The woman said it wasn't possible to be sure yet, but if she was a betting woman, she'd put money on a girl. But no guarantees. Amanda decided not to tell Rick – the woman might be wrong and they'd be able to see at the twenty-week scan. And anyway, a few weeks ago *she* had wished for a girl.

A movement on the other side of the road caught Amanda's eye and she stopped in sheer amazement as Ella emerged from the kitchen door with a basket of washing. What the – or had Rick gone to buy something for the journey, perhaps? Hope flared again. If she went over for a chat she might still see him today.

'Hi there!' Amanda pushed the buggy across the road, noticing that Ella looked anything but pleased to see her. The other woman was pale, and her clothes looked as if she'd slept in them. Had she found out that Rick…? 'Not away yet, I see.' Amanda racked her brains to remember if she was supposed to know about that morning's planned departure. But, yes, she was, Soraya had told her the other day when she'd met them on the way home from school.

'Change of plan,' said Ella, her voice dull, and Amanda frowned. What change of plan? She waited, sensing that the other woman wasn't comfortable talking about it. Where was Rick?

'Rick and Soraya have gone away for a couple of days

by themselves first.'

Amanda gaped. Rick had said nothing about this on Thursday and it didn't sound like him, wanting to go away alone with Soraya.

'Oh – that's nice,' she said lamely. There was something going on here, something she didn't know about. 'Where have they gone?'

'Up the coast a bit.' Ella's voice couldn't have been flatter, and Amanda took the hint and went on her way, her stomach churning nervously. What the hell was going on? She had to get in touch with Rick, make sure he was okay.

She hurried along and turned into the next street where she pulled out her mobile, but Rick wasn't taking calls. Exasperated, Amanda left a message. There was nothing she could do, apart from wait for him to get back to her.

By mid-afternoon Rick still hadn't called back. Amanda paced around the flat, the nervous feeling in the pit of her stomach stirring up the morning sickness. She'd tried twice more to call Rick, with the same non-result. Of course he wouldn't want to go into explanations with Soraya by his side, but he could have texted. If there was anything going on she wanted to know. Time for another attempt.

She sank into the sofa to call in comfort, and thank God, this time he answered straightaway.

'Rick! I've been trying - '

Heavy breathing filled Amanda's ear and she stopped,

the hairs on her arms rising. This wasn't Rick. 'Hello?'

'Mummy?'

A child's voice, heavy with tears. Amanda gripped the phone. 'Soraya? Where are you, sweetheart? Where's Daddy? Can you give the phone to Daddy?'

'He's in the shower. Who are you?'

'It's Amanda, sweetheart. Where are you?'

'In a hotel and I want to go to my Mummy. I was trying to phone her – how can I phone her?'

Amanda's mind raced. How indeed? 'If you, um, tap the little man picture at the bottom of the screen when we're finished, and then swipe upwards till you come to Ella's name...' This was stupid, a six-year-old who wasn't used to mobile phones would never manage that. 'Why don't you just ask your dad, Soraya?'

'He won't let me call Mummy.'

Amanda's unease was growing by the minute. Rick and Ella must have had some kind of bust-up. It would explain Ella's behaviour, but now Rick was endangering their plans. His job was to keep things ticking over nicely until Ella had her chosen child – and then leave.

'I see. Have a go, and I'll phone Daddy again in ten minutes anyway, okay? Tap the little man at the bottom and then swipe up till you see 'Ella' and tap that.'

She ended the call and sat hunched on the sofa, watching the minutes tick by on her phone. Five, seven, ten. She made the connection and listened as it rang out. And of course, he didn't pick up.

'Yog-ut,' said Jaden, toddling in from his room with a cuddly rabbit under one arm.

'I was going to make spaghetti. Don't you want

spaghetti?'

'Yog-ut.' He started to climb into his high chair, and Amanda hoisted him up and gave him what he wanted. Helping him open the tub, she came to a decision. If it was her child who was away from her, wanting to talk to Mummy, she would want to know.

Reluctantly, she connected to Ella's number. This might not be easy.

'Ella, I had Soraya on the phone a minute ago. She was trying to call you, but she ended up with me. I gather Rick was in the shower. Kids, eh?'

It sounded awkward in her own ears, but at least Ella knew now and could react as she thought fit.

'Oh... thank you. I – I'll give them another call. Rick wasn't taking calls earlier.'

Her voice was weary and alarm bells rang even more loudly in Amanda's head. This must *not* come between her and Rick. They were meant to be together; he loved her and they were having a child. Rick's child.

'Is everything all right, Ella? You sound a bit down.'

There was a pause, and Amanda held her breath. A horrible thought struck her and she gazed in horror at Jaden stirring his yoghurt. Did Ella *know*? If Rick's wife was aware that her husband was having an affair with the woman down the road... and it wasn't only the affair. Gareth... He had to stay a secret, no one could ever find out.

'I'm fine, thanks, Amanda. I miss them, that's all.' Ella's voice was still dull.

The connection broke, and Amanda dropped her phone on the table and went to fetch the laptop. It didn't sound as if Ella suspected anything, but if Rick carried on like this she would, nothing was more certain. It was time for some plain speaking, and if Rick wasn't answering his phone, an email was the next best thing. Grimly, Amanda waited for the machine to boot up.

# CHAPTER THREE

Sunday 20th – Tuesday 22nd July

Rick stared at the phone in his hand. Ella, for the tenth time at least. She was going to be furious, and who could blame her? He should never have run off – again – with Soraya. Rick squirmed, remembering the contempt in his wife's voice on Friday evening, and how he'd clenched his fists so hard his fingernails had marked his palms. He'd needed to lash out after that and he'd done it in the only way he could. Still, this wasn't the way forward. He couldn't fob her off with text messages indefinitely. Trembling, he accepted the call, wiping the palm of his free hand on the bed he was sitting on.

'Rick. Where are you? I'd like to speak to Soraya, please.'

Her voice was cold but he heard relief there too. She wanted Soraya, he had to remember that. If he gave her Soraya she would let him do anything.

'We're in a hotel outside Newquay. I know I shouldn't have left without saying anything and I'm sorry. But you can't speak to me like that, Ella. I've been thinking and I have a suggestion for you.'

He waited.

'What is it?' This time her voice was suspicious.

'Come here tomorrow and we'll talk about it then. Soraya's tired, I'm going to take her for a quick walk and then it'll be early bed for us both.' What a reasonable Daddy thing to say. Rick blinked hard. When had he turned into such a trickster? And Ella clearly wasn't taken in.

'I want to speak to Soraya before making any arrangements with you.' Frozen would be a good description of her tone now.

Rick turned to the child at the table in the corner. She was staring at him, fingers poised over her game on the iPad, fear on her face. She must have realised it was Ella on the phone and something was wrong. He patted the bed beside him. 'Want a quick word with Mummy? She'll be here tomorrow.'

Soraya knocked the chair over in her rush to get to the phone. Rick held it to her ear, his head bent close to Soraya's to hear what Ella was saying.

'Mummy? When are you coming?'

'Tomorrow at the latest. Are you okay, sweetheart?'

'I wanted you to come too. We had ice cream this afternoon and they had the strawberry kind you like.'

Rick's tension evaporated. Ice cream talk was exactly what was needed to convince Ella that Soraya was indeed okay. Sure enough, his wife's voice was oozing warmth when she replied. She had missed her vocation; this entire phone call was worthy of an Oscar.

'Yum. We'll buy some tomorrow, shall we? I'll be with you for breakfast.'

'Yay!' Soraya was one big beam.

The beam didn't last long. The girl was restless all night, tossing around in the bed beside Rick's, and he cursed himself anew for his impetuous decision to leave St Ives. Punishing Ella had turned into a bigger punishment for him. As soon as Soraya was awake – at six-thirty – she started asking when Mummy would be there, and when Ella appeared at eight Rick would happily have signed the child over to his wife there and then. Not that Soraya greeted her mother with hugs and smiles.

'You didn't come with us! Why didn't you come too?'

Ella held out her hand. 'I'm sorry. I wanted to. Shall we go for breakfast?'

Rick was left to follow on behind. He slid into his chair in the hotel dining room, where too-close-together tables removed any illusion Ella might have had about a private talk over the bacon and eggs. He saw her mouth tighten.

'I think we should have the day here with Soraya, Rick, and then go home to talk.'

Rick agreed – what else could he do? He'd blown it this time; he could tell by her face. What a pity it was she'd overheard him on the phone on Friday. But at least his affair – and thankfully she didn't know it was Amanda – was out in the open. They could plan on from there. The problem was, his blood boiled every time she looked at him, her scorn and frustration plain to see. He had to fight to keep the disdain from his own expression.

Soraya was the only one who enjoyed her day, opting for the beach instead of Rick's suggestion of the Eden Project, which made it even more difficult to play happy-

Daddy beside Ella playing happy-Mummy. They barely said a word to each other that didn't go over the medium of Soraya. At four o'clock Ella suggested they went home, and Rick couldn't agree fast enough.

When Soraya was in bed he and Ella faced each other over the kitchen table.

'Who is she, Rick?'

'No one you know.' She didn't know Amanda, or not like he did, anyway.

'Don't be so childish. I need to know what you intend doing about the adoption, that's the most important thing. And then there's the house. I want to stay here with Soraya -'

'No way.' It was a gut reaction; he could *not* leave Ella here with Gareth under the shed waiting for someone to chip away at the concrete and find – what? What did a body look like after two months under a garden shed? Sweat trickled down Rick's neck.

Ella was glaring and she was calm, too, always a sign of determination.

'Yes, way. You get the relationship you want, I get the house. And Soraya. And if you make it impossible for me to adopt her, Rick, I'll take you for every last penny you have. You'd lose the house anyway.'

Rick pressed his lips together. Keep calm, man, you have to do this. 'You, ah, you can have your adoption. I'll stay schtum till everything's finalised. But this is my home too and I don't want to leave all the work I've done here – or the garden, the shed...'

She was staring; hell, he should never have mentioned the shed.

'This is my home and Soraya's too. Plus, even when the adoption's finalised we'll still have people coming to check how we're getting on.'

'I'd be there for the visits. You could find a nice flat -'

'Don't be ridiculous. If Soraya and I went to live in a flat it would be immediately obvious to any adoption society worker there was no Daddy living with us. Here, we'd have a fighting chance of looking like a normal family even if you weren't living in. I won't have them taking her back, Rick.'

He licked sun-cracked lips. They wouldn't do that, would they? But they might. What could he say to get her and Soraya away from the house? He was still contemplating this when Ella's mobile rang.

'It's Mum. I have to take it. Don't forget we're supposed to be arriving there tomorrow.' She went out to the garden, and Rick poured a stiff drink. He had to get out of this, he had to. In a surprisingly short space of time Ella was back, and her triumphant expression told him he wasn't going to like what she was about to tell him.

'Mum and Dad are coming here for a few days. They'll arrive on Wednesday. I said you'd had to go on an unexpected business trip and I didn't want to drive all the way to Yorkshire alone with Soraya. Mum quite understood.'

Rick closed his eyes. Round one to Ella. He stood up.

'Very well. I'll go tomorrow. And you can have the house until the adoption's finalised and the initial visits are over. Then we'll talk again.'

Without giving her time to reply he left the room, taking the whisky bottle with him.

The following morning Rick was up early. First things first – what could he do about Gareth while he was away? He couldn't exactly change the lock on the shed door. If Ella got someone in to remove the concrete, Gareth would come to light straightaway.

Nothing came to mind – all he could do was trust they'd leave the shed alone. June and Steve would be into the Grandma-and-Grandpa scene; nobody would worry about a bit of concrete, would they? He would lay the wooden floor panels back on top of the concrete and hope for the best.

By ten-thirty Rick was packed and ready to leave on his 'business trip'. In reality, he was going to Amanda's and oh, how good it would be to get away from the hell he'd created here. He brought his case downstairs, where Ella was sorting through the accounts folder.

'Your credit card bill hasn't been paid yet. You splashed out in the garden centre, didn't you? Concrete and lime and heaven knows what.'

Rick retreated into indignation. 'Have you ever thought your marriage failed because you were too involved in children and unimportant things like bills from the garden centre? And it's hardly sky-high, is it? Just the stuff I needed for the shed...' He flinched in horror. There it was again, the shed...

Her face was uncomprehending. 'What is it about that shed, Rick?'

He swallowed, searching for words, then saw she didn't expect an answer. She'd said it to annoy him, but he wasn't annoyed as much as unsettled. A picture of him and Ella a few short months ago slid into his head – happy together, preparing for the adoption. At least... Ella had been happy. His own happiness hadn't matched hers, and their decline started.

'By the way, I've applied for a part-time receptionist post at the dentist opposite the station,' said Ella nonchalantly. 'I could do that when Soraya's at school. And I know Dad'll help me buy this place from you, Rick. So you be thinking about that, and we can discuss it when Mum and Dad have left.'

She swept into the living room and joined Soraya watching cartoons.

When he arrived at the flat Amanda was folding the washing, which seemed to be ninety per cent Jaden's things. She glared at him and Rick sagged. First Ella – which was in a way understandable – but now Amanda was looking at him as if he'd poisoned her favourite cat.

'You'll never guess who I've just had on the phone,' she said, shaking out a small t-shirt. 'Your dear wife. She wants me to babysit for her while she goes for job interviews. Apparently there might be one next week.'

'What did you say?'

She looked at him, a tiny smile pulling at the corner of her mouth. 'I said I'd be away visiting friends next week. And then I booked me, you, and Jaden into a B&B in Edinburgh for a few days. How about it?'

And in spite of the truly terrible situation he was in, Rick's heart began to sing.

They were going to get through this.

# Chapter Four

'Darling! Lovely to see you! And Soraya! You're just as pretty as you look on Skype!'

Ella hugged her mother, who let go almost immediately to concentrate on her prospective grandchild. Soraya submitted to being kissed, which made a good impression, though Ella knew that the little girl's restiveness might not go down well with her new grandfather, at least.

'Come in. Rick was sorry to miss you, but it's great you could come. Was the drive down okay?'

'It was lovely. I see Rick's taken your car?'

Ella blinked. All this lying. But it wasn't a lie, actually, Rick had – inconsiderately – taken the car. They hadn't even discussed it, either.

'Yes. I'll need to get you a booster seat for Soraya. I should have thought to keep hold of ours.'

Ella's father swelled visibly, the picture of pride. 'We've already got one. Can't have a new granddaughter and no car seat for her, can we?'

Soraya ran to look and was loud in her praise of the Muppets design on the booster. Ella began to relax;

maybe this wouldn't be so hard after all. If she avoided talking about Rick there shouldn't be any problems.

Her optimism took a dent at lunchtime, however.

'Wonder what poor Daddy's doing today,' said June to Soraya, while Ella was dishing out the Cornish pasties that were her father's long-time favourite.

'Don't care. Daddy's always grumpy.' Soraya dived into her pasty as soon as it arrived in front of her, and June frowned.

Ella made a mental note to instruct Soraya on her grandmother's version of table manners ASAP. Anything for a quiet life. 'Daddy's been working too hard and he's been a bit, um, distracted,' she said. 'Let's think of some places to go to while Grandma and Grandpa are here.'

After the meal Soraya took June and Steve out to see her shell garden. Steve began to help the little girl rebuild the back section, and Ella and June wandered along the flower border.

'Ella, is Rick all right?'

Ella sighed inwardly. Mum had a nose like a bloodhound, but she had no intention of telling her parents the true state of her marriage.

'He's fine. Just busy. And as you've maybe noticed, tact isn't Soraya's middle name.'

Steve was trotting towards the shed. 'Got a gardening pad? The old knees aren't used to crouching down any more.'

'There's a brown cushion on the bottom shelf,' said Ella.

He disappeared into the shed and emerged a few moments later with the cushion and a perplexed expression. 'What on earth's going on with the floor in there? The left side's wobbly as a jelly.'

'Daddy tried to make a new floor but he couldn't do it.' Soraya danced off after a bright turquoise butterfly.

'There's a concrete base underneath, but it's uneven. We'll get it lifted again,' said Ella. 'Rick thought it would be more waterproof or something. I don't know why he put the wood back down.' She went into the shed and heaved the slabs up again, propping them against the side wall. At least now people could see what they were walking over.

Steve brightened immediately. 'I'll have a go while I'm here, shall I? Be something to do while you're all being girly.'

'Daddy's silly. It's a stupid floor.' Soraya pulled Steve towards the shell garden.

'You shouldn't let her talk about Rick like that,' said June, turning back to the flower border.

Ella massaged her hairline. A tension headache was lurking, and no wonder. 'I know, but we have to cut her some slack too. Adopted kids often go through a 'testing you' phase. She's doing very well, considering.' Considering her new mother and father weren't on speaking terms and her father had twice driven off with her. Ella squinted to see if her mother was buying into the explanation. Don't rock the boat, Mum.


The following day was overcast and June suggested taking Soraya to buy a new dress for that evening's meal out. Steve folded his newspaper and winked at Ella.

'I'll leave you girls to do that. I can make a start on the shed floor.'

Ella felt as if she was the punch bag between two warring parties that morning. Her mother's idea of a dress suitable for a small girl was not the same as Soraya's, and neither was prepared to compromise. Eventually they found a mid-green tunic with a white lace border that was feminine enough for June, and Soraya was persuaded that Kermit the frog was the very same colour. They continued towards the supermarket, grandmother and granddaughter pleased with their purchase and Ella fighting another headache. Her mother was so full on. Keeping up the 'Rick on a business trip' pretence was wearing, too, and Ella couldn't imagine what June would say when she learned what was really going on. They returned home with a cheese and onion quiche for lunch, and found Steve washing his hands in the kitchen.

'Rick's no builder,' he said. 'I don't think he even levelled the ground before putting that concrete down. I've been hacking round it – should be able to lift some like that.'

Ella went out to look. The concrete was frayed round the edges as well as patchy and uneven.

'Be nice when it's finished,' she said dryly, and Steve chuckled.

'I don't promise to finish it. But anything that makes for a quicker job for the experts will be less expense for you.'

Ella was leafing through Steve's paper after lunch when a job advertisement caught her eye. School secretary in the local secondary. Now that would be well worth thinking about. She went online and filled in the application, tears pricking in her eyes. The dream of being a stay-at-home mum had taken a battering. But if – when – her marriage ended she would need the money, and this job came with school holidays.

And it would show Rick she was serious about keeping the house, too.


The overcast weather turned to heavy rain, and Ella was glad her parents were there to occupy Soraya. The four of them spent an hour at the garden centre, and came back with some new parts for Rick's drill, and a candle decoration set. With Soraya and Grandma decorating chunky candles in the dining room, Ella had some me-time, and spent most of it trawling adoption websites trying to find out what happened when a couple adopted and then split up. There were so many instances of single people adopting, surely she would be allowed to keep Soraya? The problem was, she was afraid to ask. If she mentioned it to Liz there would be a big fuss and the adoption would be delayed at best. Ella shivered. The best way forward was to arrange her life into a place where she was financially independent, and in a pleasant, settled home with her child.

Her thought of a couple of weeks ago niggled at the back of her head. *An adopted child is never your own child*... But nobody would remove a kiddie from a settled, happy home – would they? And how sick-making it had come to this. Grief for her marriage welled up inside Ella, taking its place beside the bitterness that Rick had changed so much. He'd cheated on her and deceived her

– and possibly he'd deceived himself, as well, that he'd wanted to adopt.

'Pooh! More rain,' said Soraya on Friday morning.

Ella had to agree. Being cooped up in the house wasn't her idea of a fun summer either. She'd spent the past half hour teaching Soraya their phone number, as well as Lindsay's and Owen's, as contact people in an emergency. After thirty minutes of sitting still, Soraya was rarin' to go, but the rain couldn't have been heavier. The buddleia was bereft of butterflies, and the shell garden had sunk several inches.

Steve appeared in the kitchen looking for coffee. 'The forecast's terrible all weekend. Ella, your mum and I were thinking about going over to visit Mary in Helston today, instead of on the way home. We'd come back at the beginning of the week when it's supposed to be summery again, and stay another couple of days. We want to go to the beach with Soraya and hunt for more shells. And I think you said Rick would be back next week? Be nice to catch up with him too.' He ruffled Soraya's hair and she squealed.

'Sounds like a plan,' said Ella. 'I'm not sure about Rick, but I'll call him and find out.' She smiled at her father. Rick was under the impression that the house would be guest-free by Sunday, but that didn't matter. It would do him good to realise that her life and Soraya's didn't revolve around him. And presumably he wouldn't say no to staying on with his girlfriend, whoever she was. A new thought struck Ella – did she even want Rick back here to live? It was scary how her feelings about him were changing.

'I'll have another go at the shed with the new bit,' said Steve. 'Then we'll leave in the afternoon – if it's okay with Mary.'

'What's a bit?' said Soraya, staring after him as he ran through the rain.

'It's the new metal thing for the drill that cuts through stone – he hopes,' said Ella. 'No, don't go with him, sweetheart. There might be chunks of concrete flying around in there.'

There was certainly plenty of noise when Steve started, and Ella found time to be glad that the drilling wasn't going to continue all weekend.

At half past three she and Soraya waved her parents off.

'Grandma's funny, isn't she?' said Soraya as Ella closed the front door on the rain.

Ella opened her mouth to say, 'In small doses', then closed it again. There was a lot to be said for tact around children. 'She certainly is,' she agreed. 'Now, it's been a filthy day and it's going to be a filthy night too. Let's have ourselves a lovely blobby evening with a DVD. And lemon pancakes for tea?'

Soraya ran into the kitchen. 'I want to see what Grandpa's done in the shed!'

Ella looked outside; you could barely see the shed for the rain. 'Let's wait till the morning, huh? If the shed hasn't turned into Noah's Ark and floated away by then.'

Which, when you thought about it, would be a blessing in disguise.

# CHAPTER FIVE

Sunday 27th – Monday 28th July

'Pingu! Pingu!' Jaden was warm and heavy on Rick's shoulders as they watched the Penguin Parade at Edinburgh Zoo.

'Pingu everywhere you look,' said Amanda, reaching up to squeeze the little boy's foot.

Rick leaned over and kissed her head. Being here just felt so right – him and Amanda, and Jaden who would be his boy. Things might be messy now, but it was going to be all right. They belonged together.

He hadn't contacted Ella since leaving St Ives, and she'd made no effort to call him either. Worry about what was going on at home nagged at Rick; it was like toothache, the kind that isn't bad enough to make you phone the dentist, but still jabs away at the back of your mind all the time. The news was unsettling too – horror-reports about landslides and flooding were coming from the south-west. Was Gareth still all right under the shed? What happened to a buried body when the soil was completely saturated – did it try to float, work its way to the surface? Good thing he'd put that concrete down;

it wasn't perfect but it would do the job until he got back. They were planning to leave Edinburgh tomorrow. Decision day was looming for him and Ella.

'Let's go for coffee,' said Amanda. 'I'm parched. Juice for Jaden?'

Jaden bounced up and down, and Rick gripped the small feet more firmly.

They were squeezed together in a bus on the way back to the B&B, Jaden dozing on Rick's knee, when his phone rang. Hell, it was Ella. He couldn't take the call here. He switched it off and tried to look nonchalant, cursing the fact that parking was limited at the zoo and they'd come by public transport.

He stayed outside to phone when they arrived at the B&B, apprehension twisting in his gut.

'Hi – Ella.' He wiped a stray bead of sweat from his temple. 'Sorry, I was in the car when you called. Is everything all right? The news is full of your awful weather.' He couldn't ask about the garden shed. That would be just too odd.

'Fine. And Mum and Dad are well too, thank you for asking.' There was no friendliness in her voice.

'Are they still with you?' That sounded kinder than 'have they gone yet' – didn't it? Her answer sent his heart thudding towards his boots.

'They've been visiting Mum's cousin for the weekend but they're coming back tonight for another couple of days. I thought you should know.'

'Thanks. Um – has the garden survived all that rain?'

'Oh yes. And you'll be glad to know Dad's been attacking the concrete in the shed. He bought a heavy-duty bit to drill holes in it and he's shifted a lot round the edge. He'll do some more next week.'

Rick flushed hot, and then cold sweat trickled down his brow. 'No! Tell him to leave it – it's much too strenuous for a man of his age. I'll get it fixed when I get back.'

'Which will be...?'

'Tomorrow. I'll call you when I'm back in St Ives.'

'Where are you - ?'

Rick ended the call and sprinted inside. That interfering old man. Nothing, but nothing in this life was ever easy – would he get back in time to prevent Gareth being discovered?


It was afternoon the following day when he arrived in St Ives, having driven several hours the previous evening before crashing out at a hotel south of Manchester. He'd persuaded Amanda to take Jaden to Gareth's mother in Glasgow for a couple of days. If there was going to be a problem with Gareth and the concrete, it was best she wasn't around. Something was telling him Amanda might not be happy about Gareth's resting place, and dealing with Ella and her parents would be enough hassle.

Rick drove through town, cursing the fact that Amanda's flat was so close to home. If Ella saw the car parked outside... On second thoughts he couldn't risk that. He turned back, and left the car at a supermarket near the sea front, hailing a taxi to take him to Amanda's. Rick glanced up at the sky. Cotton wool clouds were floating across immaculate powder blue – a picture postcard day. The town was full of happy tourists, and how he hoped Ella was safely on the beach with her parents and Soraya. Back in Amanda's flat, he poured a stiff drink and lifted his phone.

'Ella, hi. I'm in St Ives. I'm wondering when to come home?'

'Mum and Dad are back again. I don't think you should come while they're here, Rick.'

She couldn't have sounded cooler, and Rick winced. 'Ah. How are you all getting on? Having fun?' Shit, what a stupid thing to say. How could he get the conversation round to the shed?

'We're having brilliant fun, Rick. I'm choosing my outfit for the job interview I have on Thursday, Mum and Soraya are washing shells, and my father's knocking lumps of concrete from the shed floor as we speak. I'll let you know when my parents leave.'

The connection broke, and Rick stood there, rigid with shock. Steve was lifting the concrete *right this minute* – any second now he might come across whatever was left of Gareth. No, no, no, that could *not* be allowed to happen. Rick fled from Amanda's flat and pounded up the hill.

The garden was empty and he ran straight over the grass and burst into the shed. Broken-off pieces of concrete were all over the place and Steve was on his knees, pulling at an enormous chunk, his face red. Rick's worst fear was realised – the floor he'd laid was more than half gone and the ground beneath it was ragged and soft. It would take very little to uncover Gareth.

'Rick! What a -'

'Leave it, man! Come away – it's too much for you!'

Rick grasped Steve's arm and pulled, but the run up the hill or the nerves or something was zapping his strength. Steve shook him off, surprise on his kindly round face.

'Hey, it's not as hard as all that! Look!' Steve tugged the lump again and it broke away in his hands, bringing a wodge of sticky wet earth along with it. He tossed it to the side and to Rick's horror, there in the hole was a piece of shiny plastic. Gareth's bin bag.

Before Rick could stop him, Steve tugged it. 'Ah, you did try to line the base before you put the concrete down.'

Rick yanked the other man's arm. 'For God's *sake*, leave it alone!'

Indignation and shock filled Steve's eyes and he jerked back, pulling at the bin bag as he did so. Rick's breath caught in his throat. If the plastic tore... He tried to manhandle his father-in-law away from the hole but Steve gripped the bag harder and pushed Rick back with his other hand. The bin bag ripped open with an odd little popping sound and an almost skeletal hand appeared, shreds of God knows what still attached to the bones.

'Aargh!' Steve dropped onto all fours, straddling the hole and staring straight at the hand, gasping for breath. His face turned a mottled grey colour.

Rick grabbed him again. 'Come *away*!' Had he seen the hand? But he must have. It was over.

Steve fell across the hole, his breath strident in the confines of the shed. Black giddiness descended on Rick and he ducked his head; he must *not* pass out here... Steve's breath rattled in his throat and then cracked into horrible silence.

Rick retched. No, please no, the man was dead – was

he dead? Oh fuck he was dead; he wasn't breathing and his face was the colour of – Rick retched again and spat. Christ no – what was he supposed to do now?

Sobbing aloud, he rolled the older man away from the hole and onto the wooden half of the floor where he slapped his cheeks. 'Steve! Come on! Breathe!'

And that face, those eyes, staring at him, expressionless and empty – how very much more terrible than Gareth's they were. Rick leaned across and vomited bile on the earth floor. Should he start CPR? But Steve had seen the hand…

Panting, Rick shoved clumps of earth over Gareth's hand before whacking the chunk of concrete back on top. He stamped on earth and concrete until the floor was more or less flat, tears rolling down his cheeks. Then he pulled the wooden boards from the side and dropped them on the still uneven base.

Now for Steve. Heaving his father-in-law to his dead feet was one of the most horrible things he had ever done, but the strength of sheer panic was with Rick. He pulled Steve's left arm over his own shoulders and grasped him round the waist. Half-blinded by a mixture of tears and sweat, he stumbled forwards, pulling Steve with him. A good kick opened the shed door and they staggered out, Rick's head thumping so hard against the door frame that he fell to his knees, still clutching Steve's lifeless body. For a moment he couldn't see anything, the pain was so severe, but he forced himself to his feet, pulling Steve with him.

*Come on, come on* – get away from the shed… Steve's feet dragged over the grass as Rick lurched forwards, to the house, to the house... the kitchen door...

He didn't quite make it. Two metres from the house he fell to his knees, Steve collapsing in a heap beside him. Rick crawled forwards and thundered on the door. It opened, and Ella's face, incredulous at first before horror took over, stared down on him.

'He was stumbling over the grass, I was helping him in when he collapsed – call an ambulance!'

Ella pitched forward on her knees beside her father and gathered the grey face in her hands.

'You call! Daddy? Oh, Dad!'

On his knees beside the dead man, his hands shaking like they'd never shaken all the time he was dealing with Gareth, Rick pulled out his mobile and punched out 999.

# CHAPTER SIX

Monday 28th July

Ella crouched on the ground beside her father, her heart thudding in her ears. This couldn't be happening.

'He's not breathing – I can't feel his pulse! Rick! We should do CPR!'

Rick had dropped his mobile after giving the address to the emergency operator and was cowering on hands and knees a few yards away, panting. He gave no sign of having heard her. Ella looked round wildly – she couldn't do this; she didn't know how. Vague memories of Casualty on TV had her pushing down on her father's ribcage, *push push push push push* and now breathe into his mouth... She retched painfully but went back into her *push push push*...

'Ella? What's –? *Steve...*' June was propped in the kitchen door, her face rigid with shock.

'Mummy?' Soraya appeared behind June and then immediately turned and fled back into the house.

Ella didn't pause in her rhythm. 'Go inside, Mum. Stay with Soraya. An ambulance is coming. Rick! Come and *help* me!'

But all he did was crawl over and kneel beside Steve's head while Ella blew into the cooling lips, gagged and spat, and started again, *push push push*... It seemed like half a lifetime before they heard a siren in the distance, but help was nearly here and oh dear God had she done enough? Was Dad even alive?

An ambulance screamed up and two green-clad paramedics took over, clamping a breathing bag over Steve's mouth. Ella sat on the doorstep, panting, her heart racing as the paramedic pounded up and down on her father's chest, so much more forcefully than she had. She turned to Rick, squatting to the side, his eyes fixed on the paramedics and their patient.

'What were you thinking about? You left me to do everything!'

His eyes slewed sideways. 'He's gone, Ella.'

The older paramedic slapped pads on her father's chest. 'Clear... shocking... Sinus rhythm, let's go!'

Ella raised clasped hands to her mouth. One of the men was still operating the breathing bag, no, no, he still wasn't breathing – *Daddy, please breathe, please be okay.*

'We'll get him to hospital now. Are you coming with him?'

Ella turned to Rick. He was sheet-white, you'd think it was his father being bundled into an ambulance. 'Go and tell my mother. If she wants to come, either bring her or get her a taxi.'

She clambered into the ambulance and they wailed off, down the hill and through town. Should she have left her mother with Rick in the state he was in? Thank

heavens her mobile was in her sweatshirt pocket. Mary…
she would ask Mum's cousin to go over.

'Mary. It's Ella. Dad's been taken really bad. I think it's
his heart. I'm in the ambulance with him – can you go to
mine and help Mum?'

'Oh no. I'm on my way, Ella. Speak soon, lovey.'

Now to let them know at home… but no one answered
the landline, and both Rick's and her mother's mobiles
were switched off.

Halfway to the hospital at Truro her father's heart
stopped again, and the rest of the time was spent with
the paramedic pounding Steve's chest. And there was
nothing she could do, nothing. She couldn't even hold
his hand. Would he be in this state if she'd been better
at CPR?

At the hospital he was trolleyed away and a nurse
sent Ella to reception to 'book him in'. It didn't take long;
the place wasn't busy, and when she went back to the
room where her father was they were still doing chest
compressions. Oh no. A horrible foreboding took hold
of Ella; she couldn't control the shivers coursing through
her body, and her hands were freezing. Five minutes. Ten
minutes. Fifteen minutes, and she had known all along,
hadn't she… He wasn't going to make it.

And moments later they stopped.

'I'm sorry,' said the doctor in charge, a woman who
looked no older than Ella. 'It was a massive heart attack.
We did all we could. You can see him presently if you
want. Come and have a cup of tea first.'

It was as if she'd been out in extreme cold, and her feet
and her lips and – right inside her – were all numb. Ella

sat in the relatives' room shivering and drinking horrible tea with too much sugar while the doctor explained what had happened to her father's heart.

'Did he have any previous problems?'

Ella gripped her mug with shaking fingers. It was dreadful to be so out of control. 'He was on medication for high blood pressure, and he had a scare of some kind last year but they changed his pills and he was fine again...'

Until he came to stay with his daughter and rip up concrete floors. This was her fault, she should never have allowed him to do something so strenuous. Ella began to sob. She would never forget the mental picture of her father this past hour – her ineffectual pounding on his poor chest, the taste of those rubbery lips –

She clamped her hands over her mouth and raced for the toilets, the doctor close behind. When the spasm was over Ella rinsed her face and the doctor passed her a paper towel.

'Is there anyone who could come and get you?'

'My husband's at home with... I'll call them now. Will Dad – will he be taken to an undertaker's?'

'Yes. You can see him here before he goes to the mortuary, if you like, and your undertaker will collect him from there.'

Ella struggled to her feet. She had to call her mother, oh, what could she say to Mum?

Mary answered the house phone, and Ella closed her eyes in relief.

'Oh, Ella. June's in a terrible state. How is he?'

Ella managed to pass on the news with a lot more

control than if she'd been talking to her mother. Bless Mary. What a good thing she'd been able to drop everything and run to help.

It was nine before she arrived back home, calmer after the long taxi ride. June was huddled in the corner of the sofa, her eyes red and blotchy. As soon as she saw Ella she burst into tears.

'She didn't want to go to the hospital,' said Mary helplessly. 'She's been sitting there shaking since you called to say he had – gone.'

Ella rubbed her mother's back. 'Oh, Mum,' she said, hearing her voice break.

June wailed anew, rocking back and forth, and all Ella could do was hold her mother and rock with her. She looked at Mary.

'Soraya?' And Rick, where was Rick in all this?

'She was pretty upset. I asked Rick to take her away for a bit,' said Mary, and the words seared into Ella's head.

'Wha -' She couldn't speak; dear heavens no, where was Soraya?

Mary moved across the sofa and murmured in Ella's ear. 'June was hysterical. It wasn't good for the child, seeing her grandmother like that. I think Rick's taking her to a little friend. You'll know who.'

Ella grabbed her mobile and sat patting her mother with one hand and pulling up Rick's number with the other. And of course, he didn't answer. She fought to keep fear at bay. Surely Rick would do what he'd said, take Soraya to – Amanda? Was she home yet? Lindsay was still away… Ella gripped June's hand. She couldn't cope with this and her mother too.

'Come on, Mum,' she said firmly. 'Let's get you up to bed. You need to sleep.'

The words seemed to calm June, and she allowed Ella and Mary to take her upstairs. Ella gave her one of the sleeping pills she'd been prescribed last winter when her nerves about the adoption got the better of her. She and Mary exchanged a look of relief as June sank into the pillow, her eyes closing. Ella pushed damp hair back from her hot face and hurried through to Soraya's room. No small girl lay sleeping there tonight, and the pink suitcase was missing from the corner. So Rick had packed for Soraya – *where had he taken her?* Ella tried his mobile again, but it was still switched off, and why that should be was hard to imagine. Twisting her hands, she fought for control. This was the worst day, the worst time she could remember, and all she wanted to do was scream, loud and long. Rick wouldn't do it again – would he? Disappear with Soraya? This time he even had an excuse – Mary had asked him to go.

Ella tore downstairs, where the older woman was packing her handbag. 'What did Rick say before they left?'

Mary looked startled. 'Just that he would take her somewhere. He was very upset too. They left shortly afterwards. I'll get off home, Ella, as long as there's still a vestige of light, but I'll come back in the morning. I'm sure Rick won't be long – why don't you text him, if he isn't answering his phone?'

Ella nodded. She should have thought of that. She

went out to the car with Mary, who gave her a long hug.

'You get some sleep too, darling. Take one of your pills. June will need you strong tomorrow.'

So would Soraya, thought Ella, waving briefly as the car drove off. She was still in the hallway when the doorbell rang, and Owen stood there, his face questioning.

'Oh no – Ella, I'm so sorry,' he said, when she explained about her father. 'I thought something was wrong when I saw you outside there. I won't bother you now, but if there's anything I can do, give me a shout. Any time.'

He touched her shoulder and left. Ella closed the door behind him and leaned on it. Thank heavens he hadn't wanted to stay for tea and sympathy.

She collapsed on a kitchen chair, leaning her head on the table and sobbing quietly. No one else in the house was awake to comfort her. And her father was dead. Impossible to see further than tomorrow, when she'd have to arrange undertakers and a funeral and look after Mum and – where were Rick and Soraya?

# CHAPTER SEVEN

Tuesday 29th – Wednesday 30th July

Amanda propped herself up on one elbow and grabbed her phone from the bedside table. Thankfully, she'd put it on vibrate. She glanced at Jaden, asleep in his cot on the other side of their room in Susie's Glasgow west end flat. At last, Rick was getting back to her – she'd tried his number at least ten times yesterday.

'Well, you took your time! What -'

'He's dead, Amanda.'

It was a shaky old man's voice; she'd never heard him speak like that before. He sounded both gutted and terrified, and fear stabbed into her.

'*What?* Who?'

'Ella's dad. I – I found him in the – the garden after he collapsed and I called 999 but he died, Amanda, he died at the hospital.'

A sob followed his voice down the line and Amanda blinked. Had Rick been so close to Ella's dad? But what a shock for him, poor baby – this was the why of yesterday's non-communication.

'Oh no, Rick, that must have been terrible. How old

was he?'

'Sixty-eight, I think. Amanda, it brought it all back, you know... Gareth.'

Alarm bells shrilled in Amanda's head. If Rick was in earshot of anyone at all he shouldn't be talking about Gareth – and neither should she, with Susie on the other side of the wall.

'Don't talk about that, Rick. Will you be all right? Would it help if I came back?'

'My head's buzzing. Please come, Amanda.'

He broke the connection and Amanda stared at her phone. He wasn't coping, she could tell. Twenty to seven. She might make the mid-morning flight to Newquay, if there was a seat available. Thank heavens Jaden was young enough to sit on her lap.

The thought of Rick hurting and upset and saying who knows what to all and sundry gave Amanda no peace. She grabbed her clothes and went through to the bathroom to dress. It was understandable that a second man dying right in front of Rick would have shaken him – it was the kind of thing that didn't happen at all to most people, and now Rick had experienced it twice within a couple of months. The memory of Gareth on the bedroom floor flashed before Amanda's eyes.

She was going to have to leave the warm security of Susie's flat. Arriving here on Sunday evening, seeing how pleased Suze was to welcome her and Jaden back – it had felt like coming home. Now she would have to go back to St Ives, where Gareth was hidden somewhere – unless he was in the sea – and it was such a complicated, horrible situation. If only they could all come to live in Glasgow.

But that wouldn't work either. Amanda blinked unhappily. Suze was Gareth's mum and it would be a while before she welcomed the thought that Amanda had found another partner. The lump in her throat almost choking her, Amanda booted up the laptop and searched for a flight. But the first available seat to Newquay wasn't till the following day and she burst into tears. Nothing was going right this summer.

Amanda pushed Jaden's buggy into the arrivals hall at Newquay Cornwall Airport, glancing to right and left. She'd texted her flight times to Rick but he didn't reply, and she hadn't liked to call him. If he was with Ella and her mum, and still upset, he might say something indiscreet. She kept sending supportive messages until she realised someone might pick up his phone and see them. Now she was here and Rick was nowhere to be seen. She would have to risk a call.

'Rick – we're at Newquay Airport. Any chance of a lift home?'

'I'm not at home, Amanda.'

He sounded exhausted; Amanda had to press the phone to her ear to hear him. Frustration and weariness made her snap. 'Where the hell are you, then?'

'June was in a terrible state so I took Soraya away for a bit and she's playing up and I hardly slept. I can't pick you up, Amanda. I'll be in touch.'

'But -' She was left talking to nothing. Amanda shoved the phone into her bag and stood fighting for control. Jaden was drooping in his buggy, she was four months pregnant with Rick's child, and he expected her to hitch-hike back to St Ives. She stormed towards the exit. It would have to be a train.

Watching the scenery flash by, Jaden asleep on her lap, Amanda regained her sense of proportion. Okay, it wasn't fair that she should have the permanently shorter straw, but that would change. She would go home and provide the support he obviously needed – he could bring Soraya to her. She texted this twice, but no answer came and she gave up. Rick would get in touch when he was ready.

The flat smelled stale and there was no yoghurt in the fridge, a major catastrophe as far as Jaden was concerned. His lower lip trembled when Amanda offered him a biscuit instead, and she scooped him up and hugged him.

'Okay, sweetie pie, we'll go and buy yoghurt, will we? Yummy yoghurt in the shop for Jaden?'

Jaden clapped plump hands, and Amanda kissed him. This was such a lovely stage, when he could understand and show her what he wanted. She glanced at the calendar in the hallway, and stood still. How funny – she was sixteen weeks pregnant, and Jaden was sixteen months old. Smiling at the coincidence, Amanda hurried downstairs. The newsagent up the hill had a small supply of yoghurt.

'Did you hear about Ella Baxter's father?' The woman on the till was eager to spread the gossip.

Amanda had a brief moment of panic – was she supposed to have heard? No, she'd just got back, hadn't she? 'What happened?'

'Dropped dead at the back door yesterday. They

got help straightaway, but it was too late. Poor Ella's distraught, I hear.'

There was something unattractive about the way the woman was so avid to pass on the little sensation.

Amanda put her purse away. 'I'm sorry to hear that. Um, I don't want Jaden to hear... See you again.'

She passed Cedar Road on the way home. Now that she'd been told the terrible news, she should go by and offer her condolences, shouldn't she? She turned the buggy and continued towards Rick's house. Rick's home, to be strictly accurate.

The garden was deserted and Amanda strode up the path with the buggy. She could offer to babysit, too. She wasn't supposed to know that Rick and Soraya were away, and this way she might find out where they were.

Ella was pale, and guilt washed through Amanda. Poor soul, she had lost her father and soon she would lose her husband too. Stammering, she made her condolences and asked if she could help with Soraya. There was a long pause while Ella fumbled with a tissue, and Amanda felt more and more uncomfortable. This was horrible.

'Soraya's away with her dad for – for a bit,' said Ella at last, wiping her eyes. 'It's better for her; my mother's still here and of course she's terribly upset.'

'I can imagine. Are they nearby? And – is there anything I can do, Ella? Shopping or something? Shall I call you tomorrow morning before I go to the supermarket?

Ella appeared to pull herself together. 'Oh yes please, Amanda. That would be so helpful. I'll see you tomorrow, then.'

There was no way Amanda could think of to prolong

the conversation, and she didn't like to ask about Rick and Soraya again. She would try calling him later when Soraya would be asleep.

Thinking about Ella's dead father was a horrible reminder of her own dead husband and Amanda blinked back tears. Gareth had died, just like that, in a stupid, fluke accident, and here was another unexpected death. There was no guarantee of tomorrow for anyone. Imagine if she lost Rick too... but she didn't even have him yet, not really.

She was walking down the hill, hunched over the buggy to hide the tears, when a dull knock inside her abdomen jerked Amanda upright. Her baby – her baby had moved! She massaged firmly and was rewarded by another knock from within. Wow. How – how brilliant. Her baby was helping her at exactly the right time. That would be something very positive to tell Rick when she called. His baby was kicking. Amanda shivered in delight.

# CHAPTER EIGHT

Thursday 31st July

Ella put the house phone down. *Thank you, thank you.* Life was maybe sheer and bloody hell, but people were helping. She went through to the living room where her mother was slumped in an armchair, an untouched cup of coffee by her side. Poor Mum – she was a broken woman.

'That was Mary on the phone, Mum. She wants to take you to stay with her for a few days. I think you should go – it would be easier for you. It'll be hectic here when Rick and Soraya are back.'

Dread – and anger too – pulled at Ella's middle as she spoke. She still had no idea when Rick was planning on coming home. They'd spoken twice on the phone and he'd answered two of her texts, but all she could glean was Soraya was well and they were 'at the beach' – which could be anywhere. And he'd refused point-blank to come home while June was still there. It was so unfair of him to keep her and Soraya apart but with her mother to look after there was a limit to what Ella could do about it.

June's expression couldn't have been more listless. 'All right. Whatever's easiest. Once I have the ashes I'll think about getting back home.'

Ella sat on the arm of her mother's chair and rubbed the hunched shoulders. 'Take your time. You don't need to rush into anything.'

It was so hard. Her father, who had been so full of life and enthusiasm, would soon be reduced to 'the ashes'. Never again would she visit 'Mum and Dad', and Soraya's memories of her grandfather would be sparse at best. It was heart-breaking.

But oh, the biggest question of all, the one that had sick dread pulling at her middle, overpowering the grief – was the adoption going to work out? Rick was having an affair, and if he'd taken Soraya to be with his mistress Ella knew she would never forgive him. She wiped her eyes on the tea towel and tossed it into the washing machine. Everything was out of control – she didn't know where her child was, her husband was having an affair, and her father was dead. And the adoption agency was clueless about what was going on. What would they do if they found out?

Her mobile vibrated and Ella grabbed it, disappointment spearing into her when she saw Amanda's name on the screen and not Rick's. Still, Amanda was proving a good friend, saving her from the eyes in the supermarket like this. Eyes staring at the woman whose father died on the kitchen doorstep. Amanda knew what it was like to face those eyes, and it was kind of her to spare Ella the horror.

The shopping list was on the kitchen table, and Ella sat down to pass it on, trying to sound positive. 'You'll come in for a coffee when you get back, won't you?'

Amanda accepted, and Ella went upstairs where June was packing. She was struck, horribly, by how frail her mother looked. Death did that to you. Only now could Ella appreciate how brave Amanda had been – and still was – getting through her own tragedy with a little one to support and another on the way.

Mary arrived and Ella was glad to see a little more colour come into her mother's face as the cousins loaded June's things into the car. It would be good for Mum to be with someone of her own generation, someone who had known her all her life. And with Mum at Mary's, Ella would be able to concentrate on Rick, and getting Soraya home again.

She stood in the front door as Mary drove off, then turned back into the hallway and stopped. Not a sound, nothing moving, silence everywhere. Surely it had never been this quiet before? Or was it that after just a few short weeks of having a lively, quirky six-year-old to laugh with, she wasn't used to hearing nothing in her home? Ella closed her eyes against burning tears. How very much she missed Soraya; more than she missed her father, if she were honest. But this was the time to be active and get her girl back.

Pulling out her phone, Ella texted Rick. *Mum gone to Mary's, please come home*. She waited a few minutes, but no answer came and she bit her lip. Rick's behaviour was beyond that of a man in shock after witnessing a sudden death. Was she doing the right thing, not telling Liz that she didn't know where Soraya was? What Rick was doing almost amounted to abduction – and it wasn't the first time.

The doorbell rang and Ella flew to answer it, but it was Amanda with her shopping.

Jaden ran straight through to the living room. 'So-so-so!'

'I don't think she's here today, sweetie,' said Amanda, depositing a supermarket carrier on the table.

Ella swallowed. 'No, she's not. Look, Jaden – biscuits.'

He ran back and accepted a chocolate digestive. Amanda took him on her knee while Ella made coffee, feeling a strangely awkward silence fall. Amanda was cuddling Jaden, staring round the kitchen, not meeting Ella's eyes.

Eventually she spoke. 'How's it going, Ella?'

'Oh, Amanda, I don't know what to do!' It was out before she'd thought, a real plea from the heart, and Ella didn't miss the apprehensive expression that crossed Amanda's face. It wasn't fair, this woman's loss was so much greater than her own – she must be in bits still too.

'What is it?'

Ella clasped her hands together. 'Rick's having an affair and I don't even know where he's taken Soraya. He's in a terrible state with Dad dying like that. I don't know if I should contact the adoption people or the police or what.'

As soon as the words were out she wished them back; confidences like this didn't belong in her relationship with Amanda. But Amanda would understand. She was grieving too, and she was a mother.

Amanda's face was horrified. 'Oh no. Surely he'll be back soon, Ella. Have you heard from him since he left?'

'A couple of texts and calls. He's done this before – driven off somewhere with Soraya to get back at me after a row, but he's never been away this long. I think I should tell someone.'

'Oh, Ella, that would mean police and heaven knows what. I would wait another day, I really would. Now your mum's gone he might feel able to come back.'

Ella sat making crumbs with her biscuit. It was what she wanted to think too. She came to a decision. 'I'll text him again and tell him I'll call later and he should answer it. Then if I don't get hold of him I'll get in touch with our adoption worker.'

Amanda leaned across the table. 'But that might mean – they might cancel the adoption or something. Or delay it, anyway. I think you should wait until you've been able to talk properly to Rick – I'm sure you're worrying about nothing. It's, um, I mean – after a death in the family people don't react the way they usually do.'

She was right, thought Ella. Maybe she should give Rick until tomorrow to come home. He might even think he was being helpful, staying out of her hair like this.

Ella stood at the window as Amanda loaded Jaden into her car then sat manipulating her phone for a minute before driving off. Everyone was so accessible nowadays. With a push of a few buttons you could contact anyone, anywhere – yet she was struggling to get hold of her husband. She sat on the sofa to text. *Will phone later, please answer. Am worried about Soraya. Don't want to involve Liz or the police. Please.*

And now – there was nothing more she could do. Grimly, Ella put the coffee mugs into the dishwasher and was wiping Jaden's chocolate smear from the table when her phone rang. Her heart leapt; it was him, oh thank heavens, it was Rick. Her hands were shaking so hard she could barely take the call.

'Rick! Is everything okay?'

His voice was low but he sounded more or less normal. 'Everything's fine. Don't worry, Ella. We'll be back tomorrow morning, and I want you and Soraya to move out.'

'Let me speak to her, Rick, please.' How awful this was, she was begging to speak to her own child.

'She's in the bathroom. We'll see you tomorrow.'

'Where are - '

The connection was dead. Ella stood leaning on the table, panting. They were coming home, and she would do anything he wanted if they just came home. Rick was clearly still upset, but it was going to be all right, oh please, it must be all right.

# CHAPTER NINE

Thursday 31st July

Rick tossed his phone on the bed. Good job Amanda had warned him. The call to Ella hadn't been easy, but it was done and all things considered it had gone well. He should never have gone off with Soraya again – but it was the one way to make Ella cooperate. A few days without Soraya meant his wife would do as he wanted, and Mary'd made it all too easy for him to leave. He'd been fleeing the repercussions of Steve's death and the look on Ella's face when she yelled at him for not helping. And the frustration, and the anger, and the *pain* – his head was buzzing with pain.

And of course he should have helped Steve the moment he collapsed and not – what? Five, ten minutes later? Now Steve was dead and if the police started sniffing around they would find Gareth – or what was left of him.

If his hand was almost skeletal, what did Gareth's face look like, with those empty grey eyes? Rick's stomach heaved.

Relax, hissed the calm part of his brain. Even if the

hospital did a post-mortem on Steve, surely they would never notice that five minutes had passed before anyone started CPR. He was worrying about nothing. But he didn't know, that was the problem. And – how had he turned into some kind of adulterous mass-murderer? His brain shied away from the thought of first Gareth and now Steve... It was incomprehensible.

He glanced at Soraya, prone on her bed, colouring in with a glum face. They were in a B&B near Penzance, and as the weather had turned wet again they were stuck indoors in this crappy little bedroom that didn't even have an en suite. After just five minutes in the guest sitting room this morning the landlady came in for a chat, and that was the last thing he needed. God knows what Soraya would say if anyone started asking her questions. She wasn't happy, that was clear – it was 'When are we going home to Mummy?' every five minutes. And he couldn't think straight because his brain was buzzing. Maybe a call to Amanda would help.

'I'm going to the bathroom. I won't be a minute,' he said, and Soraya gaped at him speechlessly.

Amanda answered her phone on the first ring. 'Rick, where are you? What are you playing at?'

'I'm trying to keep my head above water, what do you think? I have to get Ella to cooperate and she will, this way. But she mustn't go to the authorities. If the police start sniffing around they might find Gareth.'

He heard her intake of breath. Shit. That was a mistake. She didn't know where Gareth was any more than the police did.

'Rick, the reason Ella's thinking about contacting

anyone is because you've done a disappearing act with Soraya. Get her back home and everything's fine. Should I talk to Ella?'

'I called her. I said we'd be back tomorrow.'

'Good.' Silence. She was obviously mulling something over, and he waited. 'Rick... what did you do with Gareth?'

Her voice was almost a whisper and he wondered if she was worried about someone hearing. But a sound from the corridor told Rick he was the one being overheard. He jerked the bathroom door open and Soraya looked up at him, her little face dreary. He clicked his phone off.

'What are you doing? Are we going home to Mummy now?' Her voice was afraid and he made an effort to pull himself together.

'It's some work I have to organise. We're going home tomorrow, so let's get you bathed and your hair washed for Mummy, shall we?'

She rose to the bait and was soon splashing in warm soapy water. Rick retreated to the corridor and called Amanda again. No way did he want her 'talking' to Ella.

'Listen. I need to persuade Ella to let me have the house. If she thinks it means she'll get her precious daughter back, she'll do it. But you keep out of this, Amanda.'

He switched off and was listening to Soraya in the bath when a disturbing thought came to mind. Sweat broke out on his forehead. Amanda wasn't stupid. And he had just told her, in almost as many words, that Gareth was somewhere in or around the house.

# PART FOUR
# END GAME

# CHAPTER ONE

Friday 1st August

It was eleven-thirty and there was still no sign of Rick and Soraya. Ella tried to keep busy, but the apprehension that had her firmly in its grasp had long since turned to fear. But he would come – he *would* come. He'd said 'tomorrow morning'. At quarter to twelve she gave up reorganising the cutlery drawer and stood at the living room window, watching for the car. It was typical of the new Rick that he was making her wait.

Minutes ticked by and at five to Ella allowed herself to formulate the thought that was lurking ever closer – what if he didn't come? What if he'd just said he would to keep her out of his hair? And how pathetic it was that she'd been reduced to this, a frightened woman waiting for her husband, helpless to do anything to bring her child home.

At five past she turned away, sick at heart. Oh, he could have been delayed for any number of reasons... traffic, Soraya playing up, a queue at the petrol station... but somehow she didn't think so. She would give him until one and then call him, but there was nothing to say he'd answer his wretched phone, was there? And now she needed a coffee like never before.

Soraya's butterfly mug in the cupboard brought tears to Ella's eyes, but she blinked them away with grim determination. She was *not* going to let Rick win here. A call was maybe too easy for him to ignore – she would text him that if he didn't appear within the next couple of hours, she'd report it to Liz… who would involve the police. But if that happened Soraya might be sent straight back to Mel when she was found. It was the perfect Catch 22 situation. Ella hugged the mug to her chest, her courage deserting her. This was horrendous – she could do nothing to find her girl.

The ringing of the doorbell had her heart rate soaring, but a glance outside revealed Amanda on the doorstep. Bless her, thought Ella as she trailed through to the hallway. She knows how tough this is and she's doing her best to be supportive.

The younger woman gave her a quick smile. 'Hi. I was passing and saw the car wasn't here. Is Rick -?'

'Heaven alone knows where. I can't believe he's doing this.' Ella stood to the side. 'Come in and have a coffee. Where's Jaden?'

'He's with a friend today. We alternate with the kids once a week.'

Silence fell as they sat at the kitchen table, steaming mugs in front of them.

Ella broke it. 'I'll give him until three,' she said, pulling out her phone and texting as quickly as she could with cold, nervous fingers. 'Then I'll call our adoption society worker. He can't do this. I'm worried about Soraya.'

Hopefully the mere thought of the authorities being involved would be enough to bring Rick to his senses.

'Oh dear, that does seem drastic. Do you think maybe he's – not well? Depressed or something? Due to your father's death?'

Amanda sounded flustered and Ella paused. Was she being too hard on Rick? No, because no matter what was going on with him, there was Soraya to consider as well. She finished her text and pressed send.

'I can't help him – or Soraya – while they're not here,' she said, feeling better now the way forward was more clear. And Amanda must be wrong – there was no reason for Rick to be so affected by Dad's death. She was the one who'd failed to resuscitate him, not Rick. She was the one who'd lost a parent – and she was well on the way towards losing her husband as well as her child. Oh please no.

Amanda was sitting with both hands encircling her mug, fingers tapping against the blue and white stripes. Ella searched for something to say; not so easy when circumstances had thrown the two of them into a closer relationship than either of them was ready for.

It was a relief when the doorbell rang and Owen's voice called, 'Anyone home? You've left the front door open!'

Ella went out to the hallway. 'Owen – come in. Thanks – I'm all over the place today. This is Amanda, Jaden's mum.'

He joined them at the table and accepted Ella's offer of coffee. 'I'm not surprised you're stressed – you've had a terrible time. How's your mother?'

'Not great. She's with her cousin in Helston. And Rick's, um, taken Soraya away for a day or two, I'm expecting them back today but…' Ella pressed her lips together, blinking hard and feeling Owen's gaze. She would burst into tears if she said another word here. It was terrifying to have such a frail hold on her self-control.

'He'll be back soon,' said Amanda, but she didn't sound convincing.

Owen moved in his chair and Ella glanced up to see him frown. 'Ella, I suppose he's okay after Monday? I wasn't at home, but Mum saw Rick support your father out of the shed and she told me later how he'd cracked his head and then fallen.'

Ella froze. It was one of those moments when the world seems to stop for an instant before continuing in a different spiral. Rick and Dad were in the *shed*… but Rick said he'd seen her father collapse on the grass…

Owen was looking at her, waiting for an answer.

'I didn't know anything about the shed – but he's been weird about it for weeks. I didn't know he'd been hurt. Oh no…'

A picture of Rick in the garden that day slid into Ella's mind. He'd banged on the kitchen door and when she opened it her father was face down on the path and Rick said, *'He was stumbling over the grass…'*

Why would Rick lie about where he'd found her father? Come to that, what was Rick doing in the shed at all? Dad had been hacking out concrete, Rick must have come here and gone straight to the shed. What an odd thing to do. Something was just very wrong here. Owen and Amanda were staring, Amanda's face apprehensive while Owen's was thoughtful.

'You look dazed, Ella. Tell me what I can do to help.'

Ella clasped trembling fingers round her mug and met his eyes. He was trained to deal with people in weird situations – he must be able to see her fear and pain. If anyone could advise her, he could.

'I'm giving Rick till three to come back,' she said in a low voice. 'If he doesn't... I might need help then.'

'And you last spoke to him...?' It was the policeman sitting opposite her now.

'Yesterday. He sounded – all right.'

'So there's no reason to think he might be ill in any way?'

Ella stared. Actually, there wasn't. Rick was punishing her for wanting to be Soraya's mum and live in this house, but that didn't count as 'ill'.

'He's upset and being awkward, that's all. Men, huh?'

He gave her a sharp look, then rose to his feet. 'Okay. Let me know, then. Thanks for the coffee.'

Ella took him to the door and returned to find Amanda putting the mugs in the dishwasher.

'Ella, is Owen a...?'

'Policeman. You can tell, can't you? He works in Newquay but he's on leave until mid-August. I only hope I don't need his professional help.' Ella struggled to stifle a yawn; she couldn't remember when she'd last felt so exhausted.

Amanda closed the dishwasher. 'I'll be off too. I'm sure Rick'll be back soon, Ella. Give me a ring if you need any more shopping.'

She hurried off, leaving Ella alone once again in the

silence of an empty house. She checked her phone, but no answering text from Rick had appeared. This was every bit as bad as waiting at the hospital, helpless as they tried to save her father. And oh, was Soraya afraid? The child must know something wasn't right. Poor little soul. It might have been better for Soraya if they'd never played racing cars that day at the adoption party. Hot tears gathered in Ella's eyes and her throat closed. How were they to get out of this mess?

She booted up the laptop to check her emails. Two spam mails, a bill, and – an email from the school she'd applied to, for the secretarial job. She'd cancelled yesterday's interview, of course, pleading a death in the family.

It was a date for another interview, this coming Wednesday. Well. At least they were interested in her application. Ella jotted the details on a note and stuck it to the fridge, new determination filling her. She would find a job and she would get her daughter back and no matter what happened to her marriage, she would do her damnedest to adopt Soraya. But before she did any of that she'd go and have a good poke in the shed, see if she could find out why Rick went there on Monday and then lied about it. He could go to hell. She wasn't going to let him bully her any longer.


The shed was messy; no one – of course – had done anything more about Steve's concrete-removing work. Ella stood in the doorway. She hadn't been in here since before her father's death, and how odd; the wooden slabs were back on top of the concrete, inches higher than they had been, turning the shed floor into a two-level affair. The wheelbarrow on the low side was half full of mud and chunks of concrete. Possibly Dad had finished his job and tried to replace the floor before feeling unwell? Ella stamped, feeling instability beneath her foot. The slabs were a metre by two metres and were supposed to slot into each other, but two of them were wobbly and uneven, unattached to the next. Had Dad rushed the job at the end, realising there was something wrong?

Ella crouched on one of the non-wobbly slabs and pressed on its neighbour. One end lifted, and she grabbed it and heaved the slab on its side. Well. Here was part of the answer; Dad hadn't nearly finished. The central mass of concrete was still intact, though the edges had been lifted all the way round. Dad must have got fed up chipping it away. She dropped the slab and it banged back into position. Someone would have to fix that one day, but not her and definitely not today. Ella glanced at her watch. Half past two. Half an hour and then she would do – what?

# Chapter Two

Friday 1st August

'This is the wrong way! You said we were going home to Mummy!'

Soraya unclicked her seat belt and Rick slowed down, frustration mingling with fear as the child stood up in the back seat.

'Sit down! We're not going the wrong way – you don't know all the roads around here. This is a better way.'

Soraya sat, but not in her car seat and Rick pulled over as soon as he had the chance. She was right, of course. They were on the A30 heading north-east, and they'd passed the exit for St Ives. He undid his own belt and twisted round to the child in the back. Her face was desperate and Rick searched for something to keep her quiet.

'We – we're going to the place you bought Mummy the weather house first. Remember?'

'And then we're going home?'

'Yes. But we're not moving until you're back in your seat.'

She shifted immediately, and Rick leaned back to

make sure she was strapped in, avoiding eye contact. He had no idea what he was doing – he'd intended going back to Ella, but as soon as the road sign for St Ives loomed over the car he'd realised he couldn't cope with a confrontation with his wife. Not yet, not today, maybe not ever. There would be messages from both Ella and Amanda on his phone when he switched it on, and God help him, he didn't know what to do. Something was different today; he felt different. Heavier.

The service station was busy with people having lunch. As well as the shop and a small restaurant there was a snack bar where a crowd of noisy bikers were hanging out eating burgers. Soraya's eyes were wide as she gazed round, and her lower lip was trembling. Rick grasped her hand.

'What would you like for lunch?'

'I want to go home for my lunch.' It was a frightened, peevish little whisper and it made Rick see red. Everyone, even this child who was nothing to do with him, was against him today.

'We're not going home yet. You can choose something here or you can go hungry.'

Soraya burst into noisy tears and he jumped in fright then stretched a hand towards her. She jerked away and ran towards the door.

'I want to go home to my Mummy! I don't want to be with you anymore.'

The bikers and the snack bar personnel were staring and to Rick's horror and embarrassment, silence fell. He wiped his face with one hand and went after Soraya, but a woman ran out from behind the snack bar and reached the girl first.

'Can I help you, sweetheart? Where's your Mummy?' She took Soraya's hand.

Tears trickled down Soraya's face, and Rick was suddenly and painfully aware of how unkempt she looked. He hadn't combed her hair that morning, and her t-shirt had more than a trace of last night's dinner down the front.

When sniffs and sobs were the only answer the woman tried again. 'Can you tell me where you live, darling?'

Rick found his voice. 'Please. It's all right. She's upset, we've had a death in the family – my wife's father. It hasn't been easy for her, has it, Soraya?'

'Is that your name, lovey?' A nod. 'And is this your daddy?' A stare. The woman turned to Rick, her expression neutral. 'Can you prove you're Soraya's father, sir?'

Two of the bikers had approached and were standing behind the woman, and Rick began to shake. They were ready to intervene if he made a run for it. For a second his mind went blank, then he pulled out his wallet. Bless Ella, she had saved the day. The photo of the three of them she'd put in his wallet was a laughing family group, Soraya in the middle with a large ice cream. He thrust it into the woman's hand and her face relaxed.

'What a lovely photo! Is this your mum, sweetheart?'

This time, she got an answer. 'That's me and my mum... and my dad and I want to go home now.'

Rick put his hand on her head, and thankfully this time she didn't pull away. 'We will go home, Soraya. But Mummy needs to get things sorted first. How about some lunch?'

'We can do you a lovely cheeseburger with chips?' said the woman. 'On the house. How about that?'

Tears spilled down Soraya's cheeks, and Rick could have shaken her.

'I wanted to go to my mummy for a long time,' she whispered, and the woman hugged her.

'I'm sure Daddy'll take you as soon as Mummy's ready for you, sweetie. Come and have some lunch.'

Soraya allowed the woman to lead her back to the snack bar and sit her on a high stool. Rick perched beside her; at least the goddamn meal was free. It was all he could be glad about here. Soraya picked listlessly at her burger, gazing at the woman, who came by every couple of minutes to make sure everything was all right. The bikers left, leaving the snack bar almost deserted, which made Soraya's non-replies to Rick's remarks more obvious. He could cheerfully have throttled her, and the tight band round his head was getting tighter by the minute. He ordered a double espresso and swallowed two paracetamol along with it, but by the time they left Rick felt as if he'd run to Land's End and back. He settled Soraya into the car and got behind the wheel.

And now what? All he knew was he couldn't go home. He needed to have a good think first, about Ella and Amanda and Steve and Gareth and the shed... He needed things clear in his head before he confronted Ella. She would go all teacher-ish with him; the very thought was making him see red. Maybe he should check his phone, see what she was thinking... and like he'd thought, there were messages galore here. She was obsessed and so was Amanda. He deleted them without reading any – a

265

little more time to worry about her daughter would make it all the more likely that Ella would agree with whatever he suggested. He twisted round to talk to Soraya.

'Okay. Mummy texted and there's a new plan. Remember the place we went to in Newquay and Mummy came to get you?' That was clever, he thought. Of course she'd remember and it was a very positive image to give her, wasn't it? Soraya nodded. 'We're going back there now, and Mummy'll be along later. Okay?'

Soraya blinked at him, her lips pressed together. Ignoring the tension in his head, Rick started the car.


The B&B had a room for them, but it was much smaller than the one they'd had last time and again there was no en suite. Misery welled up inside Rick but he booked them in and led Soraya upstairs. She had slept in the car but was wide awake again and all he could think of to keep her occupied was to go to the beach. He sat on a towel while she splashed about in shallow water. A dark cloud of dreariness settled over him as he watched her, but it wasn't long before another little girl appeared and made friends with Soraya. Rick lay back and closed his eyes – the other child's mother was there with the girls.

What was he going to do about Ella and the house and Gareth? The three went together. He would call Ella later and tell her he'd give Soraya back if she left the house. She could maybe even stay here in the B&B until they found a flat. That way, he could plan how to remove Gareth, because that had turned into an absolute necessity. With Gareth gone he could get someone in to fix the shed floor and everything would be back to normal. And *of course* –

Joy and relief broke over Rick as the solution to the entire problem flashed into his head. What had he been thinking of? No one needed to find flats and move out. With Gareth gone, Ella and Soraya could go back into the house and it would all be sorted. He wouldn't need more than a week. Could he persuade Ella to take a little holiday?

Whatever happened with the house, though, his future would still be with Amanda. And the baby. But that would sort itself automatically once he had the Gareth situation under control. He would call when they were back in the B&B, tell Ella to come and collect Soraya. Yes.

It was going to be all right... Rick rubbed his head. He was so tired it was hard to keep his eyes in focus, and disjointed thoughts of Ella and her parents were filling his head. Steve... what was it with Steve? Oh yes, he hadn't helped Steve and the poor sod had died. So it didn't matter if Steve had seen Gareth or not, did it? All he had to do was get Ella out of the house for a bit and everything would be all right.

The idea gave him new hope, and he forced himself to his feet and joined Soraya at the water's edge. Her new friend had gone, and Rick realised guiltily he should have been watching the child.

'How about an ice cream? Then we'll go back to our room and phone Mummy.'

'Ooh yes!' Soraya was distracted now and happy.

He followed her across the beach to the ice cream van, a lump rising in his throat. If things had been different he and Ella could have been a family with this kiddie, she was a sweetie even if she wasn't a boy. What had changed that? Oh yes, Gareth and the baby. His real baby. So leaving Ella was the best thing to do... If only his head would stop buzzing.

The bathroom at the B&B was free, and Rick ran a bath for Soraya, adding a generous slosh of rose petal bath foam from the basket on the window ledge. He needed a few minutes peace to phone Ella, and a bath had worked well the last time. He left her to play.

'No splashing, now, and I'll leave the doors open. Shout if you need anything.'

She was busy piling foam on her head, and he hurried back to the bedroom. Now for the phone call. He had to sound calm, firm, and positive. Ella was to come here for a week with her darling daughter, that was the new plan, but... Oh no. How could he have forgotten? June was staying with them and Steve was dead – under these circumstances Ella might not want a holiday. He would have to insist, that was all. A holiday or lose Soraya.

Phone in hand, Rick lay back on his bed, then dropped the mobile to massage his forehead. He was so tense. This headache he'd had since leaving home was getting worse; he should take another pill... What had he wanted to do? Ah yes, call Ella. Where was his phone?

He felt around the top of the bed, but the phone... no, here it was. He squinted at the screen. But he was much too tired to speak to Ella. He would have a little sleep first, then everything would be better. His eyes closed.

# CHAPTER THREE

Friday 1st August

Amanda stood outside the flats, twisting the strap of her handbag and staring back up the hill. She was home, but she didn't have the peace of mind to go inside and do some of her freelance secretarial work, the original plan for this child-free day. The thought that Ella's neighbour was a policeman who was all set to help if Rick didn't reappear... that was spooking her well and truly. And there was nothing she could do, apart from text Rick. Which was futile. If Rick didn't get in touch, Ella would call Owen and then – what?

A nauseating sensation that had nothing to do with her pregnancy gripped Amanda's gut, and she sat down on the wall by the entrance to the flats. Rick had been very odd on the phone... Gareth must be somewhere close to home. The shed. Something was shouting out to her that it was the shed. At some point, Rick had hidden Gareth there, he must have. Maybe there were bloodstains he couldn't get rid of? But Gareth hadn't bled – or had he?

And... Ella was gobsmacked when Owen told her about Rick banging his head coming out of the shed.

According to Owen, Ella's father was in there when he collapsed... Amanda's breath caught painfully. Was Gareth *still* in Ella's shed? Waiting to be buried? That would explain everything. Amanda began to shake. Had Rick stuffed Gareth into a box or a barrel and left him there? But – bodies smelled, didn't they? Or maybe the smell didn't last long? Amanda raised unsteady fingers to cold cheeks. She was getting into a state here; she would have to go inside.

A cup of tea calmed her, and she sat in the kitchen, trying to plan. If Rick didn't come back... and if Gareth was in that shed... and if Ella involved Owen... it would all come out that afternoon. Rick should know about that. Amanda made the connection and sat willing him to pick up but of course, he didn't. It was quarter to three, so in little more than fifteen minutes Ella would go to Owen, and sooner or later they'd investigate the shed. Amanda clasped her hands beneath her chin, feeling her knuckles tremble against her jaw bone. What would she do if Gareth was there?

Sudden adrenalin shooting through her – this couldn't be good for the baby – Amanda grabbed her bag and ran from the flat. It was no use, she couldn't think straight so the best thing to do was go and see what was happening. The July heat made it impossible to run up the hill, but Amanda hurried as well as she could, thankful she had a good two hours before she needed to pick Jaden up. Turning the corner into Cedar Road, she slowed down. It wouldn't do to arrive looking as if she was fleeing the devil himself.

She was lingering at the fence getting her breath back

when Ella appeared out of the shed, dusting her hands on her jeans. Amanda's heart leapt into her throat and she felt the baby stir. It's okay, baby, keep calm. And it was okay – still. Ella was no more het up than she was earlier on, so whatever she'd been doing in the shed, she hadn't found Gareth. At that moment Ella saw her and for a second they stood in silence, then Amanda managed to speak.

'I couldn't stop thinking about you and Soraya – is there any word from Rick?'

'No. Come and help me decide what to do.'

Bingo, thought Amanda, following on into the kitchen and sitting awkwardly on what had become her chair. The baby kicked again.

Ella poured two glasses of fresh orange and sat down opposite. 'I can't get away from the thought that Rick had a bang on the head and now he's acting oddly,' she said, rubbing her eyes. 'I yelled at him for being slow to help with Dad – he was so slow and dazed – suppose he's concussed? Amanda, suppose he has an accident while he's driving around with Soraya?'

The thought was sobering and Amanda could hear the doubt in her own voice. 'I'm sure you'd have noticed if he had concussion. He's probably, um... '

To Amanda's dismay Ella pounced on her hesitation.

'You see? I can't imagine what reason he could have for not getting in touch. Heaven knows how many times I've tried to call him, and I've left so many texts I've lost count. He could be unconscious for all I know, and Soraya...'

Amanda reached across the table and patted the

other woman's hand. Ella was worried about her child. She wasn't thinking about the shed or about Rick; Soraya was the important issue here, and because of Soraya, they would need to find Rick even if it did mean involving the police, that was clear.

'Have you been in contact with the adoption people?'

Tears were shining in Ella's eyes. 'I'll need to do that. We're supposed to tell them about important stuff. What'll I do if they take Soraya away?'

'No reason they would, if Rick's – ill, is there?' Amanda spoke briskly. An idea was forming in her head. 'Why don't you ask your neighbour to help trace the car – the police can do that, can't they? Then you'd have Soraya back home and you'll see how Rick is and you can take it from there.'

Amanda relaxed as she spoke. That was it. Perfect. Keep the focus on Rick's condition and Soraya's vulnerability, and no one would go near the shed. That would give her time to talk to Rick – she would *make* him tell her what he'd done with Gareth. And when she knew...

Amanda closed her eyes. When she knew she would know, that was all. Would they be able to keep the deception a secret? But they had to. But another thought was – did she really want to spend her life with the man who had done heaven knows what with Gareth and was now causing all this grief? She massaged her middle, feeling the hardness of the growing bump. The baby. Hers and – whose? Oh, it was Rick's, it must be, but a baby was no reason to stay with a man. She would never be able to trust him after this.

Ella picked up her mobile. 'You're right. I'll phone

Owen.'

Amanda sipped her juice as Ella made her call. It was a brief conversation. Ella said, 'I'm worried about Rick, Owen,' and listened for a few seconds before breaking the connection and sagging in her chair. 'He's coming over.'

Amanda swithered. Should she offer to leave, or stay on and hear what Owen had to say? She had no time to consider; Owen was at the door already. She would wait. It didn't seem to have entered Ella's head that the conversation with Owen should be private, and Amanda sat waiting to steer them away from the shed if they started talking about it. Hopefully Owen would get straight onto putting a search out for Rick's car, and nothing more. They needed to find Soraya; poor Ella's voice was growing unsteadier by the minute.

'Owen, I'm more and more worried that Rick might be concussed after Monday. He's supposed to be back here now with Soraya, and he's not answering his phone. Could the police find the car?'

Owen's eyes were searching and Amanda was suddenly glad she hadn't had him to deal with when Gareth 'disappeared'. The way he was looking at Ella was direct to say the least.

'Yes, that would be possible. Have I got this right – you didn't know about the head bang, and you didn't notice anything in particular about his behaviour afterwards?'

Two tears trickled down Ella's cheeks, and Amanda reached out and touched a shaking shoulder. Be a friend, Amanda, that's why you're here, remember?

'My dad had collapsed – none of us were behaving

normally. Thinking back, Rick was very hesitant, very shocked about Dad, and he said nothing about bringing him from the shed.'

Owen was frowning. 'What did he say?'

'He said he'd seen Dad collapse on the grass and told me to call an ambulance. But I noticed Dad wasn't breathing and started CPR, so Rick called 999.'

Amanda thought back to the call she'd had from Rick. He'd told her Ella's dad had collapsed in the garden too. It was the shed, it must be...

'Okay. How late is he?'

'He said he'd be here this morning, and when he didn't turn up I texted him to be back by three or I'd get the adoption people involved.'

'So he's only a few minutes late, if we go by three o'clock. Let's give him another ten minutes. Why are you so uneasy?'

'Oh, I don't know. We're in a rough patch and I feel he's gone off with Soraya to get back at me and now I'm worried he's not well. Why else would he lie about where he found Dad?'

'That is odd, yes...'

'I even checked the shed after you said about him banging his head but apart from a wobbly floor it's fine, and – I want Soraya back here.'

Tears were running down Ella's cheeks, and Amanda passed her a tissue, her own gut cramping at the sight of Owen's set face. This was getting dangerous, this was about the shed as well as Rick and Soraya now, and there was nothing she could do about it. Resignation filled her. She knew what Owen was going to say, and she was right.

'Tell you what, Ella. We'll get the police started on a car search, and then we'll have a look at the shed. Okay?'

Amanda stood up. She couldn't, she simply couldn't stand by while this policeman rootled round in the place Gareth might be hidden. Even if he wasn't there any more, a pair of trained eyes might notice something. What had Rick done?

'Ella, I'm sorry, but I have to collect Jaden. Will you be all right?'

Ella took her to the door. 'Thanks, Amanda, you've been a life-saver this afternoon. I'll be fine, don't worry.'

Amanda almost ran down the hill. Nothing good was going to happen here, she could feel that all the way down her gut.

# CHAPTER FOUR

Friday 1st August

Ella opened the shed door and stood back to let Owen enter, but he stood on the threshold for a long moment, just looking.

'So what's the story here?' he said at last.

Knowing the police were out looking for the car and Soraya was a huge weight off Ella's mind. How good it felt now to unload the bad feeling she'd had when the adoption became stressful and Rick retreated to the shed. But she couldn't remember exactly when he'd decided to lay concrete. And why he hadn't got someone in to do it for him was another mystery – he was usually such a perfectionist about things like that.

Owen listened without interrupting, then pressed his foot on the loose board covering the mess of stone. 'So there's still concrete under here?'

'Yes. Dad was chipping it away, and I think that must have been when he was taken ill.'

'Right. So who replaced the floor afterwards?'

Ella shrugged. 'It must have been Dad or Rick. Owen, when will we hear if they've traced the car?'

He stepped into the shed and lifted a pair of gardening gloves. 'Shouldn't be long. Ella, I'm going to have a very quick look under here if that's all right.'

Something about his manner made argument impossible. Ella stood in the doorway while Owen heaved the wooden slab up then wielded a spade.

He managed to free several chunks of concrete, and laid them on the other half of the floor. 'The earth here's pretty loose,' he said, prodding it with the spade, his brow furrowed.

Ella stood tapping her foot. Digging up the shed floor wouldn't bring Soraya home. But at least the police were out looking for the car now.

All at once Owen dropped the spade and seized a trowel from the shelf behind him. Crouching, he scraped earth to the side, looking for all the world like an archaeologist at work.

Ella leaned forward to see what he was doing. There was something plastic, and something grey and white in the hole. But – no! Oh God. It couldn't be... Her gut twisted.

Owen rose, gripped her elbow and led her firmly towards the house. Ella was shaking, shivers painful across her chest, her heart thudding at twice its usual rate.

'Were those – Owen, were those *bones* back there?' Her stomach churned at the thought.

Owen's mouth was a tight slash. 'Don't worry, finding Soraya will be top priority.'

Ella gazed at him, then felt her stomach move. She ran into the downstairs bathroom and was sick. How could there be human bones beneath the shed? Was this the reason Rick wanted to lay the concrete? What was going on?

She wiped her face with a washcloth and stared into the mirror. The woman looking back at her was pale, wide-eyed, and shocked. She'd thought the situation couldn't possibly have been more complicated but oh, how wrong that was. She trailed back to the kitchen to find Owen on his phone. He ended the call and turned to her.

'They're on their way. Are you all right?' He poured boiling water into two mugs.

Ella accepted a mug of tea and warmed her hands on it. 'I don't know what to think.'

His expression was grim. 'Could Rick have been trying to hide something?'

Ella's legs were shaking. What was he getting at?

Two police cars arrived, and Ella sat in the kitchen with a WPC while Owen took the other officers round to the shed. Her teeth chattered on the rim of the mug when she tried to drink, but the tea was lukewarm now anyway.

Time passed in a horrible blur. Ella remained in the kitchen, trying not to watch, but it was impossible to ignore the large tent being erected over the shed. Like something from the TV. The sound of drilling and hammering filled the air for a long while before subsiding into the odd scraping noise or dull thud. Rick's concrete was being removed.

Owen was still out there, speaking to the investigating officers. He must be pretty high up in his profession, thought Ella. The other officers were including him in the discussion even though he didn't belong to the St Ives force. She'd never asked him his rank, but then up until today he'd merely been a nice man, her new neighbour. Ella leaned her arms on the table and buried her head in them.

It was unbelievable. Bones in the shed – *her* shed. And – Rick's shed.

'Hey.' Owen sat down at right angles to her. 'Are you okay?'

'How long has that – whatever – been under the shed floor?'

'I can't talk about it, Ella. But – unofficially, only a few weeks.'

Ella's hands floated to her mouth. If the bones had only been there a few weeks, then Rick must have put them there. And then tried to hide them better with the concrete... *Whose bones were they?*

Fear for Soraya was heavy in Ella's gut; it was all she could do not to be sick again. And oh no – she'd have to call Liz. She could put that off no longer; the police were looking for Soraya. But it would be the beginning of the end for her as Soraya's mother. She massaged her temples, gathering strength, then lifted her phone.

'Oh, Ella, I'm so sorry.'

Tears shot into Ella's eyes. At least Liz wasn't blaming her, and it wasn't her fault, was it – but it felt as if it was.

'What'll happen when they find her?' Ella held her breath waiting for the reply. It wasn't confidence-inspiring.

'I don't know. We'll see when that happens. I'll be in

touch. Oh, and I'll contact the police about the search, too.'

That was it, then. Hot tears brimmed up in Ella's eyes and trickled down to drip off her chin. They would hardly let a child come here while bodies or skeletons or whatever were being unearthed in the back garden, even if there hadn't been the small matter of Rick's behaviour to consider too. It would be back to Auntie Mel's for Soraya if she was lucky, and Auntie Stranger's if she wasn't. Ella pounded a fist on the table. How she hated Rick now.

'Ella, can I do anything?'

Owen's voice was perfectly neutral. Was she a suspect? But of course she was, she was living in a house where bones had been discovered.

'I should call my mother too. She's at her cousin's. What can I tell her?'

'Why don't I call the cousin for you, let her know a minimum of what's going on, and tell her to keep your mother away from news reports in the meantime?' he suggested, and Ella closed her eyes in despair. Was this going to be in the news already?

He patted her shoulder. 'There are reporters out the front already.'

Ella couldn't answer him. She called up Mary's mobile and handed over her phone. Owen described what was going on very briefly, and warned against watching news bulletins that evening, then slid the mobile back across the table.

'Ella, the police need to search this place. They'll take you to the station to make a statement, and after that you can come to mine until you're allowed back in here, but that won't be today. Unless there's anywhere else you'd rather go? Amanda's?'

'No,' said Ella immediately. 'I don't know her that well. Thanks, Owen. I want to stay nearby until Soraya's found. I know it's not logical because after this I don't think I'll get her back.'

'I'm sure – I hope you will eventually,' he said heavily.

Ella felt her head droop again. Tearful, confused thoughts swirled around her mind. Impossible to imagine whose bones Rick would conceal in the garden. And when would they find him and *was Soraya all right?*

She'd thought the worst had happened, that the day could get no blacker. But the moment the head of the investigating team appeared in the kitchen doorway Ella sensed there was more bad news coming, and she was right.

'We've found your car in Newquay,' the man said. 'It was parked outside a B&B and apparently Mr Baxter and your little girl were there for a while today, but they left about five o'clock, leaving the car behind.'

Ella's lips started to tingle. Without the car, there was no easy way to find Rick. The man went on. 'We're checking CCTV cameras and we'll try to track his phone, too. We'll put out an appeal for the public to keep their eyes open. If you have a recent photo of Soraya that would help.'

The world was spinning round, no, no, she mustn't faint. Rick was on the run with Soraya. And the officer hadn't finished yet.

'We're removing the remains now, Mrs Baxter. We'll

take you to the station after that, and then bring you back here to Detective Chief Inspector Fife's home.'

Ella gaped at him. So Owen *was* one of the big shots.

'Ella. I'll come with you. Go and pack an overnight bag, and try to stay calm.'

Owen's voice was kind, but the other officers' faces were grim. Ella lurched to her feet, and the WPC appeared at her side. There would be some tough questions asked at the police station – she was the woman who hadn't noticed when her husband went so far off the rails that he'd buried a – but he wouldn't have buried a skeleton, would he, he'd have buried a body, and the biggest question of all was still there, unanswered in front of them.

Whose body?

# Chapter Five

Friday 1st August

'Wake up! I want to go to Mummy.'

Someone was shaking his arm, but weakness and dizziness were pinning him to the bed. A couple of deep breaths helped, and he forced his eyes open. Soraya's blurry face swam into view and he remembered. Hell, he'd left her in the bath.

It took a huge effort, but a moment later he was sitting on the edge of the bed, propping himself up with fingers splayed on the mattress. Soraya was fully dressed, though her hair was a damp, tousled mess.

'Right. I'll clear the bathroom.' His legs didn't belong to him but he managed to lurch along the corridor. A splash of cold water on his face helped, then Rick wiped up the mess Soraya had made on the floor and rejoined her in the bedroom. To his horror she was sitting with his phone, and he snatched it back. Shit, it was half past four.

Apprehension rising, he checked his calls. Nothing had come from Ella since the three o'clock deadline she'd given him, but there were several missed calls and a text from Amanda. He opened the text and the world swayed, nauseatingly, like an of out-of-focus horror movie. He could almost hear the music, discords heralding approaching disaster.

*Ella's involving the police. Owen's going to look at the shed. Call me.*

Rick slumped on the bed, head hanging. That was it, then. Gareth would be found – he might even have been found already. That text was sent over an hour ago. The police would be looking for him and Soraya... He had to get away from here, find somewhere to think. Penzance. He would go back to Penzance, they wouldn't think to look for him there. He lurched across the room and grabbed his case.

'Get your stuff, Soraya. We'll go in the train, it's quicker.'

'It's not quicker. I want to go in the car. You said - '

'And now I'm saying we're going in the goddamn train and I don't want to hear another word from you! Understand?'

She flinched, and he rummaged through his belongings. He needed some kind of disguise, something that would make it harder for people to identify him. Sunglasses, yes, and his cap. That would do. And something to hide as much of Soraya's face as possible. Her sunhat presented itself, and he grabbed the little girl's hairbrush.

'We'll make you a nice hairdo for Mummy. Come here.'

She retreated towards the table, her lips trembling.

'For heaven's sake, Soraya, you can't go out like that!' Two strides and he was beside her, holding her bony shoulder with one hand and manipulating the hairbrush with the other. She wriggled and sobbed as he pulled the brush through her damp hair and twisted it into one of the elastics round the handle, but she looked different with her hair under the hat. He nodded, satisfied. A quick goodbye here and off to the station, where they could merge into a crowd and be safe. And on the way he would chuck his phone into the sea.

Luck was with him downstairs. The owner's teenager checked him out, more interested in his iPad than in the departing guests. Rick didn't even need to make a detour to the sea to get rid of his phone, because they passed a section of roadworks shortly after leaving the B&B, and he dropped it into a deep muddy hole in the road.

'What was that?' Soraya was shivering. 'Are we going to Mummy?'

'Just a stone. Yes, the station's along here. See the red and white sign?'

In the train he tried to relax – he should plan now. This was surreal. He was running away from his wife, who, if Amanda was to be believed, had involved the police to search for him – and oh, what was going on with the shed? Until he knew that he'd have to be very careful. Soraya was staring out of the window in a way that made him hope she would fall asleep soon. He wasn't looking forward to the moment when she realised they weren't going home to Mummy. And what would they do when they reached Penzance? Find another B&B was the obvious answer, but it wouldn't be easy to do that and remain safely anonymous. But he couldn't sleep rough with a child under his arm. How in the name of all that was holy had he ended up like this?

Soraya slept for a good hour but was irritable when

she awoke. Fortunately for Rick she didn't realise they weren't in St Ives until they were leaving the station building in Penzance.

'Where are we? This isn't home!'

Rick had decided to jolly her along as far as possible. 'Clever girl. This is Penzance. It's not far from St Ives and Mummy's joining us here tomorrow. She phoned while you were asleep.'

Soraya shot him a look he could only describe as malevolent. 'You said - '

Rick bent and hugged her, not allowing her to squirm away. 'I know, sweetie, but your Grandma's still upset about Grandpa, and Mummy needs to help her. She said to give you lots of love. You'll see her tomorrow.'

The little girl blinked, her lips trembling. Rick took her hand. 'Come on. We'll find a nice B&B, will we?'

They wandered along Chyandour Cliff until they came to a small guesthouse whose sign was announcing vacancies, and Rick booked them in as quickly as he could. It was nothing much, but it was cheap, which was just as well, because the wad of cash he'd drawn from the ATM at Newquay would have to last him for a while. He couldn't risk using his card again if the police were looking for them. Once in their bedroom he sank down on one of the twin beds, massaging his thumping head – when had he last had a headache this bad? It was the stress, it had to be. Maybe he'd feel better if he ate something.

He forced a smile for Soraya. 'You're a big girl, aren't you? Why don't I leave you to unpack for us both while I go and fetch something to eat?'

She stared at him dumbly, her eyes huge. He tossed her the key to his suitcase but instead of catching it she allowed it to fall to the floor. Rick glared at her and left.

There was a mini-market further along the road and he stocked up with a supply of goodies – anything to keep Soraya distracted. He bought a couple of colouring-in books for her, and half a bottle of wine for him, though his head might not thank him for it.

Back in the B&B, Soraya's tearstained face brightened slightly when he went into the room. Had she been afraid he'd abandoned her forever? He gave her a tub of chocolate muesli and a banana, and she sat at the tiny desk in the corner while he switched on the equally tiny TV, turning it to prevent Soraya seeing the screen. He would watch the news – if Gareth had been found it would definitely make the bulletin at the top of the hour.

To his utter dismay that was exactly what had happened. The first item was a bomb scare in London, but then a familiar scene replaced the image of the Houses of Parliament and Rick sat frozen on his bed as he saw his own street – his own house – fill the screen. They had cordoned off the driveway. He didn't dare put the sound on in case Soraya noticed what was going on, but at least there was no picture of him or Soraya. Yet. He would catch the late news while Soraya was asleep. A sob rose in Rick's throat and he swallowed it down, painfully, before the little girl noticed anything.

He didn't need to wonder any more what was going to happen to him. Stone-cold certainty filled his head and he switched the television off. He would go to prison. He had buried a man in the garden, and he couldn't prove that Gareth's death had been an accident. Rick moaned aloud then turned it into a fit of coughing as Soraya looked round, her face full of apprehension.

'I swallowed the wrong way.' Now he was making excuses to a six-year-old.

'You aren't eating anything.'

'I was sucking a sweet. Look, I brought you some too.'

The diversion tactic worked, and Rick returned to his pondering. Would Amanda help him? He should have called her before abandoning his phone. It wouldn't be long until Gareth was identified, and… Rick began to feel sick. Amanda could deny everything. She would save her own skin first, for Jaden and the baby, and there was nothing to connect her to Gareth's death. She had driven 'Gareth' to Lamorna to start his walk, and the people in the café had confirmed that. He, in contrast, had taken the day off work and disappeared off the face of the earth from early morning until late afternoon. Burying Gareth in his own garden was a complete admission of guilt. The police would deduce he had met Gareth that day and killed him.

A picture swam before Rick's eyes. Him and Ella, this time last year, looking forward to having a little boy to love. Where had it all gone so wrong? He strode into the en suite where he sat on the toilet seat, his face buried in a bath towel, sobs shaking his shoulders.

His head was buzzing more than ever, and he swallowed a couple of paracetamol. Ella had done this to him. But he had his revenge; he had Soraya here and no one knew. He could jump off a cliff with Ella's daughter tomorrow. And – what choice did he have? They would find him eventually.

Returning to the bedroom, he gave Soraya the carton of blackcurrant juice he'd bought, and opened the bottle of wine. If this was going to be his last evening on the planet, he might as well make it a good one.

# CHAPTER SIX

Friday 1st August

'Was it okay?' Owen clicked the indicator up and pulled away from the police station in the centre of St Ives.

Ella leaned back in the passenger seat, her eyes closed, more thankful than she could say that Owen's job was based in Newquay so he hadn't been interviewing her. He was a – a friend who was also a police officer. The interview had lasted over an hour, and never in all her life had she felt so utterly bone-weary. Everything had changed; she wasn't in control of her life any more, and Soraya was gone. The pain was both dull and sharp; the constant ache of long-term fear alongside piercing shafts of an agony she'd only imagined before she had a child to love – and lose.

'I suppose so. They asked about the shed and Rick, and how much he'd changed and what he'd been doing and – I felt so stupid. If I'd talked to him more, made him tell me what was going on in his head...'

He said nothing, and she opened her eyes, squinting in the evening sunlight. They were driving along the coast road, and how macabre it was to see the tourists – families, young couples, teenagers, all happy and sun-browned, living the day, milling around on their way home from the beach. While she was in the middle of the biggest nightmare imaginable. Owen's face was grim and Ella sat straighter.

'What is it?'

'Ella, Rick's a grown man. You aren't responsible for his actions.'

She twisted in the seat to see his face. 'You know something, don't you? I thought Detective Inspector Martin knew more than he was telling me. Please tell me it's about the body and not Soraya.'

Her voice was shaking as much as her hands were. Because terrible as it sounded, the body was of secondary importance. A skeleton was beyond help. Soraya was vulnerable and needy, and the important thing was to find her.

Owen turned up the hill towards home. 'I don't have much more info than you do. They've identified the body, but the information won't be made public until the next of kin are informed. I don't know who it is either.'

Ella's world swirled before her eyes and she clenched both fists. The police knew who had been buried in her garden all those weeks. 'I thought DNA tests or whatever took days.'

'There was an SOS pendant round the person's neck,' said Owen quietly. 'So it's odds-on the identification according to that is correct.'

Ella shuddered, then stared across Cedar Road where a little crowd had gathered. Owen swung the car into his driveway to a series of flashes. 'I'm afraid we'll have the press here for a day or two. Get inside as quickly as you can, Ella. I'll have a word with them.'

Eight or nine men and women were standing around the street with cameras and microphones, and a TV van was parked further down the road. Ella stumbled towards Owen's front door, conscious that cameras were clicking, immortalising her every move.

The front door opened as Ella approached and Caroline stood back to let her in. 'Oh Ella, this is a dreadful ordeal for you. I'm glad we can help.'

Ella sank down at the kitchen table and buried her face in her hands. How completely hopeless everything seemed, and all she wanted was her girl. But Soraya wasn't her girl, was she?

Owen came in and poured them all a drink. Ella forced back her tears and sipped the wine, feeling the liquid warm its way through her gut. Thank goodness Owen was here to field the press. A missing child in combination with a skeleton under a garden shed was news, she understood that – but understanding made it no easier to cope.

Owen rummaged in fridge and cupboards, and laid cheese and a tin of crackers on the table. Ella clutched her middle. Food was the last thing she felt like.

'What happens now?' she asked.

'We eat,' he said, slicing Brie and pushing the biscuits towards her. 'You need to stay strong. The local DI is confident the body will be formally identified tomorrow. What else did they tell you?'

Ella sat making crumbs with a biscuit. Did he really not know, or was he just making her talk it through? 'They're searching in Newquay hotels, stations etc for Rick and

Soraya, and in St Ives and a few other places too. Airports have been alerted though they don't think Rick'll try to get her out of the country. And they're trying to track his phone. An appeal with photos will be put out tomorrow unless he's found.'

He nodded, and Ella forced down a piece of Brie. Soraya was conspicuous, with her long dark hair. A man with a little girl, surely someone would notice and remember? But this was the holiday season, the resorts were packed with tourists, and a lot of them were men and little girls with long dark hair. Ella twirled her wine glass. *Was Soraya all right?* Not knowing was killing her. All those years she had waited for her child, but Rick snatched the happiness away almost before it began. And how bloody dare he.

Gradually, anger replaced the helpless feeling, and Ella sat planning. She should be active here. Her husband had as good as abducted their child and this was no time to throw a wobbly. She was depending on Owen far too much. Ella pulled out her mobile and keyed in Liz's number.

'Liz, sorry to disturb you. Do you know yet what's going to happen with the adoption authorities?'

'It depends a lot on whether Rick has committed a crime, Ella. But Soraya'll go back to Mel, short term at least. I'm sorry.'

Sick at heart, Ella ended the call. Rick was not going to win here. She would fight with every bone in her body, she would divorce him as soon as she could and she would re-apply to adopt Soraya. She had found her child and she wasn't going to lose her again.

# CHAPTER SEVEN

Friday 1st August

'Book. Book!' For the third time Jaden sat up in his cot, and Amanda fought to keep her patience. But if she spent the next few minutes being anything other than calm and pleasant it would be the end of getting him to sleep quickly.

'Let's have a song. You lie down and Mummy'll sing all the songs your Grandma used to sing to me.'

Jaden lay down again, his bear under one arm and the other hand clutching Amanda's. She took a deep breath. No way would she have managed yet another reading of *Dear Zoo*, Jaden's book of the moment, without losing it completely. He always had a hard time finding sleep after an afternoon away from her. Poor baby. He needed his mum, but his mum needed him to go to sleep and give her some peace to think in.

*Climb Every Mountain* followed by *Feed the Birds* – her mother was still a big fan of musicals – and Jaden was slumbering, a sweet, happy little smile on his face. Amanda crept from the room and went to make tea. What she needed was a stiff V&T, but the baby wouldn't enjoy that. Back on the sofa, mug balanced on the beginning of her bump, she glared at her phone on the coffee table. What was happening, out there in the world? Maybe she should call Ella, but if Rick had hidden Gareth at home and the police found evidence of this... it might look odd if she was continually calling and visiting Ella. As next of kin she'd be the first to be told if the police found a body. Oh, please let Gareth be in a nice woodland grave somewhere, a place of beauty and tranquillity.

It still might be all right.

The sound of teenage voices from the street had her rushing to close the kitchen window. Heaven help her if Jaden woke up. Amanda massaged her tummy, feeling the answering kick from within. She wasn't alone, she had her babies. The doorbell shrilled out and she jumped.

It was the police. Amanda stood aside to let them in, motioning towards Jaden's room and murmuring, 'My son's asleep.'

Sergeant Jacobs and a tall man who introduced himself as Detective Inspector Martin followed her through to the living room. Amanda's brain was whirring; this was going to be important. Should her first thought be that the visit had something to do with Gareth, or should she be more worried about Rick and Soraya? It might be better to let them speak first.

She motioned the two men towards the sofa and perched on the edge of an armchair. Tense. She should look tense and nervous, that would be right no matter what, and heaven knows it wasn't difficult. Be careful, Amanda. You have two children who need you.

Sergeant Jacobs cleared his throat. 'Mrs Waters –

Amanda – I'm very sorry but we have to inform you a body has been found and we have reason to believe it's your husband's.'

Amanda swallowed. 'Oh no. Where – when?'

'It was found earlier today under a shed in the area. Along with the body we found this.'

Amanda felt her eyes widen. For a moment it was difficult to breathe. Rick had buried Gareth *under the garden shed*... That was just – sordid. She could have accepted Rick leaving Gareth in the shed for a little while... but not this.

Sergeant Jacobs put a clear plastic bag containing a stainless steel SOS pendant on the coffee table. Amanda's breath caught and her hands were shaking as she reached to touch the plastic with one finger. She'd forgotten all about the pendant. But it wouldn't make any difference, would it?

'The information inside has your husband's name and your old address. Can you identify this?'

'Yes. Gareth's – he was allergic to penicillin. I told you. I didn't think... he didn't always wear it.... Are you sure it's him?'

'A DNA test's being done to confirm the identification.'

'And this shed...?' Amanda sat with her hands clenched under her chin. This was tricky. Ella's neighbour was a policeman, and he knew she was aware that Ella was worried about her shed. Did these men know too? Should she be suspicious – or should it be a complete surprise – shock – that Gareth was under Ella's shed? Shock would be best. And there was no need to act here, she was genuinely distraught. Poor Gareth, what had he done to deserve being buried under a shed? Damn Rick to hell.

'It's at 43 Cedar Road.'

She could see they were watching her, waiting to see what her response was. She leapt to her feet. 'That's Ella's address – she was talking about the shed earlier – why was Gareth under Ella's shed?'

That was good, she could see their faces relax. DI Martin answered.

'We're investigating that. We're still looking for Mr Baxter – he may have information that would help us. Mrs Baxter has already been interviewed.'

Amanda flopped back into her chair. Think, think. She'd met 'Rick' after she came here... Holding her hands over her mouth, she looked from one man to the other.

'Do you think that *Rick* – I always thought he was a bit odd... But why would he bury... Did he *kill* Gareth?'

'We're still investigating. What made you think Mr Baxter was odd?'

'It was – he was so jumpy. He must have known Gareth was my husband because I told Ella about losing him before I even met Rick...' She couldn't remember if this was true or not, but they weren't likely to check it, were they? The two men on the sofa were gazing at her benevolently, and Amanda burst into noisy tears. A little more drama wouldn't hurt.

'I don't understand! Gareth disappeared miles from here!'

Sergeant Jacobs put the pendant back into his pocket. 'You last saw him at Lamorna, but we don't actually know where he disappeared – or died. That's what we need to find out. Is there anyone you can call to be with you?'

Amanda wiped her eyes with her sleeve. 'I'll call my – my mum-in-law. She's in Glasgow but she'll come down straightaway.'

The two men rose.

'Your husband's name won't be made public yet. We'll be in touch tomorrow,' said Detective Inspector Martin.

Amanda showed them to the door, then went back to the living room and burst into genuine tears. They didn't suspect her, but oh, what had happened to her life? Fierce longing for the old days swept through Amanda, the simple days when she was a bored stay-at-home mum with a baby, and she grabbed a sofa cushion and squeezed it to her chest. She had turned into a monster.

Gradually, the sobs subsided and she wiped her eyes. She had to make things work, for her children. All she needed to do was stick to the original plan made by her and 'James'. Hopefully Rick wouldn't drop her in it... but then she could deny everything. It would be her word against his. She'd need to get rid of her phone again, in case the police decided to investigate her. But now for Susie.

Amanda picked up her mobile then dropped it again. It would be cruel to phone at this time of night when Suze couldn't get a plane until the morning anyway. Had there been anything on the news? But if Suze had seen anything she'd have called straightaway.

It was half an hour later when Amanda was lying in bed, eyes wide open and mind still racing, that she realised what her one mistake had been.

She had told Soraya the St Christopher was Gareth's.

# CHAPTER EIGHT

Saturday 2nd August

It was after eight when Ella awoke in Owen's box room the following morning. His mother, of course, had the main guest bedroom. She reached for her phone on the chair beside the bed, and stared in disbelief. She had slept for *ten hours*. Had Owen spiked her drink? And what had Soraya been doing all that time? Panic surged through her at the thought of her child needing help, needing her mother – and in spite of everything Ella was still hoping to be Soraya's mother – and having no one but her father to depend on. The father who had buried someone in his back garden. Ella pulled on clothes and ran downstairs. Please, let there be news, let this be the day her girl was returned safely, even if social services did whisk her away again.

Caroline was at the kitchen table with her library book. 'No new news,' she said at once, getting up to put the kettle on. 'No, let me do it, Ella. It's good for me; I can't be depending on Owen for the rest of my life. He's gone to the police station to see what's happening.'

Ella dropped into a chair and accepted a mug of tea.

No news was bad news, as far as she was concerned. 'The police said yesterday they'd come and see me this morning. I should look out some photos for the appeal.'

It wasn't much, but it was all she could do to help find Soraya. She sat swiping through the images on her phone until she found two good ones – one of Soraya alone, her little face bright but not smiling, and the three of them in McDonald's a couple of weeks ago. A family group. Ella blinked furiously. This was horrible – she couldn't even call on her mother for help, and oh, poor Dad... But howling would help no one.

The sound of cars outside interrupted her thoughts, and Ella saw Owen's Ford and a police car pull up in the driveway. DI Martin went to speak to two reporters who were lingering outside, and whatever he said made them walk off towards their own vehicle. Ella sat straighter. Was there news? Hope flared painfully in her chest.

'You can go back into your house in an hour,' said DI Martin. 'They're finishing up now. We're still looking at your husband's laptop and we've taken some paperwork too. Here's your receipt for that.'

He slid a piece of paper across the table and Ella took it automatically. It wasn't important. 'Are you any closer to finding them?'

'I'm afraid not. Your husband's mobile signals end after Newquay. We're putting out an appeal this morning. Do you have any images we can use?'

Ella sent the pictures to his phone. She didn't want to sound as if she was telling him how to do his job, but... 'Um – I'm worried Rick might have concussion. Will you say something in the appeal about him maybe needing medical attention?'

He checked the images, nodding. 'That's the plan. Your car is also being checked. There are several finds – hairs and the like – being investigated. We have to rule everything out.'

Ella clenched her fists. Had Rick transported a dead body in their car? What a sick thought – and how had he managed to live with himself, knowing what he'd done? When exactly had he buried this poor person – and was it a man? Or a woman – the girlfriend? And *when* had it happened?

Ella blinked despair away as another thought struck her. This could be the reason for Rick's time off work. She should tell them about that. The police would have to talk to his colleagues, find out when Rick had been absent. She only knew what he'd told her and that was a pack of lies. Over the course of what should have been the happiest summer of their lives, her husband had turned into a lying stranger. A murderer? Why else would he have hidden a dead body?

# CHAPTER NINE

Saturday 2nd August

Rick stood in the dimness of the reception corner, the guesthouse phone jammed to his ear. It was an old-fashioned model with the receiver attached to the base station, probably to stop people walking off with it. The girl at the desk was clicking around on the computer and obviously had no intention of leaving him alone to make his call. But complaining about the lack of privacy would make him conspicuous and after all, they were letting him use their phone. Rick peered at the paper where he'd listed his contacts and keyed in Amanda's number, imagining her at home in her flat with Jaden. And his baby. Please answer, please take this, Amanda.

And she did, because of course she didn't know it was him. 'Hello?'

'Amanda, it's me, I'm - '

He could hear her breath hiss as she inhaled and then she was – not shouting, exactly, because thank God her voice was low – but he could hear the fury all the time she was speaking.

'Listen very carefully, Rick. You and I are over. *Finito*.

I had two policemen here last night breaking the news to me that Gareth's been found *under your bloody shed*. I can't even begin to tell you how I feel about that. But it's nothing to do with me. I last saw Gareth when I waved goodbye to him at Lamorna and you can't prove otherwise. Now bugger off and hand yourself in.'

The line buzzed in his ear, and Rick gripped the edge of the desk with his free hand. She'd hung up on him – he needed her help and she'd told him to bugger off. What a cow. But quick, he should say something to convince the receptionist the call had ended normally.

'Perfect. See you soon, then.' He replaced the receiver on its base and managed a grin for the girl. 'Thanks for that. I must have left my mobile on the train yesterday.'

She smiled vaguely, and Rick turned away. Least said, soonest forgotten.

Upstairs, Soraya was spooning her way through a tub of strawberry yoghurt, a little frown on her face. 'I like it better at home when it's cold from the fridge,' she said, her voice trembling. 'Is Mummy coming very soon today?'

'Very soon,' said Rick. 'That's why we're not having a proper breakfast. We'll go for a lovely walk, and then it'll be time to meet Mummy.'

She accepted this, but her expression was bleak and Rick felt his temper rise. He should have taken her home days ago, dumped her at the end of the road and disappeared. Alone, he could have left the area – he could have left the country, started a new life somewhere else. He reached for the bottle of paracetamol. The background pain in his head had gone on so long now he

303

was almost used to it, but Soraya whining every time she opened her mouth made him see stars.

He stared at the girl, scraping the sides of her yoghurt carton. She looked like – like a child nobody cared about. Her hair was a mess and her clothes were rumpled, and this, combined with her natural thinness, had turned her into a poor little wretch. Topping them both was drastic, but the thought of spending the next however many years in prison was horrendous. His life was ruined, and all because they'd started to adopt a child. Ella had changed, then the dream changed too because the child he had wasn't the child he'd have chosen. In a way you could say that Ella and Soraya between them had killed Gareth. A fresh wave of tension surged through Rick's head and he groaned. What had happened to him that he was even *thinking* like this?

'Can we go now?' Soraya's face was pale.

Rick nodded, then stopped because it hurt. Stupid girl. She only wanted to go because then they'd have started on the journey to Mummy. He shook three paracetamol into his hand and grimaced as he swallowed them with a slug of room temperature orange juice.

'You brush your teeth while I finish packing. We'll leave the cases at reception.'

Her face brightened and she ran towards the bathroom.


The bus dropped them at the top end of Lamorna Cove, and Rick grasped Soraya's hand as they started the trek downhill.

'Why did we come here?' Soraya gazed unenthusiastically down the lane stretching in front of them.

Rick groaned inwardly. Why indeed? He didn't know, but part of the reason was to somehow touch base with the man he'd buried under the shed. Which was stupid, as Gareth had never made it as far as Lamorna this summer. But the buzzing in his head was so loud he couldn't think straight, and anyway, a walk was something to do while he was deciding whether to jump off the cliff or go to the police. Could he really face prison?

'I told you. We'll have a lovely walk first, and then we're meeting Mummy in the café further down here.'

He gripped her hand and she allowed him to lead her down the narrow lane. For the first few yards they were in full sunlight and his head shrieked in protest, but shady trees and bushes soon appeared on the verge, and Rick crept along on their shadow. When they reached the cove he realised that telling Soraya about the café had been a mistake. All she wanted now was to have an ice cream and wait for Mummy, and Rick felt his temper desert him. He gripped the child's shoulder and hissed into her face.

'This not all about what you want! Come on!'

She flinched, then nodded stiffly, her eyes huge. Rick looked round. The last time he'd been here he'd been Gareth. The coastal path from Lamorna to Mousehole was a tricky one, not necessarily something you'd want to do with your six-year-old daughter. But he couldn't stop now. They would repeat Gareth's walk and he would decide whether or not to end it all. But deep inside he knew he wasn't brave enough for that. It would be prison for him.

Pulling Soraya behind him, Rick started along the path, feeling lighter in spite of his headache. It was so lovely; the ever-changing blue of the ocean as it surged and swelled, stretching on and on to be replaced by the lighter blue of the sky – the best view in the world. And this might be his last walk in freedom for – well, that would depend what they convicted him of, wouldn't it? He should memorise this scene, build it up layer by layer in his memory – something to picture during his imprisonment.

'I'm thirsty. I want my juice.' Soraya wrenched her hand free and sat down on a rock to open her rucksack.

Rick plumped down on the turf beside her. They were in full sunlight here and it was blinding. His head shrieked and he lay flat, pulling his cap across his eyes as some slight protection, and listening as Soraya grunted in her efforts to open the carton of juice. A slurping sound told him she'd succeeded, and Rick felt the world drifting away. The odd seagull cry... the sound of the waves as they crashed into the rocks... the wind rustling through the long grass beside him. Such a peaceful place, a beautiful place, sun and sea and the elements.

When the juice was finished Rick tottered to his feet and they went on. The path was almost deserted; a lot of people missed this section out because it was challenging. But the views were stunning, and even in his weakened state Rick was able to appreciate the seascape in front of him.

'I want to go back now. I want to go to Mummy.'

The same old whine, and something snapped inside Rick. He lowered his face to Soraya's. 'Just do as you're damn well told. If you don't we won't ever go back. Got that?'

The terrified expression was back, and she nodded. Rick wheeled round. On, on.

He staggered, feeling the heat on the back of his neck, oh, that sun. It was high in the sky, beating down without mercy. His head was pounding in spite of the sun cap and dark glasses, and when they came to a bend where the track crept round a rock, sickeningly close to the edge, the vague nausea in Rick's middle became acute.

'Sit down and wait,' he told Soraya. He dived behind a spur of rock and vomited violently. For a few seconds he felt better, but as soon as he straightened up the sickness returned. Rick leaned on the rock, vomiting and retching and spitting, and then gradually began to feel more normal. Apart from his head – that was still pounding. He turned back to the track and Soraya.

She was gone. And apart from this rock, there was nowhere she could be hiding. Panicking, Rick stared round, pain stabbing through his eyes as his head moved left and right. Where the hell was she? But of course she'd gone back, back to the café where Mummy was supposedly coming to meet them. He stumbled a few steps in that direction, then voices behind him made him flop down on the scrubby grass by the track and pull his cap well over his eyes.

It was a middle-aged couple and two teenage boys. Lucky parents, going hiking with their sons. Rick raised his hand in reply when they greeted him in passing, then rolled onto his front, smelling the sweetness of the warm grass and shading his eyes from that terrible sun. It was over. His legs were trembling and there was something wrong with one eye – he couldn't hurry after Soraya. She would reach the café before him and everyone there would witness whatever scene played out then. He wouldn't get away as lightly as he'd done in the snack bar yesterday, when they'd met the bikers.

He stood up, then turned left and continued along the track. He'd go on to Mousehole and contact the police there. They might even be waiting for him, if Soraya told her story at Lamorna. They might catch him up before he ever got there.

On and on he blundered, stopping every so often to look out over the blueness of the Atlantic. He should have been happy here. A family man... For long minutes he followed the path through merciless sunlight, then a blessedly shady part with bushes and trees appeared before him. Rick dropped to his knees in cool dimness and rolled into a ball. He would have a little sleep here and then he'd go on.

Darkness swirled around his head, and he sank into it.

# CHAPTER TEN

Saturday 2nd August

'They've found a body, Suze.'

Amanda waited, fingers sliding on the phone as Susie sobbed down the line. This was worse than telling her mother-in-law that Gareth had disappeared in the first place; then at least the poor soul had been able to hope her son would turn up again. Susie ranted on about Gareth having done nothing to deserve any of this, Amanda murmuring, 'I know, I know,' and fighting to keep hold of her composure. Eventually Susie's diatribe came to a halt and Amanda made her suggestion.

'I'd like to come to Glasgow if you'll have us for a bit. It isn't good for Jaden, being in the middle of this. I never know when we might meet someone and they'll say something that'd frighten him. He understands a lot now.'

Susie was silent for a moment before she spoke again. 'You can come and welcome, hen, but I'll come down to you for a few days first. I need to hear what the police have to say. Are they sure it's him?'

Jaden cried out from his cot in the middle of Amanda's

explanation, and she was glad of the excuse to end the call.

'They expect to confirm it soon. I have to see to Jaden – you book your flight and we'll talk in half an hour or so.'

Maybe it *would* be better to have Suze here to help with the police, she mused as she dressed Jaden then sat him down with a piece of toast. Suze wouldn't make a mistake about what she knew, so having her here to do most of the talking would be an advantage. Then later they could go back to Glasgow together – they could arrange the funeral in Glasgow.

The thought of what was left of Gareth being buried or cremated made her stomach churn, although the morning sickness was more or less over. She was seventeen weeks pregnant tomorrow, realised Amanda, looking at the kitchen calendar. If – no, *when* they went to Glasgow she'd need to get antenatal care organised there. But that shouldn't be a problem and a big city hospital would have the added benefit of anonymity. When Susie called back to say she'd be arriving in Newquay late that afternoon Amanda was able to sound suitably grateful.

'I'll pick you up at the airport, and I'll make sure we can talk to the police either today or tomorrow. I'm so glad you're coming, Suze.'

She was, too, thought Amanda as she smeared sun cream over Jaden's face and arms. 'Nana's coming,' she told him, and he nodded seriously. Did he understand? It would be interesting to see if he recognised Suze. She held out her hand. 'Come on, lovey. Let's go and see if Soraya's home yet.'

Jaden's face lit up. 'So-soa!'

Love surged through Amanda. What a sweetie he was.

As soon as they turned into Cedar Road Amanda saw the police cars in Ella's driveway. Oh – they were still investigating. But she could still walk past and see what there was to be seen.

No new activity was evident in Ella's garden, however, and Amanda was striding towards the corner when she heard her name. Oh no. Ella's policeman neighbour was in his garden. Reluctantly, she turned back, meeting him by the fence.

'Ella's gone into town to hire a car,' he said, looking at her in his direct way.

Amanda gripped the buggy, her brain whirling. Did he suspect anything? It seemed best to concentrate on Ella.

'Oh, I wish she'd said. I could have run her places.'

'I offered too, but she wants to be independent.'

'Will she get back into her house soon?'

'They're finishing up now. She doesn't care much about that, though, she's so worried about Soraya.'

Amanda looked at Jaden in the buggy. She knew how she'd feel if he was missing. 'I can imagine. I don't suppose they've told her it was Gareth yet?'

He stood there, his face expressionless – you could tell he was a policeman.

Amanda's middle churned anew. 'Didn't you know?' What had she done? But he must know… or was this a trap?

'I'm not on this team, you know, and I'm on leave at the moment.'

Amanda stared dumbly at Owen. What a fool she was.

'Don't worry,' he said. 'No harm done.'

'We're going to Glasgow soon,' said Amanda, trying desperately to move the conversation away from Gareth's body. 'My mum-in-law's coming down today and when we've organised things with the police we'll be off up north.'

'Good idea.'

Amanda turned the buggy round. She'd been stupid, but it would be all right. 'I'll maybe see Ella later, then, to say goodbye.'

She crossed back over the road to make it look as if she had a particular reason for walking along Cedar Road this morning, and scooted round the corner as quickly as she could.

It might actually be better if she never saw Ella again.

# Chapter Eleven

Saturday 2nd August

Ella bobbed up and down on the balls of her feet as the clerk in the car hire office completed his paperwork then handed over the key. Now she was mobile again without having to depend on the neighbours. The car was larger than their own but easy enough to manoeuvre, and she negotiated the town centre and drove up the hill without incident.

Feeling like an imposter in her own home, she walked through the ground floor rooms and on upstairs, noticing everywhere signs that things had been lifted, examined, and replaced in not quite the right places. It was horrible. The house felt nothing like home and she knew it never would again.

Impossible to go into Soraya's room. The feeling was every bit as bad as if she'd given birth to a child and raised her for six years before losing her. This ache of wanting was worse than the no-child ache had ever been. Ella couldn't sit still; she had to be active or she would fall head first into a deep, dark hole.

At least Mum was coping. After the police visit that

morning Ella had called and given her mother a brief account of what was happening. Fortunately, Mum agreed to stay in Helston. Mary wanted Ella to come for a few days too, and Ella agreed – anything was better than being alone in this house. She would pack a bag and leave as soon as she could.

Upstairs, she opened her wardrobe and rifled through its contents. Clothes belonging to a different life were hanging here, summer shirts and blouses from happier days. A stranger's clothes.

Her mobile buzzed while she was packing underwear and she fumbled it out of her handbag. Oh please, this could be – but no, it was a strange number. Hope crashed again.

'Hello?' It didn't sound like her voice.

'Hi, are you Ella Baxter? This is Jill at Lamorna Café. We've got Soraya here – she lost her Daddy and she asked us to phone you.'

The room spiralled round and Ella plumped down on the bed. Thank God, oh thank God. Soraya was okay. The relief was as painful as the fear had been and Ella began to laugh, conscious of hysteria lurking inside her. 'Oh, thank you – I've been so worried. I didn't know where they were. Can I speak to her?'

Soraya's voice was in her ear. 'Mummy? I want to come home. Where are you – Daddy said you were coming here for lunch!'

The tone was nothing but peeved and Ella's almost-hysteria vanished abruptly. 'Oh darling, I'm glad you found someone to call me. That was so clever. Daddy hasn't been well and the arrangements were a bit wrong, but I'll come and get you straightaway. Where did you lose Daddy?'

A sniff. 'On the walk. He was being silly and I ran away because I thought you were coming to the café but you weren't here.'

Another few words with Jill to make sure Soraya was kept in the café even if Rick came storming in looking for her, then Ella was running downstairs and out to the hired car. She was out of town before it occurred to her that it might have been an idea to let the police know Soraya had been found – and she should have told Owen, too. But it wasn't far to Lamorna and she could notify everyone then. Ella drove swiftly, her senses sharp as they hadn't been for days. Once at the coast she had to slow down. The road down to the cove was narrow but thankfully she didn't meet any other vehicles, and the gods were on her side today because there was a space right at the harbour.

Inside the café, the first thing Ella saw was a table near the counter where Soraya was sitting, an empty glass in front of her.

'Mummy!' The little girl slid from her chair and ran towards her. 'You weren't here, why weren't you here? But they gave me a lovely ice cream!'

Ella sat down with the child hugged on her lap, noticing that Soraya was holding on tightly too.

'Sweetie, I didn't know where to come. Daddy didn't tell me and he wasn't answering his phone. But I'm here now.' She turned to the woman behind the counter. 'Thank you so much for looking after her. I've been so worried.'

315

And now she should phone the police. But as soon as she did so the clock would start ticking. St Ives to Lamorna... she'd have thirty more minutes with her child, once that call was made. Grief swelled in Ella's throat and she kissed the hot little head leaning on her shoulder, inhaling the smell of a strange shampoo. She would take Soraya outside and explain everything first.

There was no sandy beach here, but Ella sat on a rock and watched as Soraya threw stones into the sea. This was such a lovely place, the deep blue ocean going on and on into eternity, and the paler blue of the sky above. Ella clasped her hands tightly. Please, somebody stop time while she enjoyed having a child, this child she had chosen. These would be the last minutes of peace; before the day was out Soraya would be gone from her life and the fight to get her back would have started.

'Are we going home soon?'

Ella patted the rock beside her. 'I'm not sure. I'll have to phone the police; they've been looking for you and Daddy. Liz'll be coming and I don't know what'll happen then.'

Soraya sat on the rock, her eyes dark. 'Why's Liz coming?'

This was where she destroyed her daughter's new world. 'Sweetheart, something very bad has been happening at home, something I didn't know about. Liz wants to know you're okay.'

'Did Daddy do something bad?'

Ella blotted her eyes before the tears escaped. There were no flies on Soraya. 'I'm afraid he did. The police are trying to find out what it was. Liz will explain what she wants for you, and we both know we can trust her. You might be going back to Auntie Mel's for a bit.'

Soraya's face blanched. 'I don't want to go to Auntie Mel's! I want to stay with you!'

'That's what I want too, and I'm going to work very, very hard to make sure that happens. But we – the police and I – need to get the bad stuff sorted first and that'll take a day or two.'

Her heart breaking, Ella made the call, then sat on the rock with Soraya wedged between her knees, and they gazed out over the ocean. Thirty minutes of beauty with her child in her arms; remember the feeling, Ella, remember the smell, remember the love.

DI Martin arrived with a WPC half an hour after her call. 'Rick's been found further along the coast path,' he said. 'He's unconscious. They're airlifting him to Truro.'

Ella clutched Soraya's hand. 'Did he fall?'

'I don't know. A German family found him. It wasn't until the paramedics reached him that we were alerted. WPC Gray here will go with you back to your home. We'll catch up later.'

Soraya was clinging to her, and Ella lifted the child into her arms and turned towards the car park. For the very first time she was walking along carrying her daughter, and please God this wouldn't be the last day they spent together.

# CHAPTER TWELVE

**Saturday 2nd August**

Not knowing what was going on was intolerable. Amanda played with Jaden until he went for his nap after lunch, then sat on the sofa zapping round the TV channels. There was nothing on the national news at one o'clock, and only a very short mention on the local station. *The body of a man has been found in a Cornish garden*... She didn't dare look online. And what would happen when Gareth's identity was released was anyone's guess. She'd need to discuss that with DI Martin. Amanda balled her fists and thumped the sofa. Living alone, with just a toddler for company, was unbearable today, thank God Suze would be here later. Amanda smiled wryly; she had never looked forward so much to a visit from her mother-in-law. But Suze was a good person and more important, she was family, exactly what they needed now. They could stay in Glasgow till autumn, when it would be cool enough to visit her own parents in Spain. St Ives wouldn't be home for much longer. It was horrible to think how many lives had been ruined by that stupid affair with James/Rick – she needed to get her babies right away from that, into a fresh start.

Jaden's voice called from his bedroom, and Amanda winced. His naps were getting shorter; her lovely long break in the middle of the day was a thing of the past. She lifted him, revelling in the sensation of his head snuggled under her chin. Her boy, and he loved his mum; this was what she had to defend. If the truth came out she would end up in prison and Jaden would be sent to Suze in Glasgow. And probably the new baby would too, eventually. Suze would take them, Amanda knew. But that wasn't going to happen; she wouldn't let it.

So she had to know what was going on.


There were two cars in Ella's driveway and Amanda slowed down. Neither was obviously a police vehicle but then they didn't always drive around in panda cars. Maybe this was a bad idea, she didn't want to barge into a roomful of people. But there didn't seem to be any other way to find out what was going on.

She trudged up the path rang the bell, her heart thumping. To her dismay it was Owen who opened the door, but before Amanda could say anything Soraya ran out.

'Jaden! Come and play!'

Jaden was struggling to get out of his buggy, grey eyes shining and his face one big beam. Owen stood back silently, and Amanda stepped inside.

'Is Ella all right? And Rick?'

Soraya took Jaden's hand. 'Daddy's in hospital. Come on, Jaden. We can play in the living room.'

Ella appeared in the kitchen doorway and gave Amanda a hunted look. The pain in the other woman's eyes brought tears to Amanda's.

'Ella, I'm so sorry,' she whispered, and to her enormous surprise Ella hugged her tightly.

'*You're* sorry – it's me who should be saying that,' she said, her voice tight. 'They've told me it was Gareth. Amanda, I don't know what to say. I've no idea how Rick was connected to your husband. The police are investigating but so far there's nothing.'

Amanda wished with all her heart she'd stayed at home. 'Soraya said Rick's in hospital?' She could hear the fear in her own voice. If he was in hospital he wouldn't have been interviewed yet – would he?

'Yes. Come in, Owen's made coffee. And this is Liz, our adoption worker, and Mel from foster care. And you know DI Martin?'

Amanda sat down opposite Mel, feeling like the biggest imposter on the planet. This was exactly what she hadn't wanted to happen. Ella poured her a coffee, and Amanda saw how the other woman's hands were shaking. An awkward silence fell. Amanda blinked at her coffee, noticing how sunlight from outside was casting mug-shaped shadows on the kitchen table. Eventually Ella spoke, her voice unsteady. 'Rick's in Truro. They're operating; it's a brain haemorrhage and it's not looking good. They're talking about brain damage.'

For a moment Amanda couldn't breathe. First Gareth, then Rick… '*No* – what happened?'

Ella gave her a queer look and Amanda ducked her head. She'd sounded over-concerned there; she should be more careful. Fear chilled through her, and the baby kicked in protest. Silence fell again, broken by the sudden blaring of the television in the living room. Jaden's bubbly laugh rang out.

'A bang on the head may have caused his injury,' said DI Martin. 'We're hoping he'll wake up enough to tell us what happened with your husband.'

Amanda nodded. How horrible, now she had to hope Rick was never able to speak to them. But at least they didn't know how Rick and Gareth were connected. She should say as little as possible now. If only she'd stayed at home.

'I see,' she said at last. 'You're busy, Ella. I'll leave you to get on with things.' She was about to get up when Liz spoke.

'If you can stay another five minutes while I explain to Ella what's going to happen with Soraya it would be helpful. Your little boy's being a good distraction through there.'

Amanda slumped back into her chair, and Liz turned to Ella.

'Until this case is closed she'll be going back to Mel's, Ella. I'm so sorry, but you'll understand we can't do anything else.'

'And afterwards?' Ella's face was white.

'That depends. If Rick was involved in this death, he won't be allowed to adopt.'

'My marriage is over.' There was determination in Ella's voice. 'I want Soraya.'

'What are you talking about? What's happening? I don't want to go to Auntie Mel's, I've got a forever mummy now!' Soraya was in the doorway, her eyes huge and her face almost as white as Ella's.

Amanda choked back a sob. This was awful. Jaden's voice from the other room gave her an excuse and she went through to pick him up, rocking him in her arms. And she who had been instrumental in a man's death could rock her child, while Ella, who had done nothing wrong, was about to have hers taken away.

Amanda stood in the hallway, listening as Ella spoke to Soraya.

'Darling – you remember I told you Rick had done something bad? Well, I have to help the police find out what happened, and that will take a bit of time. Another thing is, because of what Rick did, I don't want to live here anymore. So I'm going to look for a nice new home and I'm hoping very hard that you can join me there some day. But until it's all settled you'll be staying with Auntie Mel.'

Amanda could see into the kitchen. Soraya's face was tear-blotched and red. 'I don't want to go! What did he do? Will you come every day? And can Jaden come too?'

'I don't know what Rick did but the police will find out. I'll see you as often as they let me but I don't know anything about that yet. Auntie Mel will keep us right about it.'

Amanda closed her eyes. It would be the biggest relief ever to get right away from the whole situation here.

A chair scraped back, and Mel spoke. 'Come on, sweetie. Let's pack your case and then we'll be home in time for tea.'

'I want my shells but if I take them the others'll get

them!' Soraya was crying loudly now, and Amanda buried her face in Jaden's neck. They had done this, she and Rick, and she would have to live with that.

# CHAPTER THIRTEEN

Sunday 3rd August

The house was silent. Ella walked through the kitchen, into the dining room – hard to remember the last time they'd dined in here; probably at the beginning of May, before Soraya started visiting – and across the hallway into the living room. There were so many little knick-knacks lying around, so many memories of her marriage. And this was the famous first day of the rest of her life.

She glanced out to the back garden. The shed, still in its police tent… and the shell garden, bereft of most of the seashells. Only the buddleia looked as usual, butterflies bobbing around in their colourful dance.

Thank goodness she was going to Helston to stay with Mum and Mary, albeit a day later than originally planned. The thought of spending another night in her bed here made Ella feel sick. No, no – she would get the house cleared and on the market ASAP – if that was possible without Rick. If it wasn't she would rent it out.

The photo on top of the television caught her eye – her, Rick and Soraya the day the little girl first came to spend a night. The happy family that had never been, in reality, and there was no way back from what Rick had done. Ella lifted the photo and stared. She and Soraya were standing close, sharing the same space and touching, but Rick was a few centimetres away, at a distance. The gap had been there long before she was aware of it. Ella eased the photo from its frame and went for the scissors. Two good snips and she was holding a lovely photo of her and her girl, with a tiny bit of Rick's arm at the side. She would touch it up and have one made for Soraya too, if they'd let her have it. God bless Photoshop.

Tears welled up and Ella blinked determinedly. Liz would be here soon with information about how – and if – she could proceed as a single adopter. It was important to make a good impression in the face of adversity, but oh, this was tough. She was back to making a good impression on her adoption worker. Back to assessment and back to panel, too – if she was lucky. If she wasn't it would be the end for her and Soraya. The doorbell rang, and Ella stuck her chin out. This was it, the new beginning. Or maybe the end.

'Are you okay? And how's Rick?' Liz came in and sat in her usual place.

'I'm fine. Rick's still unconscious and they're not happy with him. His sister's on her way. I'll be starting divorce proceedings tomorrow no matter what, though. Liz, do I have any chance of getting Soraya?'

Ella held her breath. The hope was unbearable, but how very much worse it would be to have Liz dash it forever.

'You do, but it won't be a quick fix. You'll need to get your living situation regulated, including your income, and then we'll be back at the assessment leading to home study stage. Realistically, we're looking at six months at least. And no guarantees. I'm not even sure you'll be able to visit her until your application's gone through. The circumstances are – unusual, to say the least. We'll sort that out next week.'

Ella stared at her hands on the table. What were six months, after all, if she had her girl back at the end of them? A shitty fucking horrible long time, that was what.

'Ella, I called Mel today and as an exception we're going there this afternoon. We need to make sure Soraya understands what's going on. You'll be able to make your goodbyes properly. Yesterday was chaotic.'

For a moment Ella couldn't speak. Oh, what a painful kind of joy this was. She was to be allowed to say goodbye properly. With no guarantees. But at least there would be a goodbye before she left her girl to be cared for by others.

Ella ran upstairs and rummaged in her jewellery box. Here it was; the butterfly brooch she'd worn as a little girl. A delicate gold base, and vivid turquoise enamel. She would give it to Soraya whether she was allowed to or not.


'For me? Is it gold?'

They were upstairs in Soraya's bedroom. It was hers alone now as her foster-sister had been adopted, and Ella was glad to see Soraya's shells safely spread out on the chest of drawers.

She fastened the brooch on the little girl's sweatshirt.

'Yes. It's on loan. We'll hope very, very hard that you can come to a new forever home with me, maybe next springtime. Then we'll get you one of your own and you can give me this one back.'

'And if I can't come?'

'Then you have a forever butterfly to remind you I love you.'

Soraya nodded slowly, fingering the brooch. 'Honest truth?'

'Honest truth.'

'Are you ready up there?' Liz's voice called from downstairs.

Ella took Soraya's hand. She'd been allowed exactly five minutes.

They were crossing the upstairs landing when Soraya pulled her arm. 'You know when I found that gold chain at Amanda's? She *did* say it was her husband's. But it wasn't, was it?'

'No,' said Ella. But whatever that meant, it was completely unimportant today. She led Soraya downstairs and hugged her hard, inhaling deeply, not trusting herself to say more. And she got into Liz's car and waved as they drove off, and as soon as they turned the corner she howled.

# CHAPTER FOURTEEN

Two years later

The house phone rang out, and Ella cursed, the mud pack spread over half her face. How to ruin an expensive beauty treatment. Heck, no, she would finish her face pack first. It wouldn't be anything important on that phone, and she could call back if need be.

Twenty minutes later and suitably rejuvenated, she lifted the phone and took it to the window seat. As always, the view took her breath away. The vastness of the Atlantic was spread before her eyes, the rugged Cornish coastline contrasting starkly with the blue-green-white of the ocean. Walking up and down four flights of stairs every time she went in and out was worth it for this view.

The missed call was a strange number... or was it? On an impulse Ella booted up the laptop and checked the area code. Oh. Shetland. Nobody except Rick's sister would be calling her from Shetland. Heaviness descended into Ella's stomach as she pressed connect.

'Oh, Ella, thank you for calling back. How are you?'

Ella closed her eyes. Did they really need to exchange

pleasantries? But it was easier to play along. 'Fine, thanks. You?'

'Pete and I are fine, but I thought you should know Rick's not doing so well. He had a chest infection last week and now his kidneys… He's not going to make it, Ella.'

Ella stared at the sea far below. What was she supposed to say – did she even care what happened to Rick? Yes, in a way she did, but it wasn't the kind of caring that made her feel good. It had been a relief when Marianne and Pete took Rick to a nursing home in far-away Shetland. He had never recovered consciousness and in a terrible way Ella was glad.

'I'm sorry,' she said at last. 'Was there anything you needed me to do?' Hopefully that sounded polite enough while telling Marianne that she didn't want to be involved.

'No, no. I realise you won't come all this way to the funeral. Will I phone you when… or would you prefer a card?'

Ella balked at the thought of an 'I'm sorry for your loss' phone call. But none of this was Marianne's fault. 'Give me a call,' she said slowly. 'Then I'll let the police know. The case is still open although they've never found out anything more. Take care, Marianne.'

She replaced the handset and wiped her face on her sleeve. The case would most likely be closed when Rick died. Uncertainty would reign forever; what a horrible end to the worst time of her life. But now she should put on her glad rags.

She was spraying perfume behind her ears when she heard a key in the flat door.

'We bought a cake! Double choc with raspberry ripple cream, and ice cream to go with it! And I've got a present for you!'

Soraya hefted a large plastic bag onto the kitchen table, beaming. And oh, how bittersweet this was. Ella knew she couldn't share the news of Rick, not today. She hugged Soraya hard and turned to smile at Owen, who was unpacking not only ice cream but also champagne.

He stuck the bottle into the cooler and winked at her. 'One year today, huh?'

'I can't believe I've had a beautiful daughter for a whole year. The best year ever.' Ella opened the cake box while Soraya went for plates.

'Can we put a candle on it, Mummy?'

Owen poured champagne into two glasses and grape and elder into a third. His eyes met hers, and Ella knew he'd seen the shadow behind the joy. But this was Soraya's day; the shadow would keep. She turned to the little girl.

'So what's this present? Shouldn't you be getting the presents?'

Soraya jumped up and down. 'It sort of is for me too. Owen told me you had a secret for me, and we made it into a better one for you.' She handed over a small velvet box.

Wondering, Ella looked from Owen to Soraya to the little box. She had arranged to have a butterfly brooch made for Soraya, with her name on the back. The child was still wearing Ella's brooch.

'We got the new one made for you instead,' said Soraya, and Ella lifted the delicate blue enamel butterfly and examined it. *Ella and Soraya* was engraved on the back, and the date of the adoption. Ella hugged Soraya to her chest, closing her eyes to keep the tears in. To think she could have lost this treasure.

'Thank you,' she whispered. She could never say thank you enough for her girl.

'I wanted to keep your old one, you see,' said Soraya, pulling back and staring into Ella's face. 'Because it reminds me you love me. Can we cut the cake now?'


Amanda fought her way up Buchanan Street, Glasgow wind and rain making it almost impossible to control her umbrella. Working at weekends was the downside to her job in a city centre stationery shop. On the other hand, it gave her the odd day off during the week, and Suze was always happy to babysit. Amanda reached the underground station and descended thankfully out of the rain.

The orange train rattled its way round to Hillhead, where Amanda got off. The rain had stopped, and she hurried past red tenements in Highburgh Road. This was the best part of the day, going home to her kids. She would never forget how nearly she had lost them; thinking about it still made her shiver. Gareth and the old life were gone, but she still had her children.

What she no longer had was confidence that she was safe. If Rick ever woke up... There was no way to know what was happening with him. She'd called Ella once, a few weeks after Rick's operation, to be told he was still unconscious and Soraya was still in foster care, and something in the other woman's voice had prevented Amanda ever phoning again.

Life here was good, but the black uncertainty hanging over her head was always there, ready to pounce, and sometimes it stalked her at night, too. You heard all the time about people who were in a coma for years, and then they woke up and started talking. If Rick did that, the police would investigate.

Amanda shook her umbrella before going inside. Any time at all, there could be a knock at the door and a policeman would be standing there, waiting to take her away. The fear was a permanent weight in her middle.

'Mum! Nana's making spaghetti for tea!'

Amanda ruffled Jaden's hair, smiling wryly at the Glasgow accent. But this was a good place to bring up your kids.

'Where's my Jasmin?' she called.

Jasi always hid when she arrived; it was their special game. Amanda would search and search and eventually find her daughter, in the same place every time, behind the living room curtains.

'Where's Jasi? Not in the kitchen... and not behind the sofa... and – oh! Yes... *there* she is!'

Amanda seized the child to shrieks of laughter and held her close. And how thankful she was to be able to hold her daughter, this amazing wriggling creature with the shock of dark hair, and grey eyes.

Just like her daddy's.

THE END

If you enjoyed *Chosen Child*, you might be interested to read Linda Huber's other novels:

## The Paradise Trees

*He had found exactly the right spot in the woods. A little clearing, green and dim, encircled by tall trees. A magical, mystery place. He would bring his lovely Helen here... This time, it was going to be perfect.*

When Alicia Bryson returns to her estranged father's home in a tiny Yorkshire village, she feels burdened by his illness. Her hometown brings back memories of a miserable and violent childhood, and Alicia worries that her young daughter Jenny's summer will be filled with a similar sense of unhappiness.

The town is exactly as she remembered it, the people, the buildings, even the woods. But Alicia's arrival has not gone unnoticed.

Someone is watching her every move. Someone who has a plan of his own. Someone who will not stop until the people he loves most can rest together, in Paradise.

# The Cold Cold Sea

*They stared at each other, and Maggie felt the tightness in her middle expand as it shifted, burning its way up... Painful sobs rose in her throat as Colin, his face expressionless now, reached for his mobile and dialled 999.*

When three-year-old Olivia disappears, her parents are overwhelmed with grief. Weeks go by and Olivia's mother refuses to leave the cottage, staring out at the turbulent sea and praying it didn't claim her precious daughter's life.

Not far away, another mother watches proudly as her daughter starts school. Jennifer has loved Hailey for five years, but the child is suddenly moody and difficult, and there's a niggling worry that Jennifer cannot shake off. As she struggles to maintain control there are gaps in her story that even she can't explain.

Time is running out for Maggie at the cottage, and also for Jennifer and Hailey. No-one can underestimate a mother's love for her child, and no-one can predict the lengths one will go to, to protect her family.

# The Attic Room

*A father's secret. A mother's lie. A family mystery.*

An unexpected phone call – and Nina's life takes a disturbing twist. Who is John Moore? And how does he know her name?

Nina travels south to see the house she inherited, but sinister letters arrive and she finds herself in the middle of a police investigation. With her identity called into question, Nina uncovers a shocking crime. But what, exactly, happened in the attic room, all those years ago? The answer could lie close to home.

The arrival of her ten-year-old daughter compounds Nina's problems, but her tormentor strikes before she can react. Searching for the truth about the Moore family puts both Nina and her child into grave danger.

Printed in Great Britain
by Amazon